Also by Jadesola James

Watch for
Redeemed by His New York Cinderella,
coming soon from
Jadesola James and Harlequin Presents!

The Sweetest Charade features brief depictions of drug abuse and references to cheating.

THE SWEETEST CHARADE

JADESOLA JAMES

carina
press

carina
press®

Recycling programs
for this product may
not exist in your area.

ISBN-13: 978-1-335-47523-7

The Sweetest Charade

First published in 2021. This edition published in 2021.

Copyright © 2021 by Jadesola James

For questions and comments about the quality of this book, please contact us at CustomerService@Harlequin.com.

Carina Press
22 Adelaide St. West, 40th Floor
Toronto, Ontario M5H 4E3, Canada
www.CarinaPress.com

Printed in U.S.A.

To Dr. Gary,
who told me I could write a book in the first place,
and to my husband, John,
who cheered me on while I did.

THE SWEETEST CHARADE

Chapter One

Professor Alexander Abbott-Hill was not vain enough to think that his class of undergraduates had suddenly taken an interest in the history of commuter travel because of his skill as an instructor, but *something* was going on.

All twenty-two students tramped in on time, dressed in their usual athleisure, toting glass water bottles and Starbucks coffee cups. They slid into their seats with uncharacteristic alertness, opening their tablets and laptop computers almost as if they intended to *listen* this time. Pleased, Alexander greeted them with none of the irritation he usually felt at the presence of the electronic devices.

"How was everyone's weekend?" he asked as he powered up the instructor's station.

"Not as good as yours, I bet," someone murmured from approximately the second row, and the titters that followed that show of wit made Alexander roll his eyes. What passed for irony with this generation...

"What, because I was up reading your midterms? I couldn't think of a better use of time myself," he retorted, and pulled up his slides for the day. "All right, everyone log in. We're starting with your reading on Robert Moses..."

The class went on and grew—well, stranger and stranger. Instead of being half-asleep, students were texting and scrolling and whispering. Oddly, Alexander seemed to be the object of scrutiny. Two girls whispered fervently in the back with round eyes fixed on him. One actually pointed at him, then at her phone. A young man in a lacrosse jersey gestured in his general direction, waving his hands not-too-subtly while talking to his tablemates, who gaped.

After a subtle check to see if his fly was open, Alexander gave up thirty minutes into his lecture and confronted them directly. "Is there something going on?"

Silence.

"Everyone seems very preoccupied this morning." He shot a significant look at the young lady who'd been sharing her screen earlier. "Is there something going on in the news that I missed? Has someone died?"

"Um, no," she said, blushing and staring down at the tabletop.

"Have I got anything on my face?" He tried to inject a little humor. "I know I'm fully dressed."

At *that*, there was an explosion of mirth in the back. "Now you are," he thought he heard a student mumble, but he couldn't be sure. His patience was wearing thin anyway.

"*Look*," he said. "We have forty minutes left. Either everyone gets it together, or you dump your phones up here. Your choice."

His students managed to calm themselves, thank goodness, and Alexander finished his lecture feeling more than a little ruffled. His students filed out relatively meekly, shooting looks at him over their shoulders. Some were still whispering. Alexander headed for his office, riding the waves of his own irritation.

"Something is definitely in the air," he announced as he opened the door. His teaching assistant, Natalia, was seated at the desktop they shared, squinting at something on the screen. "My class just now? Completely distracted. You'd think Kennedy was shot just this morning."

To his horror, Natalia turned and goggled in the way his students had that morning. She tugged at her nose ring nervously.

"*What?*" he exploded.

"Um. Dr. Abbott-Hill, have you had a chance to see—"

They were interrupted by a ringing phone. Alexander raised a finger, shot her a "don't move!" look and picked it up.

"Alexander Abbott-Hill."

"Hello, Dr. Abbott-Hill." A woman's voice floated smoothly over the line. "This is Theresa, from the office of the dean of humanities; he'd like to ask if you have any time this morning?"

"Oh. Well, I've just gotten out of my eight-thirty class—"

"Yes, I know. That's why we're calling *now*."

"When would you want to—"

"Now, if possible."

"Right this moment?"

"Yes, please, if you can. It's quite urgent. Thank you," she trilled, and was gone with a click.

Christ, what a morning. "We'll finish this later," Alexander said to Natalia, who clapped her jaw shut and nodded. He slipped his tweed blazer over his shoulders and raked his fingers through his hair. "I'm going to see Wayne."

"I thought that might be Theresa. She always cuts you off when you're speaking," observed Natalia.

Alexander just shook his head and left.

The walk to Wayne McDermott's office was fairly short, just the next building over, and the crispness of autumn was sweet and soothing. He took deep breaths of the earth-scented air, and arrived at his supervisor's office in a decidedly better state of mind. He was ushered in by Theresa, who smiled serenely at him; the dean was seated at his large mahogany desk, frowning at his desktop screen. Alexander eased himself into one of the two burgundy leather chairs that flanked the desk and waited for the man to speak.

He took his time.

"Dr. Abbott-Hill."

"Alexander, please." He desperately wanted to roll his eyes whenever one of the senior faculty approached him with such formality. As the only child of a former faculty member—and a prominent one at that—he'd practically grown up on this campus. He hadn't liked Wayne McDermott then either, and the man always found a way to take a subtle dig at the fact that he was nowhere near the scholar his father had been.

Dean McDermott grunted. "I'll get right to it. I asked you to come"—*summoned me*, Alexander thought—"because something has been brought to my attention, and I wanted to address it immediately."

"Yes?"

"I thought it best that it come from me. Your dad would have wanted it that way," he added, magnanimously.

Despite the seriousness of the conversation Alexander

had to stifle a smile. His father couldn't *stand* the man. "Appreciated, sir. I'm sure you're right."

"Social media," the dean began grandly, straining the confines of his button-down shirt, "is a tool which is used fairly broadly in our departments. We want to give you young folks the freedom to get the word out, as it were, to the general public and academic world about what we're doing. However, when it's used inappropriately…" He trailed off. "Do you understand what I'm getting at, Alex?"

Alexander, he corrected mentally. Alex had been the little boy coloring on the floor of his father's office, eating the cheese sandwiches the older man had packed for both of them that morning, waiting for him to get out of class so that they could go to their big, silent home and crawl into their beds. "I completely agree, but I'm a little confused as to why—"

"You are a vibrant and talented young man, a credit to your father, and I'm sure that you have a swinging social life. However, I would prefer that you keep it separate from your academic accounts."

"I'm not sure what you mean—"

"After all," Dean McDermott continued as if he hadn't heard Alexander, "your evaluations have given you enough of an issue this year, haven't they? And with tenure approaching…"

Alexander's heart began to hammer, even as he felt a flash of anger. His student evaluations last semester had been the worst out of increasingly lackluster reviews. "Boring," "No relevance to real life," and "too old-school," had been some of the tidbits that stood out particularly in his mind. Irritation at the students aside, it hurt. He truly loved his subject, and it was painful knowing that his enthusiasm wasn't enough to carry his class along.

Dean McDermott interrupted his thoughts. "Good man. I'm glad we understand each other." He stood up, and extended his hand.

Wordlessly, Alexander stood and shook it. The dean didn't release it immediately; instead he squeezed it and smiled at Alexander, a toothy man-to-man smile that was disconcerting at best. He ran a hand over his thinning hair, and Alexander thought he detected a wink.

"You won't mind my saying she's absolutely gorgeous, absolutely—" The dean whistled softly between his teeth. "You're a lucky bastard. They didn't make them like that when I was an associate. If they did I'd never have left teaching—it's obviously gotten sexier since my day."

What the—?

Alexander found himself slapped on the shoulder and outside in the hallway in moments. Dean McDermott ambled off in the other direction, presumably in search of coffee or a bathroom, scratching his stomach through his shirt as he went. "I want that picture down within the hour," he called over his shoulder. "There's a good man."

"What on earth?" Alexander muttered, and headed back to the department, a bit quicker this time, a sense of foreboding building with every step. When he opened the door, Natalia was exactly where he'd left her, still gawping at the computer. "Natalia, what in God's name is going on?"

"You've gotten almost *four thousand* new followers since last night," she breathed. "And the comments on the photo…"

"What photo?" As he spoke he leaned over her shoulder—he obviously wasn't going to get any sense out of her by asking any questions. He pulled his tortoise-shells up to his forehead in order to see better; when he did, he sucked in a breath.

Natalia was on the photo-blogging site he used, looking at the account of someone named Delysia Daniels. *So no one hacked me, then.* The photo Natalia pointed at was slightly out-of-focus, a black-and-white filtered affair featuring a couple cuddling on a mess of tangled white sheets. The man's torso was slim but muscled, decorated with a smattering of dark hair. Thankfully, a sheet covered the essentials.

Beside the subject was another person, presumably female, and looking at her in such an intimate position made Alexander's mouth go dry despite himself. It took only a few seconds to register the details: a gleam of oil on warm skin, the substantial curve of a bare hip and leg.

A hand, not her own, gripped her thigh possessively. Everything else was cropped out. The caption read:

Every night spent with you is a marvel, @shhistorian.

@shhistorian. Southampton Historian. *His* username.

"It's very artistic," Natalia chirped in. Her voice sounded like it was coming from very far away. He blinked rapidly, forced himself to focus.

His eyes met hers and she blushed hard.

"She tagged you in the photo," she rattled on hurriedly, fingering the keys nervously. "People are *flooding* you with comments. Dang, Dr. Abbott-Hill. I didn't know you were seeing anyone, you're not even *following* her."

"Why would I—"

"I mean, Delysia *Daniels*?" Natalia's voice graduated to a squeak. He'd never seen his sensible TA like this; she was fairly sparkling with excitement. "I mean, congratulations. I know, it's kind of personal. But still—"

"Wait, you think that's *me*?"

"She tagged you in the photo!"

At that, Alexander groped blindly for an office chair. His face was burning. If she thought that was him—well, it could be any dark-haired man with his skin tone, really. "Untag it," he ordered.

"But, Dr. Abbott-Hill—"

"Actually no, I'll do it myself." He took in a deep breath, trying to hide the hammering of his pulse, summoning his usual calm. "Please go to the library, and pick up some blue books for History 226's exam tonight."

"But—"

"*Now*, Natalia. And shut the door behind you."

Natalia pouted. She logged out, slid her chair back and left the room. It took Alexander a full minute to compose himself before he logged into his account.

The thing was made primarily to remind his students about assignments and department events, as well as acting as a photo journal for some of the primary documents, studies and projects he was working on. The last photo he'd posted was of him posing cheerfully with a local Audubon Society representative at Southampton's History Day.

At the bottom of the screen was the notification he was looking for: @thereal_Delysia_Daniels had indeed tagged him in a photo, in *that* photo.

He clicked, and there it was again, large as ever, with a comments section at least as long as his latest historical bibliography. He swiftly untagged himself, then scrutinized Delysia Daniels's account.

She was a...model, of some sort? She was attractive, he supposed, in a very filtered sort of way, with glossy piles of black hair and smooth skin that stretched over round dimpled cheeks when she smiled, which was often, revealing a mouth of milk-white, slightly crooked teeth.

Her account mostly featured her romping round the Greater New York area with a set of people that were very expensively dressed, if a little dead about the eyes. She also seemed to be the spokesperson for a bewildering variety of products. She had over a million followers who all seemed to comment on her every move, her clothes, her body parts, her jewelry, what she was eating, drinking, dancing to, and the comments on the *picture*—

@oatsnhoney123: Damn, that's hot. Well done Delysia ! ;)

@thomasjprince: He's grabbing on her thigh lyke...you gotta wonder what happened after that... :-O

@wonderfulwoman99: Delysia !!! Deets!!! Who is heeeeee??

@collegegyrljess: He teaches at my school, his classes are boring af. But I'd hit it now that I've seen it.

Alexander felt dizzy, hot, cold, and wanted to throw up all at the same time. No wonder his students had been so distracted this morning. And the *dean*...oh, *man*. He clicked through her profile, looking for any information, any information at all...and there it was! A booking number for an agent. He pulled his cell from his inner pocket and dialed the number swiftly.

He had to get a retraction on this, and he needed one *now*.

The line was promptly answered, which both surprised and startled him. "Integrity Talent, how can I direct your call?"

"Oh. I—Good morning. I'd like to speak to someone about a matter concerning Ms. Delysia Daniels, if possible?"

"Are you an agent?"

"No, I'm a—"

"Are you a publisher, a journalist, a potential sponsor, or—"

"No," Alexander sputtered. "I'm a—a—civilian. Ms. Daniels posted something about me on her social media account, and it is untrue. I need her to—retract this."

There was a long pause. Then—

"I'll connect you to our legal department."

Alexander groaned.

The source of Alexander's would-be retraction, Delysia Daniels, was cruising at 37,000 feet over the Grand Canyon on a flight back from Los Angeles to New York, and having a *marvelous* time.

American Airlines had contacted her weeks ago, offering the flight in exchange for a "candid review" on her photo-blog account. While this domestic flight was nothing compared to the trip a competitor had footed to Amsterdam two months ago, she certainly wasn't about to complain. She was fuzzy round the edges with the ice-cold Krug she'd had in the first-class lounge at LAX, and sushi she'd described as "so fresh, it might have still been wiggling" made a comfortable dent in her stomach.

She was now three hours into the flight and swaddled in the softest pair of knit lounge pants she'd ever worn (courtesy gift from a swanky English company, which she had yet to feature) and a cashmere-lined blanket and socks. Were she not working she'd have popped half a Valium so she could enjoy this experience in sleepy bliss, but she needed to take notes along the way.

Delysia pulled out her courtesy preview model of a new smartphone and began recording, automatically tilting the screen to capture her face at the most flattering angle. Despite years of dieting on and off, cryolipolysis sessions, and firming facials, that childish roundness she inherited from her mother refused to budge. She'd already filmed her "Mile-High Minute-Long Beauty Routine" featuring honey, coffee grounds, and frozen La Mer cream in the tiny bathroom; it'd garnered two thousand views already. Once she posted this, she'd be free to sleep or veg until they landed at JFK.

"Hey, everyone, American Airlines is spoiling me rotten right now, and I am loving it. I never thought I'd say that about a domestic flight, but here I am," she gushed in the husky, hushed tones she reserved for social media. "I don't want to disturb my cabin-mates—" She panned the camera quickly round the space, taking in the masked businessmen—and *possibly* one rapper—who sat to her right and left, respectively. She was sure her followers would try to ID them anyway; she never had to. "—but I just wanted to check in. See you all in New York!"

She blew a lip gloss–tinted kiss at the camera and took a moment to add a couple shots of the food she'd enjoyed during the first hour of the flight, her bookmarked copy of Wole Soyinka's *The Open Sore of a Continent* (mostly for the fans in Nigeria; she found his prose completely confusing) and her slippered feet, propped up in front of a frozen still of *Sabrina*, which she watched every time she had a flight.

"Ms. Daniels, is the Wi-Fi working all right for you?" A flight attendant materialized out of the air somewhere round her left elbow and she stifled a smile. The man had recognized her and had been trailing her since she'd gotten on. She was fairly sure he'd sweet-talked his way into her section.

"It's perfect, just posted about how lovely you all are," she said, then swiftly did so before he could ask for a picture. "Could I be annoying and ask for another bottle of Perrier? My skin just dries out so fast."

"Of course, Ms. Daniels." He was gone in an instant, and Delysia concentrated back on her cell.

There was the usual flood of comments from her latest posts; no time to reply to those, ever; there was always an intern to do that. Same with direct messages. Her work email was no less busy, but unlike her comments section, she had to look through these—she didn't trust anyone else to handle her business for her, not in today's age.

At the top of the pile was an email from her legal team; *that* should be interesting. Who was suing her now? Delysia pushed an armful of copper bracelets up to her elbow and opened the email, squinting through her mascaraed lashes. Words were jumping out at her, but in this champagne-soaked context they didn't really make sense. Something about…potential libel, and Southampton University? Out on Long Island somewhere? What?

She shook her head and logged off. This was why she

tried to unplug on long flights—God knew it was the only time she ever had where she wasn't documenting every moment for the world to see. If it weren't for the fact that she had to review the Wi-Fi on this flight, she'd never have checked her phone.

I'll call when I land, get details then. Delysia put away her phone, popped in her cordless headphones, and smiled sleepily as she snuggled deep into her nest of blankets to watch Audrey Hepburn lose her head over William Holden, while Humphrey Bogart's craggy face hovered in the background, just waiting for her to fall in love with.

However calculating she had to be on the ground, she could be as sentimental as she wanted to be here, shielded from the eyes of the world.

Chapter Two

When his phone rang in his office Thursday morning, Alexander was jolted out of a deep reverie. He tipped his coffee cup onto a library copy of *Dining Car Line to the Pacific*, swore eloquently, fumbled for the slim device, and held it to his ear. "Hello?" he said, leaping to his feet to intercept the coffee stream with the handkerchief in his inner pocket. The book managed to escape with only the tip of a corner wet.

"Alexander Abbott-Hill, please!" The person on the other end sounded as if she were at a party of some sort; he could hear voices in the background, pop music, clinking of glass.

"Speaking." Alexander fought back some irritation, mopping away at his desk. Why did people insist on making calls in the noisiest places? "How can I help you, please?"

"My name is Faye. I represent Delysia Daniels?" He heard the muffled sound of a door being shut. Then, blessedly, it grew more quiet. Not completely quiet, but enough. "I understand we have a bit of an issue with how you're being represented on her social media?" She had a high-pitched voice that rivaled Dean McDermott's secretary and possessed that annoying habit of speaking in questions.

"Represented?" He was dumbfounded. "I have no idea who she is, Ms.… Faye? I was tagged incorrectly on her account and need her to clarify the error. It's beginning to affect my reputation."

Faye exhaled. "Yes, I am aware that you are an academic of some standing in the community? Delysia is *quite* sorry? She thought you were someone else, and these handles can be so similar sometimes, no? When the two of you meet, I'm sure you can work things out? And—"

"I'm sorry?"

"Yes, that's what I'm calling to set up, dear? Delysia is free tomorrow night, miraculously—not till eight, but it is a Friday, and I'd want to straighten this out as fast as possible if I were you, yes? Reputation, and all that? I'll send you the details? Via email? And confirm by text message? Can DM if you want? No? Well, Delysia will be expecting you tomorrow? And really, we are *both* so sorry."

She hung up, leaving Alexander staring at his phone with what he was sure was an idiotic expression. He managed to haul his jaw up and stood to go home. His nerves were officially shot for the night; he wouldn't be able to get a bit of work done. He was barely out of the car when he received a text message—an eight PM calendar request for a meeting at a place called the SoHo Lounge. He looked at the address and groaned. Lower Manhattan, close to Little Italy. He hated going into the city, especially on a weekend.

"Ten thousand followers!" Natalia exploded as soon as Alexander walked into his office.

He looked at her askance.

"Oh, I follow you on social media *now*," Natalia said with absolutely no embarrassment. "Now that it's actually worth it."

Alexander groaned and went to his desk chair. "It's incredibly embarrassing. The dean knows about it. My students know about it, and they think it's me in that photo."

"Yeah, well, anyone who knows you…" She trailed off. "I mean, I knew it was a fake the minute I saw it."

He ignored that. "And this…lady, who owns the account, she wants to meet me tomorrow so we can talk about some kind of retraction—"

"Wait, you're meeting Delysia *Daniels*? In person?" Natalia's eyes widened. "When? Where?"

"Goodness, tomorrow evening, and in SoHo of all places. Somewhere called—" He had to pull out his phone in order to check. "The SoHo Lounge?"

Natalia's slack-jawed expression showed that yes, indeed, she'd heard of it. "It's members only," she said, and her voice was faint. "She's getting you in on *her* account."

Okay? Alexander didn't even bother hiding his eyeroll. "The whole lot of them are insufferable. Her publicist is one of the silliest women I've ever spoken to, and that photo—"

Natalia's expression rearranged itself into a slightly sharky smile. "I'll reiterate. I knew there was no way it was you. That guy was *hot*."

"You're not helping," Alexander said, and irritably. "Do I have any messages?"

"Two people called, asking about that train project of yours. Some European company that specializes in designer storage systems, and someone from Amtrak."

"Amtrak?" That did pique his interest, and quickly.

"Yes! Looks like your account got some traffic from the whole Delysia thing, and I guess people saw your train restoration project and thought it was a thing you've got actual money for. Here—" Natalia passed him a note-pad with two names and numbers on them.

"Thank you." He'd have to call them later. Amtrak? He felt his interest grow despite himself; this was the first good news of the day.

"Do you want to see?" Natalia twisted round. She logged in and navigated deftly to Alexander's page. @shhistorian had gone from having about eight hundred followers to having over ten thousand.

"Goodness," Alexander said blandly.

"You're getting a ton of exposure." She clicked here, there, pointing as she went. "People are engaging with your content, you know. Even all the boring historical stuff."

"I'll ignore that." Alexander resolved mentally to be as firm as possible with the young woman he was meet-ing tomorrow. "It will be over soon."

"What are you wearing?"

"I'm sorry, what?"

"To the SoHo Lounge!"

"My work clothes, I'll be coming from the univer-sity," Alexander said. The entire conversation was grow-ing increasingly irritating. "Why, is there a dress code for the place?"

"No, not really, but…"

"Then I'll be wearing work clothes."

Natalia opened her mouth and closed it, then opened it again and closed it. She cleared her throat before speak-ing again. "Should I arrange a car? Can you *find* SoHo?"

"Don't push it, Natalia."

* * *

By the time Alexander bid a tired Natalia good night and left campus, dusk was falling and the chill that would soon take over days as well as nights had crept in, wrapping Southampton in a smoky blanket of crisp autumn air. He could see a hint of his breath as he got off the train, and dug through his messenger bag for a well-worn pair of work gloves.

His ancient white Jaguar, a gift from his late father at his first graduation, was parked in the lot, but Alexander wouldn't be driving home for at least an hour—he had his train to attend to.

Well, not an *entire* train, he corrected himself mentally. When people asked Alexander if he had any hobbies, a short "train study and collecting" was usually sufficient to make them lose interest. People, he knew, immediately pictured him going home to a wood-paneled den to play with replicas, and perhaps paint them or build them by hand. The reality was that he did restoration.

The Abbott-Hill family train had long since been lost to creditors or sold off in pieces over the years. What was left in storage at the Southampton yard were two cars, the family lounge car and a sleeper. Since his father's death Alexander had been restoring them on and off. He unlocked and entered the sleeper, switching on the lantern he kept inside for the purpose.

Soft light illuminated the interior, revealing the part of the car he was working on; a series of cushioned seats built into one wall and facing two enormous windows which were now of course boarded up. They were upholstered in blue brocade nested in fine walnut wood. Alexander had finally located material that matched it in a little fabric shop in Boston and was working on it now. His tools were already here: bundles of stuffing, the crooked upholsterers needle, a seam ripper, scissors. He sat cross-legged on the floor and began to work.

Calm relaxed his shoulders, smoothed out the lines in his forehead. This was exactly what he needed after his hellish day. He took a deep breath that smelled of wood polish and dust and knelt to get to work.

He wasn't sure exactly what drew him to this kind of work. He'd hated it when he was younger. His father had spent almost every waking moment on the restoration, ignoring the fact that he'd never have any reason to use an actual train. But when he died…well, Alexander found himself coming back. Why, he still wasn't sure.

Well, you're not really good for anything else, are you? Even as a little boy, Alexander could not remember wanting to do anything else but teach. *You're turning into your father.* And a rather inferior version, if his evaluations were anything to go by. At home precariously close to the weekend, no dates, no friends over, no plans except to reupholster a vintage window seat. There was nothing wrong with that, he countered mentally. If nothing else, he deserved some peace in his life.

And anyway, tomorrow he'd have to be at that *place*. The SoHo Lounge. He shuddered a little.

Chapter Three

Friday evening found Delysia on her usual rounds. The weekends were her busiest. New York City never slept, and Friday to Sunday was when it was fairly pulsing, throbbing with a life that overtook the other four days combined. Weekends were for partying hard, meeting out-of-town contacts and most importantly, growing her texting, posting, virtual army of acolytes.

The social scene in New York was responsible for her success, and she took her engagement with her thousands of followers as seriously as her contemporaries took their nine-to-fives. Her diary resembled a carefully planned military campaign: names, dates, addresses, locations and times were all plotted out with scientific efficiency. Faye was possibly the best investment she'd ever made once she committed to being a social media socialite years ago.

Delysia's meeting with—what was his name again?—was low on her list of priorities for the evening. She knew that Faye had a proposal for the two of them, and she planned to glance over it in line, or in the car, or when she was using the ladies', or whatever. She had bigger things on her mind. Fellow influencer-slash-rival Eden Kim and her twin brother, Nicky, were celebrating their birthdays that very night in a converted opera house in Hell's Kitchen. Rumor had it that the girl had managed to swing Cirque du Soleil to perform.

Delysia had also dated Nicky a few years ago but she didn't want to dwell on *that* at the moment.

Maybe I should take this guy with me. Delysia needed to arrive with just enough of a splash to be conspicuous without being an obnoxious scene-stealer, and being seen at the SoHo Lounge beforehand with the guy all her followers were speculating about was just the thing to do it. She'd arrive late, she thought, and *just* tousled enough…

If she really thought, deeply and truly, about how shallow and silly it all sounded, Delysia might have hated herself.

In fact, the young woman who'd come to New York from Dubai six years ago to attend medical school probably would have scoffed at all this, and despised her for it. She'd long since managed to push those thoughts to the back of her mind, though. She'd be more than willing to have a few nobodies think her an idiot if her future was secure. She could study at any age; *this* she couldn't do forever. And her critics would never pay her bills, would they?

She glanced at her ever-present phone. Eight-ten. The evening would begin with a photo shoot in the new Cadillac XT6, rendered in her favorite shade, deep purple. She was supposed to meet with the professor at eight, but the car hadn't even arrived yet, and the darned photo shoot would be sure to take longer than expected. Oh, well, he'd have a drink and enjoy the scenery—it was the SoHo Lounge, after all.

She glanced at herself in the mirror to reassure herself that yes, she did look as good as she thought she did. She wore a tailored suit of silver brocade, embroidered with flowers of the same hue as the luxury SUV on loan tonight. She wore her shoulder-length curls loose and wild, gleaming with the designer hair products she'd been gifted days before from a celebrity stylist who worked out of L.A. Shoot. She needed to post about that…

She wrapped up her extensive makeup job with a swipe of violet lip gloss and held her phone up to her face. "Hey, everyone," she said brightly, "just about to head out—going to be driving a Cadillac for the first time! I'm ridiculously excited." She ran her fingers through her hair, dimpling at the camera. "Bjorn Handel Hair has got me covered for the ride—my hair's been so ridiculously frizzy lately. I'm committed to laying down that flatiron for at least a couple weeks, though. I'll post what products I used—maybe a tutorial video? Tell me what you think, okay? See you out there!" She blew a kiss, posted, and yes—that was the rep from Cadillac calling her. She slung her thoroughly impractical Versace mini-purse over her shoulder and clattered down the stairs.

The goon they'd sent to guard the Caddy was there, arms crossed, looking decidedly bored—this was probably on par for a Friday night for him. "Hi, how are you?" she greeted cheerily.

He opened the driver's door. "License?"

Well, okay. Not even a word about being forty-five minutes late. She handed it over, although she knew he had her paperwork already; Porsche had practically run a federal-level background check before offering her the sponsorship.

He squinted at it suspiciously then at her. "This doesn't look like you."

"Well, it was six years ago." And pre-expensive hair products, makeup, and a serious skin routine.

He grunted and gestured that she step in, then gave her a terse overview of the vehicle's functions. "No funny business and no speeding," he snapped, and climbed into the back seat. "You'll drive up till the next block, record whatever you need to, and then I'm taking over."

That hadn't been the agreement with Porsche at all, but whatever. She nodded and began to set up the portable tripod that came everywhere with her. It folded just enough to fit in her purse.

"What's that?" he barked.

"It's a tripod. I need to record myself pulling out, and addressing my—" God, *fans* sounded obnoxious, especially with the way the guy was looking at her. Who the hell did he think he was anyway? "Audience."

"No equipment, miss. I can do it for you."

Seething, Delysia pre-set it, then handed it to him. She recorded a brief but cheery message asking her fans to meet her at SoHo Lounge, then pulled out. She and the driver switched as planned, and Delysia had time to play with filters and write a perky message even though she felt anything but. Her driver eyed her through the rearview mirror, but said nothing.

Ten minutes into the ride he made a call, speaking through a tiny headpiece tucked in his ear; Delysia's ears perked up. Was that Tigrinya? Yes, it was! How funny. She usually ran across a lot of other Eritreans in DC, but almost never in New York. It took some work to understand him—his Tigrinya was peppered with slang that was definitely *not* a part of her conservative mother's vocabulary, but she got the gist of it.

"...driving a celebrity? Hardly. I've never heard of

her," the man was saying to his companion. He paused, then he laughed. "One of those girls that spend all their time showing their breasts online or whatever. Never puts their phone down. Yeah, I know...doesn't take any sort of talent anymore. This one's not even pretty. One baby and she'll go fat..."

Color rushed up to Delysia's face, clashing, she was sure, with both the suit and the Cadillac. She felt frozen in her seat. She'd heard criticism of social media influencers before, both in print and in person; this was hardly the first time. Still, to hear it coming from a stranger's mouth and in her mother's language...

He went on, giving a very colorful description of her breasts, her ass, the way she walked, what he'd caught a glimpse of when she bent over to get in the car, and her general demeanor to his companion while Delysia's face grew hotter and hotter. She wedged herself into a corner of the vehicle, biting her lower lip till she tasted blood.

Are you an idiot, girl? Record! She pressed the red button with trembling fingers. She should expose the asshole to her followers to get him *fired* at least, if nothing else, and possibly curse him out in kind when they arrived. But this—*this*...

Anyone who listened to this and understood Tigrinya would know exactly what vile things he was calling her. It didn't sound quite as bad translated to English. And the trouble was, she wasn't quite sure her mother wouldn't agree with him.

Forget him, she told herself. *You have a job to do.* She stuck her ear-pods in her ears, downloaded the proposal that Faye had forwarded for her and the professor she was meeting, and forced herself to read. Being hurt wouldn't pay her bills. Still, her skin felt hot, and she was fighting back tears. She didn't retain a word of what she read.

When they finally reached the SoHo Lounge, Delysia couldn't look the driver in the eye. She completely forgot about posing with the Cadillac, about taking pictures. When he handed her her bag and his fingers closed round the key ring, she looked up and met his eyes. The revulsion she felt took her breath away.

"Thank you for a very pleasant ride," she said in Tigrinya.

His face contorted in shock. "But—"

"Never assume you know who is listening," she spat out.

"What kind of Eritrean girl is named Delysia Daniels?"

Delysia ignored this and turned and walked up the sidewalk as fast as she could. A line of stragglers were hanging out in the front of the lounge, hoping to be invited in by someone on the list.

"Is that—?"

"Delysia Daniels?"

"Delysia! Hey, girl!"

Delysia's face flattened out into a sweet, slightly shy smile that had long since become automatic in public, then lifted a manicured hand to wave. No matter that it still trembled slightly. Her phone vibrated in her inner pocket; she reached into her jacket and pulled it out, picked it up.

"Delysia!" Faye, and as unceremonious as usual. "Are you there yet?"

"Just got here."

The woman let out an outraged squawk. "It's eight forty-five!"

"I know, Faye. Cadillac was late. Long story."

"Are you aware I asked you to be there at eight and he's likely been stuck outside, waiting for you?"

Delysia was aware. In fact, yesterday, in her wine-soaked state, the thought of leaving a geeky, bespectacled professor in a line of clubbers, shivering indignantly into his tweeds or whatever, had seemed a little funny. Now she felt none of that amusement; she just felt tired. "Oh. I guess I forgot."

"You can't afford to forget this guy, Delly. He's furious and probably well within his rights to sue." Delysia could hear the rush of a subway train; her frugal manager avoided taxis. "I'm on my way, myself."

"Well, has he called you looking for me?"

"No! Is he outside?"

Delysia scanned the throng outside the door, but none of the swankily dressed folks in line fit the description of him she'd made up in her head. "I don't think so."

Faye groaned. "He's left, then. Ask the doorman and get your butt in there, and prepare to grovel." She hung up without any further ceremony.

Delysia tucked her phone in her bag and tripped up to the doorman. "Hey, Will?"

He nodded at her over his clipboard.

"I'm meeting a guy here tonight. Alexander Hill? Dr. Alexander Hill?"

To her surprise Will nodded. "*Abbott*-Hill," he corrected, "and yes, ma'am. He arrived about an hour ago. Christian took him up to the Sky Bar."

"The Sky…" Delysia was truly dumbfounded. The Sky Bar? After four years she still hadn't gotten the clearance to go up there; it was as VIP as it could get. "What the—? Is he a member here?"

"He's an Abbott-Hill, ma'am." Will lifted a bushy eyebrow. "One of *the* Abbott-Hills? That Long Island family? The one that makes our farm-to-table house wine?"

"Is he a *member*, though?" Delysia was frankly confused. She'd heard of the Abbott-Hills, of course. Aside from the high-priced wine, there was one who was a socialite—a real one, not a social media one—and a couple who were, perhaps, in politics? They were important in a vague, dynastic, name-on-buildings sort of way. Faye knew more, anyway. *And you should, too.* She mentally cursed the Cadillac driver. She'd have been all caught up if he hadn't distracted her.

"He doesn't need to be a member, miss," Will said in disbelief. "He's an *Abbott-Hill*."

"But the *Sky* Bar?"

"Well, Christian wasn't going to leave him in the actual *bar*. That guy could probably buy this club and everything in it."

"You're exaggerating."

"Here—" And Will typed something into his tablet, then nodded. "Had to put you in the notes. They wouldn't let you in otherwise. Have a nice night, miss."

Flabbergasted, Delysia straightened her clothes, sent Faye a text telling her where she was going, and headed for the large glass elevators on the far end of the lounge. The SoHo Lounge featured a restaurant, a club, a lounge, and three indoor pools, all scattered strategically between swanky residences that hadn't had an opening to the general public since 1982.

The Sky Bar was the jewel in the tower. It was roofed in glass and had floor-to-ceiling windows that gave one the feeling of being a bird perched atop a skyscraper. A lush indoor garden combined with old-world-style seating that could have easily come from an English manor completed the eclectic look. The Sky Bar wasn't a bar at all, not in the traditional sense. It was made for leisurely meals and quiet reflection, a place where the truly rich and famous could drop their armor and be themselves. Influencers like her didn't have a prayer of getting into a place like that, ever, but because of Alexander Abbott-Hill…

"Here, Ms. Daniels," said the attendant. The ride up had been so smooth she'd barely noticed when the elevator stopped. "Please keep in mind that photographs are not allowed on this floor."

Fighting back a blush, she nodded.

"You're at the center table, middle of the palm trees. Your party has already arrived."

"Thank you." All she could see from this distance was a brown blazer hugging reasonably broad shoulders, and a full head of very dark hair. He was talking animatedly to a middle-aged man in a blue suit; they shook hands, and the older gentleman walked away. Delysia squared her slim shoulders and headed over.

"Dr. Abbott-Hill?" she asked.

When he saw her he rose to his feet in a single gesture, offering her a welcoming nod. Up close she registered dark hair, almost black, as tightly curled as her own. Looks-wise he could have been any of the guys she'd grown up with in her community back in Dubai, and that sort of startled her; she'd been expecting a nerdy-looking hipster. His calm eyes held an unpredictable mix of browns, both light and dark, his lashes were just on the side of long, and his full mouth was compressed. He looked as if he possessed very little humor. His crisp white shirt, covered by a dilapidated tweed blazer, was pretty academic, as well. He was precisely the type of professor one dealt with exasperatedly during the semester but had naughty thoughts about in drunken, idle weekend hours.

"I hope you haven't been waiting too long?"

"I have, actually. About an hour." Oh boy, he was annoyed. Great. Out of the corner of her eye, she saw Faye emerge from the elevator, looking as if she'd been struck by lightning. She managed to run smack into the man that Alexander had been speaking to, who apologized profusely before heading into the lift.

Faye made it over by that time, out of breath. Her cropped blond hair looked as if she'd been through a gale of wind and one of her jacket lapels was standing up as if in salute. "Was that Senator Abbott-Hill?" she puffed.

Alexander's brow creased. "Why, yes, he's my cousin. Do sit down," he added, and pulled out a chair for Faye. "You must be…"

Senator Abbott-Hill, mouthed Faye to Delysia, then sat and shot Alexander her sweetest smile. "I'm Faye. And this is Delysia Daniels," she purred, as if she were offering up the best jewel in her harem. Delysia, to her irritation, felt color creeping up in her cheeks. Alexander looked polite, but it was clear he didn't care who she was. Sort of like that driver. All of a sudden, she felt tired; all she wanted to do was go home, soak in a hot bath, and turn her phone off, for once.

"Did you read the proposal, Delysia?" Faye asked, shaking out her napkin and placing it on her lap.

"I—no. Kind of."

"Do it now, if you don't mind, and then we can discuss. In the meantime—Alexander," Faye said, and shot a sweet smile in his direction. "Do tell me about the senator…"

* * *

By the time their entrees arrived, Alexander had a headache.

Faye had not shut up and her voice was no less grating in person. Delysia was quiet and kept her eyes firmly on the mackerel *rillette* on her plate. This muteness was so far off from her online persona that he was intrigued despite his irritation. Any direct attempts to draw her out were met with one-word answers. Perhaps she wasn't feeling well.

"We wanted to apologize," Faye finally said after the wine had been poured. She'd had a bottle of his family brand ordered for the table ahead of time, much to his embarrassment. "Apologize in person, that is. It's so difficult to keep track of these things, especially when you're posting at the speed of light!" Faye's laugh trilled so high it turned heads.

"While that's nice to know," Alexander said, his face still like stone, "I would appreciate a retraction, or some sort of statement saying that…person wasn't me. I'm sure you meant no harm," he added, "but my academic community is fairly conservative, and this is casting me in a certain light."

To his surprise Delysia colored and looked up, making eye contact with him for the first time that evening. They were large and liquid-dark, and he was struck by the guardedness in them. "What sort of light?" she asked quickly.

"It's attention I would prefer not to have," Alexander said after a moment of consideration.

Faye seemed all too glad to jump in. "It's attention, though! And publicity. You *have* gained a total of ten thousand followers in less than forty-eight hours. You can't buy that sort of publicity."

"Publicity for what? I'm in *academia*, Faye. And my students have trouble enough paying attention without thinking I'm draping myself half-naked on the internet just for a laugh. My supervisor complained. It is essential we get this out of the way."

"Alex—may I call you Alex?"

"I prefer Alexander."

"Well, *Alexander*—"

"Faye, he's not going to want to do it. Just leave it alone," Delysia cut in. She was staring down at her mackerel again, and suddenly Alexander felt sorry for her. Fine lines around her full mouth said otherwise, but she suddenly looked very young to him, like the latte-toting girls who traipsed into his class every day.

"Doesn't want to do what?" Alexander asked, and both women fell quiet.

"Faye drew up a…proposal of sorts, like she said earlier," Delysia said. Her voice was so quiet now that he had to strain to hear her. "That's why we asked you to dinner. And frankly, I'm wondering if it's even a good—"

"She's wondering," Faye cut in, "if I should even be here." Her eyes had been darting back and forth between them, and now they narrowed as if she had just realized something. She stood and gathered her phone, her large handbag, and a stack of file folders. "You know, I'm just going to leave you two alone and let Delysia tell you all about it. Keep an open mind," she added, and in a flurry of gusto and perfume, she was gone.

Alexander let out a breath. "Is she always like that?"

"Worse," Delysia said, and dryly. She nervously tapped her fingertips on the tabletop, then reached for her wineglass and took a long sip. Alexander said nothing;

he was never one to mind long silences, but it seemed to agitate his dinner partner.

"Faye saw the potential for a profitable partnership for both of us because of my mistake," Delysia finally said. "I'll explain because I promised I would, but please— I'll give you your retraction, whatever you want. I just want this to go away."

"Very well," Alexander said, slowly. "I'm listening."

"You're a historian, right? Of American travel?"

"I am."

"Well—" She sighed and apparently decided to take the plunge. "If we did it, I'd need your help. And your train." She bit her lip. "I also feel kind of stupid."

"Why?"

"Faye was going on and on about how important—" There was a faint flush on her cheeks. Quite becoming, he thought a little distractedly. "I didn't realize how closely you were connected with the Abbott-Hills. I've heard of them, of course, but you looked—" And here, she paused. "You look really normal."

Oh. Alexander shifted in his chair. "Ah. Yes. Well. I'm only a poor relation," he explained, "and a distant one at that." Not that it made much of a difference within the Southampton community. An entire wing of the library was named after his father, for God's sake, and every faculty member who'd been there more than thirty years had seen Alexander in short pants and a Tigger T-shirt, at some point.

Come to think of it, he rather liked that Delysia Daniels had no idea who he was.

She was staring at him, still, then looked back at her phone, then back up at him. "It all makes sense now," she muttered.

"What makes sense?"

"Faye's proposal. Our proposal. Oh, let me just read the damn thing out loud to you."

"Haven't you reviewed this yourself?"

"Barely. I was busy on the way over here. Long story." She took a deep breath, then spoke rapidly, reading off her phone.

In exchange for the appearance of a fling with a member of one of the first families on the East Coast, she said, she would market his sole passion and investment—luxury train travel—in a way that could potentially reach thousands of the young, beautiful, and rich. Plus…

"Amtrak reached out to me. Well, Faye. They want me—us—to design a four-city Northeast rail trip through Boston, New York City, Philadelphia, and DC that will stop for night and day excursions in the hottest spots along the way."

"They called me, too, although I haven't had time to get back to them," Alexander remembered. "How would that work?"

"Well, I've got the sponsors already, or I will. I'd just need the help from you in planning. The trip has got to be as luxurious as we can make it, and include all of those elements you're always talking about on your account page. Like, a vintage sort of thing. Think a luxury cruise, but by rail."

"Vintage," he repeated. He couldn't keep the skepticism from bleeding into his voice, and Delysia sat up in her chair.

"Say what you will, but there's a historical precedent for this—I've seen it on your page!" she burst out.

"Well…" He knew that at least was true.

"I know you think it's a stupid idea. That's why I

didn't want to mention it," she said, and those twin circles of red were back in her cheeks. "If I'd read it carefully before this, I'd never had dragged you out here. Listen—"

She took a deep breath, and the words came pouring out.

"People do this because they want an escape, Dr. Abbott-Hill," she said. "They go on my page and they see this incredibly curated form of my life. It's all filtered, and beautifully lit, and it's therapeutic in and of itself. When I was younger I'd spend hours following the lives of stars and people that looked so incredibly gorgeous to me. It felt good, because what was around me—wasn't."

They were silent for a moment, and Delysia continued, a new softness in her face. "Everyone wants to be recognized, and everyone wants to be important, right? Being an influencer sort of validates your existence and your choices." She slowed down. "This trip will be so beautiful, so luxurious it'll be like stepping back in time. Think of picking up a novel and reading it and allowing yourself to get lost in all the details—the food, the music, the glamour."

Alexander was surprised to find himself holding his breath. Her husky voice, as well as those large, arresting eyes in that lovely face, had captivated him despite himself. He caught himself after a moment of staring. Troubled, he picked up his water glass.

"You should lecture my students," he said dryly, and took a sip of water. He cleared his throat, trying to regain his composure.

Delysia smiled, and there it was—the spark that he knew had captured the internet. "I know I have to appeal to the academic side," she said. "So you could also think of it as a way to educate, too? I mean, how much of an audience does your work get outside of folks who are already looking for information on the subject?"

"Not much," Alexander admitted.

"I'm not saying there suddenly would be an influx of undergraduates who want to study railway history, but…"

"Heaven forbid." He allowed himself a smile. "Then I'd have to teach them."

"It'd be a way to finish that train you're renovating," Delysia pointed out. "And use it. We'd get financing for all that. Plus, I don't know if you're tenured already, but this can't hurt with that either."

"You seem to know quite a bit about the academic process."

"I dropped out of medical school to pursue internet entrepreneurship full-time." Alexander's eyebrows climbed, but she shook her head as if to put an end to that line of conversation. "Anyway, that's just my ten cents," she said. "I don't think you'd be interested in the idea and I'd have told Faye that if I'd read it carefully. However…" Her voice trailed off. "I really *am* sorry I tagged you in that photo."

"That's all right," Alexander said. His head was still spinning as he processed everything that Delysia had just told him. "It's not a bad idea," he admitted. "In fact, some folks would consider it an opportunity. And I'm not talking about influencers, I'm talking about folks in my field. I'm just concerned about one thing…"

She lifted her brows and her wineglass.

"This photo… They think we're together, and that's not exactly true, is it? In fact, I would seriously doubt the veracity, or the possibility, of such a young lady as yourself dating a stodgy old professor like me."

"There's no way you actually believe that," Delysia said dryly, and he fought back a grin.

"Perhaps not, but it's a modest thing to say."

"Modesty doesn't exist in my line of business."

He saw her visibly hesitate and was quick to jump in. "Oh, please just say it. I think we're at the point where we can speak candidly."

"Well," Delysia said, drawing out her words, "my take on it? Say nothing, and let the images speak for themselves."

"Images?"

"Images. Photographs of us talking, and planning, and spending time together, and perhaps if we grow comfortable enough, sometimes spent in close quarters, little moments of intimacy. People will take the smallest image and run away with it. Their imagination will transform it into something tailor-made for them. And honestly, what makes something like this the most enchanting isn't the setting, or the food, or the wine. It's the potential for romance. And if we give them that backdrop, well, anything is possible."

There was something about the soft musicality of her voice that drew Alexander in despite himself, although the speed with which she'd come up with that answer made him wonder if she'd done this before, and exactly how cynical this life might make a girl like her. The lighting was low in the Sky Bar at this hour, and it felt enshrined in a soft, warm cocoon of intimacy. Alexander felt strangely lulled by her company. He had arrived incredibly agitated, but now he felt content enough to sit back and survey his dining companion, and carefully, from the top of her curly head to her small high-heeled shoes. She gave him that odd shy smile and lifted her wineglass.

"I must compliment you on your family's wine, by the way," she said, and he laughed, reached out, and took it from her. Their fingers connected with a friction of warmth and he lifted the glass to his own lips and took a long sip.

He tilted his head, considering. "I think…2011, it tastes like."

"Very good!"

"It was a good year." For wine, anyway. It had also been the year his father had died.

When Alexander passed her the glass back, she was staring at him with a mixture of surprise and amusement. "So is that a yes?" she asked.

"Well, I'm not so sure," Alexander said. "But I do know that you're a lot more convincing than that publicist of yours."

Delysia laughed out loud. "Faye is a good one to have in your corner once you get used to her. And whether or not you tell me yes, you've already caused a stir tonight. At least ten people in this room just took note of the Abbott-Hill family heir drinking wine out of my glass. And they'll see us leave together," she added. "If that is, in fact, your plan."

"It's rather late," Alexander said.

"I'm headed to a birthday party after this. Perhaps you'd like to join me? Think of it as a test. If you enjoy tonight, maybe we can negotiate. If not, I'll post a retraction in the morning."

Alexander was more surprised than she was at his

next words. "That sounds reasonable. Let me take care of the check and we can be on our way."

"Faye would kill me for that." Delysia smiled. "Don't worry, this is all part of my business expenses."

"Fair enough," said Alexander. "Let's head out."

Despite the fact that he was still a stranger to her, Delysia was oddly grateful for Alexander's steadying hand, hovering just at the small of her back without actually touching her. The wine she drank at dinner had been both heavy and sweet, and she felt a little light-headed. *I'm tired*, she realized with an inward sigh. She wasn't even sure where the rigmarole she had told Alexander that evening came from, but there was something about his gentle sternness that seemed to bring it out. Most of the time it was hard for her to believe her own nonsense, but something about him made her want to uncover something real about what she did, something palpable, something that she could say others would get out of it.

They rode down in the elevator in silence, Delysia sneaking peeks at his profile the entire time. When they reached the first floor of the SoHo Lounge, Delysia gestured at a side door she used more often than not. "We can get a car here," she said, mostly to fill the silence, "and head over to the party. It'll be fun."

"Very well," Alexander said. "Am I dressed appropriately? I have a graduate assistant who is horrified at the fact that I was coming to this place in my work clothes."

"You singlehandedly managed to get up into the Sky Bar just by showing up. I doubt that your clothes are going to matter anywhere in this city." And Alexander looked good. Quite good, although she wasn't going to open her mouth and say that. He was just tall enough to clear her head even in her heels, and broad-shouldered, narrow-hipped, with his trousers hanging low enough to showcase a flat torso.

Alexander looked like he wanted to ask her something, but they had already reached the glass doors discreetly placed at the end of the hall. Alexander pushed one open and motioned for Delysia to go through. The minute she did and he followed, a flash of light bulbs blinded them both.

He fumbled for his shades, but Delysia was less prepared. She stumbled on the landing and Alexander caught her quickly, wrapping an arm around her waist and drawing her instinctively close to him. It took only one dizzy moment for her to register lean muscle and the good, clean smells of brandy, laundered wool, and soap. It was disconcerting, at best.

Alexander had her up on her feet in a moment, and his palm came up to the side of her face, shielding her eyes.

"Faye did her work well," said Delysia, more than a little irritably. She rummaged through her pocketbook until she pulled out an enormous pair of sunglasses.

"Are you all right?" He was still holding her—not inappropriately, but closely enough to make something in her chest constrict. It had been a long time since a man had held her in a context outside of nightclub dancing. She lifted her eyes behind the shades; their faces were very close together. She could see little details now she hadn't seen before, like a tiny scar next to his mouth, a hint of what might be fading summer freckles on his cheeks, a subtle dent in his chin.

His hand not only shielded her eyes but created a strange sense of privacy, as if he created a partition from the madness going on in front of them. "Is this what you meant by images?" he said, and his voice was low, almost as much as hers had been earlier. There was laughter in it, but there was a serious note there, too, that made her stomach flip.

Delysia allowed her lips to curve up into a smile, one more mischievous than she had allowed to slide all evening. Suddenly she was feeling better, much more like herself.

"Let's see how well you can do, then," she breathed out, a little mockingly. "Dr. *Abbott*-Hill." She didn't know where the words had come from or what on *earth* must have been in that wine to get her to say them, but she took a step forward and leaned in, touching her forehead to his and lowering her lashes.

"Is this all right, Delysia?" she heard him murmur in that odd accent of his. It wasn't quite English, wasn't quite New York, an odd mix of both, but was strangely sexy. She pressed her thighs together and cleared her throat.

She nodded. She didn't trust her voice.

Delysia heard shouts and whooping, but it was all just background noise at the moment because she was being kissed, very sweetly, tenderly, deliberately. He kissed her as if they weren't virtual strangers who were basing this on some stupid deal. He kissed her as if they weren't standing in the doorway of the hottest spot in SoHo, and she was suddenly, violently, hungry for more.

It was probably a *terrible* idea to have kissed her like that, Alexander reflected, and sneaked a look at Delysia's profile for what seemed like the hundredth time that evening. The two of them were ensconced in the back seat of an SUV they practically needed a ladder to scale ("custom, elevated," Delysia had explained) and driving downtown at what he felt was an alarming rate, given that they were technically still within city limits.

He cleared his throat, then instantly regretted it as he actually had nothing to say. Delysia's silence was making him nervous.

She turned and focused on his face without actually meeting his eyes, and when crimson undertones deepened the smooth copper of her skin, he understood.

She's embarrassed.

Well, he could understand that, perhaps. He certainly hadn't intended to kiss her as deeply as he had, especially following his conversation with Dean McDermott the day before. However, when Delysia had whispered those words to him in that half-challenging, half-flirtatious tone—

Let's see how well you can do, then.

His body warmed at the memory. It had been a very long time since he'd kissed anyone, and when he had, it was after weeks of careful courtship, not in a moment of heated impulse.

Wayne will understand, he'd reasoned before kissing her, thinking momentarily of the prickly Dean of Students. After all, Delysia was supposed to be his girlfriend, yes? University policy could hardly keep him from engaging in displays of affection with his *partner* on social media...

That was the last thing he remembered thinking before kissing her, drawing her close. Now all that remained of the moment was the sweet, subtle scent of her clinging to his clothing and hands.

He opened his mouth to ask her if she had been offended by how enthusiastically he'd taken on his role, but stopped short when she leaned forward, pointing. "There it is."

Alexander wasn't quite sure what "it" was. He could see a couple of bodegas, a Laundromat, and the heavy facade of what looked to be one of the district's older factories, replete with scaffolding, boarded windows, peeling paint. "Are you sure—"

"Yeap," Delysia responded, and hopped out of her side of the car.

"Yes," Alexander corrected automatically, and took the opportunity to glance down at his watch.

"Excuse me?"

"Yes," he repeated. Delysia stared, then shook her head and began rifling in her bag. It was nearly ten thirty, and now that he was outside the car he could hear faint vibrations that hinted ominously at loud music and heaven forbid, dancing. He sighed inwardly, tried not to think of his comfortably saggy corduroy sofa, or the monitor he'd rigged to his laptop so he could stream one of the deliciously long historical documentaries he favored and veg to his heart's content. He ducked out of the car, watched longingly as it drove off.

When he turned back to Delysia, he caught her hiding a smile. "What?" he demanded.

"Nothing," she said, and gestured. "Shall we go?"

The doorman at this particular club had presumably never heard of the Abbott-Hills as the bouncer at the SoHo Lounge had. He gave Alexander and his tweed blazer a dubious look, then removed his sunglasses to peer down at Alexander's ID. Beside him Delysia bit her lip, then reached down and took his hand in one quick motion. He caught another whiff of her perfume as she tossed her curls back.

"He's with me," she said airily, and nudged him. Alexander took the wordless hint and wrapped an arm around her waist, drawing her close; he felt Delysia's warm body tense, then relax into his until there was no space left. He chose not to dwell on how well their bodies fit together, and resolved to keep his lips to himself for the rest of the night.

The inside of the building was like nothing he'd ever seen before—and with Delysia stopping every thirty seconds to greet some remarkably well-dressed person who *insisted* they take a photo, he had time to look around. The floor was raw, unfinished wood, splashed with paint in various colors; the walls were dark and gloomy, draped with chiffon in shades of gray and mauve. Chiffon also hung from floor to ceiling in strategic places, creating gauzy rooms for revelers to duck in and out of, and he could see shadowy figures engaged in all kinds of activity—drinking, dancing, and in some cases making out. His fingers tightened on Delysia's waist almost instinctively, and she did not pull away.

Instead, she drew closer, pulled out her phone and scrolled. When she found what she was looking for, she thrust her phone under his nose.

"The birthday girl tagged herself at the bar," she said low, into his ear. Although it was the quietest sound in the room it stood out to him more than a scream would have. "Let's go say hello, buy her a shot—then we can leave."

Alexander nodded; the lights and noise had him completely overwhelmed. The last outing he'd been on with even a hint of a party atmosphere had been his cousin's, a vineyard wedding out on Long Island. This was a Roman orgy in comparison.

His new companion—girlfriend, he could say, he supposed—gave him a shy half-smile, and they headed off in the direction of the bar. It became difficult not to gape—the party was absolutely bizarre. Servers covered from crown to toes in elaborate body paint circled round with canapés on heavy, Victorian silver trays.

Delysia stopped one and instructed Alexander to take a snap of it from above. "Your arms are longer." She paused for a moment, watched him take the tray, lift it up, and peer under it. "Whatever are you looking for?"

"A name!" called Alexander over the music.

"A name?"

"Yes, or a stamp, or a hallmark…" Feeling rather silly at his impulse, he handed the tray back to the server. "I thought it might be an antique," he said sheepishly.

Delysia stared for a full moment before her mouth began to twitch. "I can *guarantee* you they're from Party City."

"Oh, let's just move on," said Alexander, more than a little embarrassed. He spoke a little rapidly, to cover up his misstep. "I had no idea…"

She looked at him, lifting her brows quizzically.

"All this," Alexander said, gesturing a little weakly.

He paused to peer at the rafters. Most of the ceiling above their heads had been removed so attendees could look up to the second floor through a network of rusting steel beams. Contortionists hung from them, draped in silk and chiffon to match the hangings on the walls, folding their long arms, legs, and torsos into elegant shapes that changed each time the thrumming bass announced a new song. Soft gray-blue and white lighting, cutting through a veil of bluish smoke that smelled bewilderingly of burned sugar, completed the scene.

"Is this what it's like for you? All the time, I mean?" Alexander had come across influencers, of course, online. They invariably seemed to be young women with long hair and carefully painted-on faces shilling everything from weight-loss teas to holiday pajamas, and posting videos in which they danced side by side with what he assumed were popular celebrities, or teaching their adoring public how to draw on their eyebrows, or—whatever.

This was an entirely new experience. Delysia and her comrades seemed to have created a moving, teeming underground of excess, celebrating luxury in all its forms. He was as fascinated as he was out place; yes, he studied luxury for a living, but this was something he'd never encountered, not in fifteen years of scholarship.

Delysia was smiling another one of those tiny smiles that didn't reach her eyes. "Commitment is the first step to success, and we've committed. Our audience eats it up."

"Indeed." The sight of a macaw balanced delicately on a server's shoulder scattered Alexander's wits completely. How was this *hygienic*? Weren't there *laws*?

He started when Delysia placed a hand on his arm and leaned in again. "The Kims are a little ostentatious when it comes to parties," she said. "Are you claustrophobic at all? You look a little peaky."

He opened his mouth to tell her he didn't think himself claustrophobic until tonight, then shut it and shook his head instead. He couldn't compete with the noise.

A man on stilts with a diapered monkey on his shoulder and a tray of shot glasses alight with blue flame bent to offer them each one; Alexander shook his head vigorously, but Delysia took one, blew out the flame, and downed it almost thoughtfully. "Not bad."

"What is it?"

"It's a flaming blue ball," she said with a straight face, and laughed. "I should have taken a picture."

Alexander shuddered. He definitely could use a drink, but not a flaming—yeah. Definitely *not* one of those.

The bar took up a wall as long as a city block, and bartenders dressed as Gothic harlequins leaned over the polished glass countertop, taking orders and serving up drinks. Delysia squinted through her lashes before pointing at a throng of people clustering round a young woman seated atop a cornflower-blue chaise. A mime was topping up her champagne glass. She wore a glittery mini-dress and a tiara, of all things, her hair piled up high behind it. Curious, he squinted into the darkness. He'd done a bit of research on jewels some time ago, but he couldn't tell which…

"It's on loan from the Met," Delysia said.

"What is?" Alexander said, confused.

"Her tiara. See that guy over there?" She gestured at a large man, soberly dressed in a black turtleneck and charcoal slacks, arms crossed. "That's the visible bodyguard. There have to be at least three more, hidden in the crowd and flagging the exits. Eden took photographs with them earlier—do you follow her account? You should, it'll help you keep up with the party."

Alexander just stared at her; really, there were no words. Delysia laughed out loud, the gesture quite transforming her face. Then she set her jaw and liberated a second flaming blue ball from a passing server.

"I'm going to need this if we're going to get through tonight," she said grimly, and downed it. Alexander stared at her. Then, he reached over her shoulder, plucked his own, blew, and downed the shot.

It was his turn to laugh at Delysia's shocked face. He could not laugh too hard, though—he was already trying to keep from choking to death on his flaming blue ball.

Delysia felt just a *bit* more relaxed after Alexander downed that ridiculous drink in the most awkward way possible; it dissolved some unnamed thing, an uncomfortable tension that had hovered between them since their meeting at the SoHo Lounge. He had a sense of humor, however small it was, and it allowed her to meet his eyes for the first time since they'd left SoHo.

"Will you talk me through it, then?" he asked, after placing his shot glass down carefully on one of the trays he'd examined earlier and mouthing a *thank you* to the server. They'd fallen almost into a rhythmic way of moving, his hand resting on her lower back, steering her through the crowd with surprising skill. He'd stopped gawping within moments of their arrival—she suspected he was too well-mannered for that—and had graduated to nodding politely and offering a hand whenever she stopped to speak to somebody.

Now, determined to reach Eden and Nicky so she could exchange cheek kisses, make some small talk, and take a photo with them so she could go home, Delysia lifted her elbows and began power-walking through the crowd in earnest. They were so well fed, liquored up, and mellowed out from the smoke and strobe lights that they parted for her rather amicably.

When they reached the front of the little group of people surrounding Eden Kim, Delysia leaned on the bar, took a breath, and ordered a gin and tonic. She really didn't like the taste of gin, so she was counting on that to slow her down—the two blue balls she'd had in quick succession along with the wine she'd had at dinner weren't likely to make for the best life choices. She felt Alexander at her side, a quiet presence that she found oddly reassuring beside herself. She had her little entourage of fellow influencers and wannabes that she usually paired with for nights out like this one, but she hadn't called any of them for this…test drive of sorts with Alexander Abbott-Hill.

She took a tiny glance at him. Even in profile he looked calm, at peace, though completely out of place. She felt a sudden flash of envy at the ease with which he moved through her spaces. He probably had no idea how special that quiet self-assurance was in a world that was desperate to please, to maintain an aesthetic on which their livelihood depended.

"Can I get you anything?" she asked. He shook his dark head and placed a card on the counter; she reached out and handed it back. "No paying for drinks. I told you, business expense."

"Are you having fun?" he asked after a moment.

Delysia did look at him then. She could see a great deal of the top of his head from where she was perched on her high bar stool, and wondered in a wild, irrational moment what his hair must be like when it was unbridled, free, not-so-carefully brushed into place. Her fingers actually drifted down toward it, to her horror. She dropped them to her neck instead, fingering the pendant that nestled in the middle of her clavicle.

"I'm at work," she said finally, not sure how else to answer the question. She should be having a good time, but she wasn't, was she?

At that moment her drink arrived; she took a grateful sip and peered ahead of them. Only two other people stood in the makeshift line and they'd be able to greet Eden and she could go home, shower this bizarre evening off her…

"You came, Del?"

At the sound of a male voice that wasn't Alexander's, Delysia nearly stumbled off of her perch. She could feel her face contort in horror, and she very deliberately did not look in the direction the greeting was coming from before she spoke. "Hello, Nicky."

She could feel rather than see Alexander look first at her, and then at their new companion, Nicholas James Kim. Twin brother and second half of Eden's influencer empire—and in Delysia's case, virginity-taker and smasher of hearts.

It was impossible to see Nicky, to hear his voice, and not instantly become awash with a bombardment of images that came one after the other, rapid-fire, as if a film director of stupid mistakes had chosen to collate them in a movie trailer of the worst decisions she'd made romantically so far.

There was the party where she'd met him four years ago, when she was just starting out: he'd gotten her over the one-thousand-followers mark by leaving a comment on one of her blog posts. Fans of his assumed they were together, and like this ruse with Alexander, they'd done nothing to correct it—except in their case, Delysia had fallen for him, and she'd fallen fast.

There were months of lots of flirting and semi-dirty texting; a hand job in the back of a Hummer after a drunken night at a casino in Jersey; and finally, her sleeping with him for the first time and waking up, sore and uncomfortable, to him taking soft-filter selfies of them in bed.

There had been six more months of dating and the triumphant win of a joint endorsement with Supreme and Tony Hawk before it had all culminated in a tearful, ugly, humiliating meltdown at JFK when she'd accused him of harboring a girl in his apartment in Seoul. A fan had DM'd her an anonymous tip.

The truth had been worse than if he'd cheated on her. He had actually been in the process of hiring the K-pop star Kay Jay to take her place, cutting her out of the deal.

Words had been exchanged, nasty words. He'd changed his status to single, and posted a live video of himself at a Knicks game two hours later. They had finally agreed to somewhat of a truce a couple of years later after Kay Jay had gone to rehab, and repeated meetings at Instagrammable events in the city made it better for their brands to make up rather than remain archenemies. Nicky now treated her with the absentminded sort of kindness that enraged Delysia as much as it wounded her.

Other than that stupid, staged picture that had started this whole thing with Alexander in the first place, she hadn't had any male contact since then, and hadn't wanted it either.

Delysia usually managed a chilly cordiality, but tonight she was altogether too flustered to sound angry. Nicky capitalized on this and leaned in, pecking her softly on the mouth rather than the cheek-kisses that were more common for their set.

She could feel Alexander stiffen behind her, and she pulled back, cheeks hot.

"You've obviously already been at the Grey Goose,"

she said tartly. "Nicholas Kim, meet Alexander Abbott-Hill. He's my—"

"Badly dressed escort," Alexander said with the sort of dry humor that usually only worked in books, or in British theater. He extended a hand; Delysia watched as the two men shook, feeling rather as if she was in some sort of a terrible dream where time was slowing down. Nicky was tall, and bulky thanks to hours of CrossFit and a diet of Red Bull and protein shakes. She'd spent hours in the past tracing that muscle with her fingers and tongue; now she shrank from it.

Nicky looked at Delysia, then at Alexander, then back at Delysia, as if they were two halves of a particularly tricky equation he was keen to solve. "You're not—" he began, then stopped, probably because there was no way to say "an influencer" without sounding like a total idiot. "Haven't seen you before," he finally settled on.

"I would think not," Alexander agreed. "I teach history at Southampton."

"Ah!" Nicky raised his brows. "How did you two meet?"

Alexander opened his mouth to answer but Delysia cut in. "He's a member at the SoHo Lounge." They would have to make up a cover story later, but this would do for now.

She saw an interested gleam in Nicky's eye at the mention of the club; even *he* hadn't managed to nab a membership yet. "SoHo Lounge, huh? Abbott-*Hill,* did you say? You wouldn't happen to be related to—"

"Nicky is Eden's twin and they work at content creation together, Alexander," Delysia cut in, loudly. She slid off her barstool. If she was going to face Nicky Kim, she'd rather do it standing up.

"Happy birthday," Alexander said. "No tiara for you?"

Nicky's dark brown eyes narrowed as if he suspected he was being insulted. Then he smiled. "I leave the tiara-wearing to my sister. Eden!" he called over the heads of the people standing next to them. "Del's here, with her new boyfriend Alex—"

"Alexander," he corrected politely.

Nicky ignored him. Eden's eyes widened, and she waved them over.

"Oh, you sneaky girl—I didn't know you were coming until I saw your story post," she gushed effusively, scanning Alexander all the while and gauging his age, his status, and the net worth of his outfit. Her eyes fell on the frayed cuffs peeping out from his sleeves and they widened again. To distract her Delysia began a little gushing of her own.

"The tiara—which one was it, again? I cannot believe you managed to land this. Can I touch it, or will Kevin Costner over there tase me?"

"You'd better believe he will. I'm wearing a tracker, if you can believe it," Eden said, and held out her wrist. Among the usual assortment of bangles and tennis bracelets was a slim black band with a tiny red light. "They know what a desperate person I am, I guess. Not to be trusted."

The girls laughed insincerely; an awkward silence fell. Delysia cleared her throat and picked up her glass. "What kind of tiara is it? Are those pearls?"

"Conch shells," said Alexander and Eden at the same time, and all of them looked at Alexander, surprised.

He looked embarrassed for a moment, then cleared his throat. "I thought they were pearls at first." He had to yell to be heard over the music. "But they aren't."

"How the hell did you know that?" Eden demanded.

"Last year I wrote a paper on the history of luxury for the *Business Historians Quarterly* and focused on the Met's collection of jewelry," he said. "I got to know a few of the pieces very intimately. This one is actually on loan from the British Museum, so you've performed quite a coup. It's rumored to have belonged to Maria Carolina, Queen of Naples…" He trailed off as they continued to stare. "How in heaven's name did you manage to pull this off?" It was the first time that evening Alexander had shown any real enthusiasm. Delysia could see the awkwardness wearing off, see his eyes brightening.

"I'm working in collaboration with their education program. I chose it because I figured conch shells would be a good tie-in to my charity this evening," Eden said a little faintly.

"What charity is that?"

"Save the Whales. I just *loved* SeaWorld as a child."

"Did you?"

Was that sarcasm? Delysia would not, *could not* look at Alexander at that moment. She also didn't know whether to laugh or run screaming from the room.

"I see you've got the necklace too, and the earrings," Alexander said after a slight pause, and leaned in dangerously close to Eden's cleavage to examine the piece without touching it. "Seahorses, dolphins, mermaids, and scallop shells, all carved in. Master artist, really, and surprisingly clean provenance…" He stepped back. "Well done. Happy birthday. Delysia, have you got anything else to do, or are you ready to go?" He rounded up, turning away from Eden. Nicky's eyebrows had risen till they nearly disappeared into the coif at the front of his hair.

"No," Delysia gasped out, feeling a little short of air,

stifling a wild desire to laugh. "Maybe we could take a turn around the floor? Get some food?"

"Yes, you can't leave yet!" Eden found her voice in time to rally. "The show will start in ten minutes."

"Okay. Well, we'll better get to where we can see—" Delysia gabbled. She gripped Alexander's hand in hers, tugged hard, and bolted without looking back. She didn't stop until they were ensconced in the middle of the throbbing dance floor, where strobe lights were collecting in one blinding spotlight above their heads, where the trapeze artists would begin the show.

"Are you all right, Delysia?" came Alexander's voice out of the darkness.

"I'm fine," she said in a strangled voice that wasn't quite hers. She wasn't fine, of course; this was terrible, and she had to do something to calm herself down. Her arms, of their own volition, crept up around his neck. "Eden's watching. I'm going to kiss you," she announced, because she supposed he deserved some warning. The oddest look crossed his face, but he didn't protest. And she didn't even care to see if Eden was still watching, or if Nicky had followed them, before she stood on her toes and slanted her mouth against the soft, warm skin of his cheek. She could have kissed him on the mouth, as he had with her not two hours before, but she, quite frankly, chickened out.

You have officially lost your mind.

Chapter Four

Delysia woke the next morning with a stomachache and a pounding head brought on by too much wine, sushi, and the internal conviction that yes, she had been a very silly girl the night before. She'd finally shut her phone off at three AM to get some peace. When had her followers become so *nosy*? One hint, one whisper of her involvement with someone, and they'd all gone wild.

She sat up, caught a glimpse of her reflection in the mirror on the wall opposite her bed, and cringed. She was completely naked—her clothes lay in a heap at the foot of her bed—and she hadn't braided and wrapped her hair as usual the night before. It spurted in wild corkscrew curls in every direction. Mascara, lip gloss, and eyeliner were smeared all over her bone-white pillowcases and sheets; her linen duvet hadn't escaped the makeup assault either.

Delysia closed her eyes tight against a wave of regret-tinged nausea and tried to concentrate on the smell of the lavender that lingered in her linens. All she could see was the mental replay of a very tipsy evening.

She'd gone to Eden's party, all right. Alexander had gone with her, a bit of a misfit at her elbow, with his spurts of odd conversation, the opposite of a person that was in the know. No one knew who he was, but everyone knew who his family was. Eden had been no exception, and her attempts at flirting with Alexander—as well as the presence of Nicky, which had shaken her more than she thought possible—had brought out the worst in Delysia.

She'd kissed Alexander twice—oh Jesus, they'd kissed *twice*. Once on the cheek in a dark, secluded corner of the party, and that first time, of course, in the doorway of the SoHo Lounge, with an intensity that still made her tingle. All for show, she told herself. But in her horny, wine-addled state she'd been disappointed when his hands *didn't* wander…

Yes, she'd been *very* silly. She pressed her hands to her cheeks, remembering the look on his face when she'd planted the kiss on his cheek. Had he been expecting her to kiss him on the mouth, the way she'd dared him to earlier? Why, if this was strictly for business, had shyness paralyzed her, in front of the two people who would have been best at spreading the word?

The shrill, invasive sound of her landline ringing jolted her out of her trance. When she jumped she managed to tangle herself into her sheets, and fell completely on the floor with a thud.

Cursing, she managed to wriggle free from her blanket prison and headed over to the phone. "Hello?" she said.

"Good morning, is this Delysia?" The voice was familiar, male. Delysia was discomfited to feel her heartbeat increase, and her free hand crept down to cover her breasts (as much as possible, anyway). She didn't care how silly it was.

"Yes, it's me."

"I just wanted to check and see if you were all right," said Alexander mildly. "I've been outside for about forty-five minutes and Faye was kind enough to give me your landline. Perhaps your battery has died?"

Delysia swore, and loudly. She looked at the digital clock on the wall and swore again.

"Oh, dear," Alexander said. He sounded a little amused. "Do you need a little time?"

Shit, shit, shit, shit. Delysia vaguely remembered agreeing to meet with Alexander that morning to go over the details of the trip they were to plan, and hash out a rollout strategy for social media. However, that had been before most of the drinking, dancing, and snuggling that had taken place at Eden's party.

Alexander sounded as if they'd agreed to meet for bagels. She couldn't believe how blasé he was, to be honest.

"Alexander, I'm so sorry," Delysia said. "I'm afraid I overslept. Can you give me fifteen minutes?" It was on the tip of her tongue to invite him to come up, but she held back. She wasn't quite ready for that yet, and probably never would be.

"Of course," Alexander said. His voice held no traces of animosity. Delysia hung up the phone without saying anything more and scurried for the shower. It had been a long time since she had met someone *that* polite, male or female.

Delysia showered in record time, going over the details for the day in her head. She and Alexander were set to drive out to Long Island, at his suggestion: "…you can take a look at the Pullman cars I'm restoring, and then have lunch at mine. We will really be able to hash out some details in peace without dealing with the Starbucks crowd."

When she hesitated, he'd cleared his throat. "I'll invite Faye, if you want."

"No, no need," Delysia had said hurriedly. She trusted him, she guessed, but her stomach was still churning. His being a virtual stranger aside, Delysia was more than a little apprehensive at the thought of going with Alexander to what was sure to be some tony place out in the Hamptons, but Faye was enthusiastic. It would make some great fodder for social media. "You haven't been out to Long Island since that *Great Gatsby* fete last winter!" she'd said when Delysia called her to give her the address.

Delysia took a look at the outfit she had ready for that day. Before she'd met Alexander, this Saturday had been reserved for a boozy brunch in Brooklyn with a group of girls who worked for MAC Cosmetics. However, the distressed overalls, red-bottom stilettos, and Fair Isle tube top she'd planned seemed not quite right for a late morning out in Southampton with a history professor. A rummage produced a simple pair of jeans, brown riding boots she hadn't had a chance to wear yet, and a crisp blue button-up.

She twisted her wet curls up into a loose bun on top of her head and put on a swipe of clear lip gloss, grabbed the same Versace purse she'd had last night, and finally switched on her phone.

The notifications pouring in sounded like a tinny, electronic hailstorm. It was almost automatic; when her phone switched on, she had to transform from being a sleepy, hungover girl with regrets about the night before to a peppy online socialite whose face glowed with fun. She logged into her account and made a cheery comment about heading out to Southampton for the day, then took a makeup- and filter-free selfie.

It took about ten minutes to work through the stack of notifications, and another five to look over the correspondence that Faye had sent that morning. Alexander had been quick. He had already signed the proposal form that Delysia had left with him last night, along with making a few minor adjustments.

When she arrived outside, squinting into the morning sun, she spotted Alexander waving at her from the interior of a large white Jaguar parked at the curb. When she pulled open the door, she offered him what she hoped was a casual smile and slid into the front seat of the car. The interior smelled like it had been freshly detailed; it was pristine, and walnut paneling gleamed along the dashboard and doors. It looked very well taken care of, and very expensive.

"This was my father's," Alexander said as if he'd read her mind. "I lusted after it for years, and when I finally got my doctorate he relented and passed it on. It was the last gift he gave me before he died."

"It's quite a gift." Delysia reached out to touch the dashboard with slim, purple polished fingers. She still couldn't quite look at Alexander, but he seemed perfectly at ease, not bothered at all by the fact that they'd kissed the night before. Perhaps she shouldn't be bothered either. "I'm sorry I was late."

"It's fine, we have the full day." He looked over at her and offered that slight, guarded smile of his. "No paparazzi this morning?"

"There *never* is any paparazzi," she said, fighting a blush. Then she laughed. "I'm not a real celebrity. They don't come unless Faye calls and pays them. Last night was as set up as setup gets."

"Everyone seemed to know who you were, though. Both at the door and at the party."

"Well, social media—it's a new type of celebrity." She felt a little bit uncomfortable dissecting her livelihood with Alexander. "I think the sociologists at Southampton University might have a better idea of how to describe my work. I honestly don't always understand it myself."

"Fair enough." Alexander navigated into midmorning traffic with ease. He wore a cotton shirt with frayed cuffs, worn down from what looked like years of washing, and a pair of brown cords, thin and faded at the knees. "You look very nice," he said. "I'm afraid this is my usual weekend look when I'm working on the Pullman cars…there is water in the back if you want it," he added with all the formality of a five-star Uber driver.

"No, that's okay. I had something before I came down."

"Isn't rent really expensive in this part of the city? I can't imagine living in Brooklyn."

Oh, can't you? At her estimate it would take about forty-five minutes to get to Long Island from here, just the border, not to mention the boonies where he probably lived, and she couldn't imagine making this sort of small talk all the way there.

"You know what?" she said, and she turned abruptly so that she was facing him.

Alexander raised his eyebrows.

"Let's not pretend that we are actually in this to become the best of friends," Delysia said, then tempered the blunt statement with a dimpled smile. "What I mean is, I find small talk pretty painful and I'm sure you do, too."

Alexander laughed out loud. "I'm in academia. Small talk is part of my job."

"Yes, I know," Delysia replied, "but despite that you somehow managed to get into the most exclusive room of the SoHo Lounge last night. Want to share how that happened?"

"I honestly have no idea," Alexander said. "I showed my driver's license and the next thing I knew some big fellow in a shiny suit was walking me upstairs and offering me drinks."

"And your cousin was already there," Delysia pointed out. "Your cousin, the *senator*."

"Right." His brow furrowed. "He's a member, apparently. I suppose that explains it."

"Huh." He looked sincere, anyway. It was on the tip of Delysia's tongue to ask about precisely *what* it meant to be an Abbott-Hill, but she held back. For now.

Delysia busied herself angling her mobile over where their knees sat side by side, separated by the gearshift. Alexander's hand rested on it, strong and tan and covered with curling dark hair that matched the golds and siennas and sand-colored strands, mixed in with the black on his head. She took an overhead shot of their knees close together, captioned it *guess who? I'm close!* into her account. She turned off notifications for the time being, and focused her attention on her companion.

"Is that for us?" he asked.

"Yes, I've posted it just now."

"At least we're dressed this time," he said dryly, and despite herself Delysia began to giggle. He looked over and gave her one of his lightning-quick smiles; it was like a flash of sun hitting the water, breathlessly bright, and then it was gone.

He's handsome. It wasn't the first time she'd thought that. She shifted uncomfortably.

"Who was that photo of, anyway?" Alexander asked.

"It was a model I met on a movie set a couple weeks ago. I just put it up to tease everyone. I had no idea I'd attached the wrong handle to it until the next day." She blew a tendril of hair out of her face. "You must have been horrified."

"You have no idea."

"Well, I'm sorry," she said, and gave him the most wheedling smile in her arsenal. "It all worked out well, though, no?"

"That's yet to be seen, isn't it?"

"Well, I'm an eternal optimist."

"I'm beginning to see that."

Once they hit the bridge, Alexander asked if he could put on a podcast, "for work." Delysia, eager to avoid awkward conversation, had agreed immediately. The episode featured two Englishmen who seemed determined to out-reference each other when it came to... classic Greek myth? Delysia tried hard to follow for all of five minutes, then promptly curled up on the leather seat and fell asleep.

When she was woken by Alexander's gentle hand on her shoulder, she sat up and blinked rapidly, feeling like she'd been transported to some other world—from a postcard, perhaps, or the front of a puzzle box. The Hill house was mostly white and gray stone, pillared, and shrouded by trees so old and so heavily foliaged that branches sagged to the ground. Alexander was parked on a dirt driveway that looked like it could accommodate at least six cars.

"Is this where you live?" Delysia yawned and rubbed her eyes.

"It is."

"I thought your parents were dead," she blurted out, and then could have kicked herself for being so tactless.

"They are. I moved in afterward, to take care of the house. And the train's about a ten-minute ride from here. I'll get your door." And Alexander ducked out into the crisp fall air. He didn't even meet her eye, so she could look apologetic, at least.

She shouldered her bag and followed him up the walk. Faye was standing at the door, much to Delysia's surprise. She was wearing what Delysia supposed was her version of a Hamptons Housewife look: jodhpurs, a black cashmere turtleneck that clung to her bony frame, a thick argyle scarf, and bright yellow Hunter boots.

When she saw Delysia her eyes widened. "You're late," she snapped.

"What are you doing here?" Delysia demanded.

"Alex asked me."

"Alexander," he corrected politely, and gestured that they should move forward into a large, marble-tiled foyer. The interior was full of light from large windows that decorated the entryway. Alexander pulled his brogues off, replacing them with a pair of shapeless wool slippers sitting at the door. Delysia reached for her own boots, but he shook her head. "Don't bother. The floors are wood and it's freezing here… I usually don't turn on the heat till Christmas. I'm going to light a fire, though, so we'll get a bit of extra warmth. This way."

The interior of the house was opulent, although in the shabbiest way possible; faded oriental rugs and dated, heavy wood furniture decorated the space, along with framed photographs of people who Delysia assumed were the Abbott-Hill family ancestors. The dining room was an enormous space with a large fireplace big enough for three small children to sit in side by side. Alexander got the fire going, left and reappeared with crackers, cheese, wine, fruit, bread. Faye pulled out her laptop. Delysia, who was shivering, gratefully accepted the offer of a faded wool shawl.

"This doesn't seem much your style, Alexander," teased Faye.

He chuckled. "It's not. Don't worry—it wasn't my mother's," he said quickly to Delysia. "That would have been a bit morbid, I think. Augusta Savage stayed here a few weeks out of the year in the '60s, when my grandparents owned the house. She hated the cold. They're usually in mothballs, but I pulled out a few for the Smithsonian last year. They didn't want that one."

He returned back to his computer. Delysia and Faye stared at each other, at him, and at the shawl.

Delysia draped it around her shoulders and said not one word.

Faye lost no time whipping the two into shape. "I," she declared, "have created a virtual storyboard that breaks the trip up into days and nights. There's places for the train to stop so folks can get off, venues to visit, meals, activities on board…every minute needs to be accounted for."

"Ports?" Alexander repeated. Both women stared at him.

"What, did you expect us to sit and listen to you lecture for a week?" Faye demanded after a beat, but in good humor.

"I beg your—"

"There'll be one stop in every city," Delysia said patiently, before they started to squabble, "with something to do in each. Boston, New York City, Philadelphia and Washington, DC. I'm thinking about restaurants, lounges, clubs, and getting a sense of the local nightlife. There will be some people we'll be obligated to visit, and record ourselves visiting, for merching purposes. They give up the goodies; we get them the likes, make them look like their product is essential for the lifestyle we're trying to portray…"

"That may not be everyone's speed," Alexander said tactfully. "I'd like this to be an opportunity to educate some of these young people, as well."

"Not your speed, you mean," Faye butted in. "With all due respect, Alexander, I've studied your career, and read the stuff you post online—your history blogging, I mean. And this trip can't all be the opera and bibliographic lectures."

"I do realize it's not as…sexy," Alexander said acidly. "I just think…"

"There will be a balance of both," Delysia cut in to ease the tension, although secretly she agreed with Faye. Alexander frowned, but he held back and poured Delysia a glass of wine instead. She took a long sip. "Thanks. And that's how it works, unfortunately. My mother calls it digital prostitution," she quipped.

"Making Faye our madam in this situation, I suppose," Alexander said dryly. The two women stared at him; his mouth twitched. "Figuratively speaking, of course."

Delysia reached out and patted his arm with a manicured hand. "You'll get used to it, I promise," she said

lightly, although part of it stung. "Think of it as being…
a courtesan of luxury."

"Interesting." Alexander lifted his brows. The word
hung in the air for a moment; Delysia felt his eyes steady
on her face. Faye looked at him, then her, then smirked
just enough to make Delysia blush, and hard.

"Let's do this," she said after clearing her throat.

The three fell to work. There were more details than
they realized, which popped out as they went along.
Tiresome, unromantic details. Timing, for example, and
scheduling caterers to meet the train, and maintenance,
and working with Amtrak's scheduling, and necessary
permissions, and more. Letters had to be procured from
each of their sponsors, to submit to Southampton University for Alexander's two-week leave of absence. Tax
forms had to be completed. Spirited ideas became long
to-do lists. Alexander refilled the cheese tray twice. Faye
opened a third bottle of wine.

"I've never heard of many of these people you're
bringing on board," Alexander murmured.

"Well, you've got plenty of time to do the research.
Thank God we're going to get official planners for all
this," Delysia groaned. Her shoes had come off after all,
and she was sprawled in the captain's chair at the head
of the table, her feet propped on another. Faye was busily importing tasks into a shared calendar for the group,
and Alexander was fiddling with a pen and staring into
the fire, a thoughtful look on his thin face.

"What?" Faye demanded through a mouthful of pop-
corn.

"Nothing. I do need to take Delysia out to the Pullman, though, and it will be dark soon. Perhaps we should
call it an evening."

Faye made a noncommittal noise without looking up from her screen. "Sounds good."

Alexander stood, looming over Delysia for a moment before extending a hand to help her up in one of those oddly old-fashioned gestures of his. Were he a certain type, she would have thought it was an excuse to touch her, but his grip when he took her hand was warm and impersonal, and he let go as soon as she was steady on her feet. When she managed to look away, she saw Faye looking speculatively. She swore inwardly.

"Let's go," she said briskly, eager to escape the prying eyes of her manager.

"Yes, let's," Faye purred, gathering her belongings with more speed than she thought the woman capable of. "I drove for once, so you don't need to worry about me. You two have *fun*." She pointedly ignored Delysia's glare.

The two were soon ensconced in the Jaguar, headed for the train station. Delysia was grateful for the warmth of the car after the chilly house; her companion, however, seemed impervious to cold. She rubbed her hands together, tucked them under her arms.

"You'll have to bring a jacket if we come again," he said mildly. "I'll give you my sweater when we get to the train. It's very cold there, but I'm used to it."

Delysia's first instinct was to protest, but she shut her mouth. It was cold, in a way that she just never felt in the city. And this was only October!

"You're probably also quite hungry," he added.

"Oh, no, I'm fine—" she began to protest, but her stomach growled as if determined to reveal her lie, and he flashed her that odd smile of his again. "Brooklyn is a long way off," he observed. "I'd have raided the fridge, but we haven't had proper food there since my parents' silver anniversary. And that was catered," he added as an afterthought. "Do you care for soup, at all? I'll order something and have it delivered."

"To the *train* station?"

He grinned. "I've done it before. I may not be a social media guru, but I've more than mastered the dark occult of the UberEats order."

"Oh. Soup is fine, thanks."

"Any preferences?"

"Um, no. I'm not picky."

"I'll surprise you then."

True to word, they were at the station in minutes, and after parking Alexander was leading her through a courtyard and a small patch of woods, to a series of tracks in the back. It was well within view of the main station, so it *shouldn't* have felt as spooky as it did, but there was something about the chilly dusk and quiet landscape that made her shiver in a way that had little to do with cold. It felt—old, with that odd haunted vibe Alexander's house had given off.

Alexander kept glancing over at her; his face was concerned. "Perhaps I should have loaned you a coat," he said, and in a moment he stopped and pulled off his sweater. Delysia caught a flash of taut, tanned stomach and the waistband of black boxer shorts before he tugged his thermals down and handed her the sweater.

She began to protest, but he cut her off in a decidedly professor-ish manner. "Put it on," he said briskly. "You're already catching your death out here and I promise I don't have cooties."

Delysia opened her mouth to argue further, but he

moved toward her as if to jerk it over her head himself. "Okay!" she huffed, and pulled it on. That smell of soap and lemon starch that she'd inhaled while held against his tweeds last night engulfed her senses again, and she suddenly felt not only warmer, but flushed. She tugged the sleeves down to cover her hands.

Alexander, completely oblivious, was striding up to a stationary train car and fiddling with a massive lock. "This is the lounge," he said, excitement bleeding into his voice already, "and that there's the sleeper, over there. It was modeled after Queen Elizabeth's, has a full bath and seating area…"

His words blended to a comforting drone as his voice blew over them both, warm and quick. He lighted an old-fashioned lantern at the door, handed it to her. "Mind your step. Now—"

A faint buzzing interrupted him; he pulled out his phone with a quizzical expression. "Oh, food is here. Would you mind?"

Delysia shook her head, and Alexander legged it back toward the main station, leaving her alone with the car.

Delysia hadn't had such an odd afternoon in a long while, nor such a quiet one; seeing this only seemed to add to the surrealness of the world she'd entered. Walking into the train car was like going back in time, or at the very least creeping unnoticed onto a stage or movie set. The warm yellow circle of light illuminated rich upholstered seats, gleaming walnut wood, plush carpet. Even dusty and faded with age, one could tell this had once been the height of luxury. She carefully placed the lantern down on a round table and walked the length of the car, pausing to touch mustard-yellow velvet drapes with her fingertips.

"It's something, isn't it?" a hushed voice came from the doorway, and she turned to see Alexander standing there, paper bag in hand. She nodded.

"Feel free to look around," he said, and busied himself spreading napkins on one of the car's many card tables, and taking out four Styrofoam containers of steaming soup. "You said to surprise you, so I just got four types," he continued. "Sweet potato, tomato cream, barley, and Italian wedding."

"I love Italian wedding soup," Delysia said absent-mindedly. She tried to peer out of a window, but she couldn't see anything; it was boarded up. She touched the windowsill; she could not see the elegant scrolling in the dim light, but she could feel it beneath her fingers.

"It's all original paneling," Alexander said, cracking open what she presumed was the Italian wedding soup. He opened a foot-cabinet beneath the table and pulled out thick white bowls, spoons, mugs. It was obvious he'd done this before. He gestured for her to join him and she did, ignoring the flatware and choosing to sip directly from the Styrofoam cup. Alexander poured a stream of tomato soup into one of the proper bowls, then picked up a thin silver spoon.

"The doorman," said Delysia, after a beat to enjoy the hot, seasoned richness of the soup, "told me last night that you probably could buy half of Manhattan. He didn't tell me you owned a *train*."

Alexander laughed. "I'm not sure where he got that information. I inherited a sleeper and a lounge car," he corrected, "and it's all that's left of a fairly large fleet."

"Your family owned a whole fleet?"

"Kind of." He chewed his lip for a moment. "It was a pride thing, really. My father's people were—comfortable.

They were all in business, traveled a bit, and…well, you know how it was during those times, traveling for us."

"I know," Delysia said, taking a long sip of soup, eyes on his face.

"The Abbott-Hills invested heavily in railroad travel early in the century and maintained a whole fleet of private and luxury cars, among other things. Was meant to be specifically for private use and the use of other Black families in their circles, so they wouldn't have to deal with all of that, but they lost most of their investment when the railroads wouldn't give them equal use, and folks started relying more on automobiles. My parents used these cars for Christmas Eve train rides—a *Polar Express* type of thing, but the maintenance ate up the profits."

"And yet you kept them anyway," she mumbled through a mini meatball.

"It's a hobby for me. My father worked on the restoration when he was alive." He looked a little embarrassed. "The history meant a lot to him, and he sort of passed it on to me. We were—my mother died rather early, and we were alone for a lot of my life."

"I'm sorry," Delysia said softly. Her parents had been separated since she was young as well, but more by circumstance than tragedy. "That must have been hard."

Alexander gave a self-deprecating shrug. "It was more for him than me, I think. I was fine. I had a slightly odd upbringing, but I was fine. I'd probably have to get rid of them eventually, or donate them. They rust if not in use. Among…other things."

"Okay." Another pause, and one long enough for her to really look at him. He was close without crowding her, perched on the padded couch they shared; his body radiated warmth that was just as filling, as comforting as the soup. She barely knew him, but he felt—simple. Safe. Time seemed to slow down around Alexander, but only because he had no need to hurry. With anyone else she'd want to fill in the silence with chatter, banter, jokes. Silence felt comfortable with Alexander Abbott-Hill.

"So—so," she said after a long moment of sipping soup and gazing at the faded opulence, doing its best to dazzle her in the weak light, "this is what nights like this will be on board?"

He half-turned and treated her to one of those slow, vulpine smiles that made her tummy flip despite herself. It wasn't lust, at least not all of it; that she recognized and never panicked over. This was more…liking their closeness, and liking it very much.

"Does the prospect bore you very much?"

"It seems…nice. Restful. Long as there's Wi-Fi," she added.

He rolled his eyes, but the amusement didn't fade from his face. She could feel those dark eyes tracing her face, lingering on her mouth. "This will be our suite, if I can get it refurbished in time."

"Our…" Her traitorous mind suddenly conjured up an image of them kissing in that club doorway, lit up completely with the harshest of bulbs—Faye had sent her a short video. She'd looked tense and skittish, but Alexander…he'd been cradling her close, tenderly even, and kissing her as if they were alone—and had the entire night ahead of them.

"Um—" She almost upset her poor abused Styrofoam cup, barely felt it when Alexander pressed a napkin into her hand. "We probably should talk about that. I mean, arrangements for—"

"Arrangements for exactly how far we plan to go with the ruse," Alexander said patiently.

"Yes!"

"I was hoping to leave that up to you," he said, and leaned back in the seat, fixing calm dark eyes on her face. "Were you offended when I kissed you, Delysia?"

The way he said her name gave her an oddly disturbing thrill.

"I mean, we've talked about almost every legal aspect of this arrangement, thanks to Faye," he continued, "but I don't want to do anything that makes you uncomfortable. I asked, yes, but that—you seemed…"

"I get it." She was grateful for the dim light; her ears were burning. "No. I mean, it wasn't a big deal. It's less than what I posted on Instagram."

"Oh, that wasn't me, so I can't hold it against you. But, seriously—I don't want you to be uncomfortable around me or think I'm going to…pounce on you all the time."

"No." Her fingers sought out hair to twist round the tips, but damn it, she'd pinned it up. "I mean, you surprised me, but I said *yes*. And I obviously—" She laughed, a little nervously. "I did it again, so it couldn't have been that disgusting to me. I'm a friendly drinker."

Alexander looked like he was suppressing a smile. Delysia ran her tongue round the inside of her mouth; it was suddenly dry. "I don't get the impression, though, that you're the type for excessive PDA," she said.

"It *has* been a while," Alexander said dryly, "but you're right. Listen, Delysia. Let's keep it simple. Admit nothing, deny nothing. I'll follow your lead."

The words hung in the air between them, heavy and tempting. Delysia focused on his mouth in a near-hypnotic state; she couldn't look away. It was the only decadent thing about his face, she thought. Full, but not so much as to make it unmasculine, fleshy, and the warmest she'd ever kissed. Oh, God. She wanted to kiss him again, and now.

"Maybe some arm holding, some hand-in-hand?" she mumbled, dropping her eyes.

He grinned. "My parents didn't even do that much. Different generation. But yes—again, I'll follow your lead—within reason, of course. You can do whatever you want with me," and the words hung in the air, heavy.

I have a damned dirty mind. Delysia gave herself a hard mental shake—she would *not* let it go there—and shot her companion a bright smile. "Done."

"And for the record," he said, in those odd clipped tones he favored. She still couldn't tell what it was— Long Island, Boston, England? "It *was* nice. Yesterday, I mean."

"Stop it," she mumbled, finally gave up and lifted her hands to her face. "God."

He laughed and began cleaning up their soup mess, tossing Styrofoam packages into a plastic bag reserved for that purpose. "Let's get you back to Brooklyn."

Chapter Five

The next few weeks were an intensely paced tangle of activity, between school, Delysia's engagements, which Alexander was now very much a part of, and planning what they chose to call the *Gilded Express*.

The date, once solidified, fell precariously close to Thanksgiving. He'd learned much about what was possible through social media, including manipulating the most mundane images imaginable—eating a ham-and-mustard sandwich, for example—to look like something incredibly exciting, carefree, enviable—sexy even, if that's what they wanted. However, he had not yet managed to make grading papers look like anything but the misery it was.

At least his students seemed more engaged. Delysia, true to her word, had included Alexander in nearly every part of her very public—and head-spinningly busy—life. Today, a cloudy Sunday that smelled like snow, he was at her home for an impromptu photo shoot.

"Hey," Delysia greeted Alexander once she buzzed him up, more than a little out of breath, as if she'd rushed out of the shower or dressed quickly. Perhaps it was because he was meeting her at home, but it was one of the few times he'd seen her less than put together. She wore faded leggings, baggy at the knee, and a threadbare MIT sweatshirt that was frayed round the neckline and cuffs. She'd cut the neck out of her sweatshirt, and one slim shoulder poked out. Most of the hair he could see was wrapped tightly round a formidable-looking set of metal rollers. The rest was wrapped in a scarf of kente cloth.

"Don't say anything," she said immediately in a tone that was half-pleading, half-exasperated. "I overslept." She'd requested that he come over that day to film a "how we met" segment for her page in response to fans flooding both their spaces.

Alexander mimed zipping his lips. If Delysia wasn't late, she was almost late, and he'd grown used to it in their weeks of working together. "Not a word," he said cheerfully.

It all was rather…odd, for lack of a better word. Alexander had spent the first week or so as Delysia's boyfriend trying madly to keep up with the correspondence as well as juggle his teaching duties, and finally had broken down after the third sleepless night. When he'd finally confided in Delysia and Faye, they'd laughed in his face.

"Are you trying to keep up with all that yourself? You poor thing," Faye laughed. "I can assign someone to run the account for you, if you want."

"No, that won't be necessary, thank you." A part of him resisted. He wasn't like Delysia, or like her fellow influencers—he was in academia, and he was doing this strictly for the benefit of his career. This was temporary, he reminded himself. After the trip was over and she was back full-time at Southampton, this charade would dissolve, and he'd be back to normal. Hopefully, with a few more opportunities, but generally back to normal.

After thinking it over he handed the whole lot over to Natalia to manage, with the addition of a stipend, of course, which she claimed rather triumphantly. At least he knew he could trust her to ensure that some historical content made it in among the fluff.

The second hurdle to clear had been rather an embarrassing one. The week after the Kim party, he'd found himself invited to yet another "thing": this time, a birthday party at the Brooklyn Botanical Garden for influencer Callie Rose. There'd been an excruciating photo shoot involving scooters and skateboards, lawn games, and an absolutely raucous picnic catered by a man he vaguely remembered from late-night viewings of the Food Network while grading papers.

After, the group had changed clothes, piled into a fleet of party buses, and headed into the city for an evening of drinking and dancing, at yet another converted nightclub, this time in Harlem. There were toasts, and posing, and a trip that should have taken a bit over an hour took two, with all the stopping to pose and stage "moments" that included everything from dancing with the driver to poking their heads out of a moonroof, in the hammiest way imaginable.

Alexander had been grateful that the Kim twins were not among the celebrants that night. He'd been wary of them since Eden's birthday party. Delysia had been animated, and warm, and cheerful, snuggling against Alexander with an almost deferential shyness that hinted at an intimacy she was too modest to show. It was masterful theater really.

Aside from the ruse, Alexander could not understand how Delysia managed to keep this type of schedule. It would have been different if he thought she'd actually enjoyed it—and for the most part, she looked like she did—but there were moments where a wistfulness crossed her face, a wistfulness that made him wonder about things he probably had no right to ask. They were at that stage where he was not yet certain what was off-limits. They were playing lovers, but they weren't even friends.

Did he even want Delysia Daniels as a friend? He wasn't sure what he could possibly offer her in that capacity. He wasn't sure what he could offer anyone like Delysia, except monetary value with an expiration date.

Afterward, when he'd been panting from dehydration and a lack of sleep, the caravan had set off for pancakes at a greasy diner in Williamsburg. He'd watched longingly from the window as the night sky softened to gray then peach as his companions consumed piles of food and drank even more, stopping to document *everything*.

He was seriously considering giving the group the slip when Callie, who was sitting in her fiancé's lap and scrolling on her phone, let out a shriek, then a laugh. "Oh my God!"

"What?" said Delysia.

"Alexander," Callie said, pressing her hand on her mouth to cover the giggles, "someone got you. At my party. And the club. And the party bus—holy shit, you've been memed—"

Around them, people pulled out their phones, going to Callie's account, demanding to know where. Alexander was confused. He knew what a meme was, of course, but why would he be—

"Oh my God," Delysia murmured under the cover of all the hilarity, then scooted over in their booth, closer to him, pressed against his side in a way that quickly was feeling familiar. He registered the sweet spiciness of her skin, even after hours out, before she produced her phone. "Look."

He'd held it up, squinted at it. There was him, in the club they'd been in only hours earlier. He was leaning against a wall, arms crossed, eyes half-closed, and his expression—

"Oh, dear," he murmured, and everyone at the table exploded in mirth.

"The caption, read the caption," gasped one of the influencers, a yogini from Chicago who also dabbled in ceramics, if Alexander remembered correctly.

He looked. There wasn't one, there were several, all under the same picture:

When my trainer catches me doing half reps

Annoying Uncle: where my hug at??? Me:

When someone u hate is breathing

It hurts to live

Alexander was *horrified.*

To make it worse, there were more memes, screenshot and shared by enterprising followers. In every single picture he was in, he looked like he was in excruciating pain. There was one in the club, another during the croquet match on the lawn when his eyes were half-closed, yet another when a minor celebrity he *still* didn't recognize was yammering at him as they were all having drinks…

"Nicky is going to be *livid,*" said Callie with perhaps a little too much glee. "My friend, you are trending."

* * *

Faye had not been impressed, not in the least. "What were you *thinking*?" She'd almost lost her trademark cool at their next planning meeting. "Always assume cameras are around, Alexander!"

"I wasn't annoyed," he protested. "That's just my face!"

"You don't look annoyed so much as bored. And that's worse. Annoyed I can spin." She inhaled, puffing her cheeks out. "You clearly need some work."

The incident resulted in a crash course on camera-readiness, led by Faye, acting as his Henry Higgins in a Dries Van Noten jacket and an unlit Virginia Slim tucked behind her ear, rather than the pipe. "Starchy is fine," she lectured, "but bored is stuck-up. You don't need to grin—that would look idiotic. A neutrally pleasant look is ideal." Sensing that Alexander would not be able to parrot some of the more popular social media stars, she trotted out classic icons instead. Barack Obama. Fred Rogers. Tom Hanks. Bob Ross. Kate Middleton—

"Kate Middleton? Really, Kate *Middleton*? Why on earth would I want to be like her?"

"The woman's a gem. If you can still smile after pa-parazzi nearly run you over…" Faye's eyes took on a bit of a faraway look, and then she snapped back to atten-tion. "Anyway. Look at their pictures, Alexander. They can be sitting next to most reprehensible people in the world, and that pleasant half-smile never moves. It's classy. Diplomatic. Photogenic. *Un-meme-able*."

Doggedly Alexander studied this advice as if it was for his tenure review, honing a "pleasant half-smile" in the mirror while he shaved, during conference calls, in the pharmacy, in the supermarket. He initiated small talk with strangers, practiced the wide, then narrow-eyed slow-nod that Faye demonstrated. He made murmurs in the right places, tilted his head back when he chuckled. He forced himself to listen deeply, no matter how inane the subject. He struck up conversations with students in the commons, on the Green, in line at Starbucks. He got some odd looks, sure, but at least he knew *his* face was pleasant.

He still burned with humiliation when he remembered how they'd all laughed that night—Delysia included. She'd tried to hide it, but her cheeks had puffed out, and her eyes had been the brightest he'd ever seen them. She'd been genuinely amused, and Alexander, even after years of achievement, was reduced back to the schoolroom, with the pretty girl laughing at his awkwardness.

It wasn't a great feeling. And now, he was in Delysia's home for the first time, poised to test his newly acquired skills.

"Right! Yes, so…" Delysia stepped aside to let him enter. Her fingers had gone to her hair again, twisting the ends of her curls in that nervous tic he was beginning to recognize. He could feel the nervousness emanating from her almost palpably, and he wondered at it. Delysia's personality online was so vibrant that the difference was startling when he related with her face-to-face. She stumbled over her words at times, and was almost skittish when looking him in the eye.

He moved forward, smiling as he did so.

"Hey," he said, simply.

It'd been a while since the birthday party, and he'd learned enough for Faye to decide that it "might be nice" for them to make a recording at Delysia's place as a couple, and later, do a tour of his. Alexander had recoiled at the idea of letting the entire internet into his home, but Faye steamrolled his misgivings with her usual efficiency.

"You have summer tourists tramping through the place every year," she said briskly. "How is this different?"

"It's—" He could not explain why it was different without sounding like a complete snob, so he tried another way. "It's falling apart—"

"That adds to its charm. Very *Downton Abbey*, after the war. Genteel poverty and all that."

They had squabbled until Delysia cut in. "We'll do my place first," she'd said crisply. "Everyone on my channel is more familiar with it anyway. We can decide what we want to do with Alexander's place later. Maybe a tour of the vineyards instead?"

Both acquiesced, if a bit grumpily, and now Alexander was here.

As if she'd jumped into his thoughts, his phone rang loudly. He glanced at the face before picking it up. "Hello, Faye. Yes, I'm here. No…she didn't tell me…"

When he hung up, he turned to Delysia, lifting an eyebrow. "She wanted to make sure I was wearing the sweater."

Delysia laughed, breaking a little bit of the tension. "From our trip to Williamsburg? That sweater shop was fun."

"If you want to call it that." He, unfortunately, could remember every detail of the trip. The "shop," if one could call it that, was on the outskirts of Williamsburg, in one of those hideous converted buildings that (in his humble opinion) should have been torn down in the '70s.

The place had featured raw-wood floors, one sweater per table and, inexplicably, a giant ebony sculpture of a foot. The most shocking thing about the place—besides the price of the perfectly ordinary cashmere sweaters—had been the line outside, curving round the block. They'd gotten ahead of everyone, as the shop had been expecting Delysia, and Alexander had been treated to goggling teens and young adults, snapping away at them with their phones.

Alexander had been horrified, but Delysia played it cool as ice cream. She'd tucked a hand in Alexander's coat pocket, buried her face in the side of his neck, letting her curls spill becomingly over his shoulder.

"Is my beret still straight?" she'd murmured into the skin of his neck. He'd felt that touch of warm lips surge low and hot, despite his annoyance at the crowd, and shifted. Delysia was overwhelming still, although he'd grown used to her snuggles and touches for the cameras—all warm softness and scent. It was one of those times when they felt far too real.

"You know, Catherine Middleton and Prince William weren't even pictured kissing until their wedding day," he'd said through his teeth, more grumpily than he'd intended. "All this canoodling is completely unnecessary."

In answer Delysia's arm had slipped around his waist, beneath his coat, and he'd felt the muscles of his abdomen tense in response, involuntarily. "You've had her on the brain since Faye brought her up in that session on photographers," she'd jeered. "New idol, maybe?"

Alexander had ignored that one. "Oh, mother of God, I think that's a student of mine in line."

"An even better reason to not look in that direction. Look at me as if you adore me," Delysia had said with that low laugh of hers, and then his face was very close to hers. He had registered details that had become fixed in his brain over the past several weeks—the full mouth, the near-dimple in the left cheek, the faded freckles on honey-smooth and copper-tinted skin.

Kiss her. They hadn't since that first night, only kept their contact in public restricted to nuzzles, snuggles, all fairly innocuous. He'd be lying if he said he hadn't thought about how good kissing her had felt, but he didn't know what Delysia thought about it, and on top of that, he could not be the type of guy who just took advantage of situations because it felt *good*.

He'd cleared his throat and Delysia's lashes had dropped, hiding her eyes, and the moment had passed.

"I can't believe your life is like this," he'd said finally, almost inaudibly. Delysia had smiled again, but that time she pulled away.

The black crew-neck cashmere sweater with tortoise-shell buttons they purchased after an excruciating forty minutes posing for pictures and taking selfies in the shop looked like at least three of the ones he had in his closet already, but the price was ruinous. Anyway, he'd been spotted teaching in the sweater at Southampton a week later, a student had said online. Delysia had borrowed the thing and worn it on a few outings of her own, and people had pointed that out, as well.

"But it's a sweater," murmured Alexander, at a loss for words at this point.

"It cements the narrative! My followers are very eagle-eyed."

"In a stalkerish sort of way."

"Well." She couldn't argue with that.

Now, Alexander followed Delysia into a very small,

very clean apartment with an open-plan kitchen, painted a flat white, with the polished wood floors that were synonymous with New York City buildings. Her furniture was of the Ikea variety, in shades of gray and cream, and limited to a sofa, a small leather chair, and a desk with envelopes piled neatly on it. That was all. No pictures, no photographs, no figurines, no wall hangings. It reminded him of a dorm, or faculty housing at Southampton, at the beginning of the semester, before people had a chance to get their rooms together.

Alexander was surprised at the Spartan surroundings. They seemed completely out of keeping with Delysia's personality. However, she kept walking, threw open the door of a room to the right. "Give me a minute, I've got to bring in some things," she called.

"Do you need any help?"

"Oh, sure."

The doorway led to a small bedroom, as simply decorated as the rest of the apartment. Delysia was pulling a pile of things out of her closet, and Alexander hurried to help her. There was a beautiful woven tapestry in shades of rust and chocolate brown that he remembered from her live videos; a battered brass lamp that had been polished to a high shine; two or three plush pillows that echoed the shades in the tapestry; a small, carved wooden table.

They took the bundles out to the living room, and Delysia busily set up a corner of the sofa, mounting the tapestry directly behind it. "Can you grab two mugs from the kitchen?"

Alexander nodded and went. Her kitchen was oddly clean and cool, as if she rarely used it. He took down two white ceramic mugs and returned to a cozy, intimate setup in warm, soothing colors, with Delysia's tripod directly facing it. It was so artfully arranged, such a change from the rest of the apartment that he exclaimed.

"This is amazing," he said, reaching out to touch the tapestry with a finger.

"It's from Abu Dhabi." She paused as if considering what she wanted to say next. "I grew up there."

Surprised, Alexander wanted to ask her more, but she stepped away nimbly and began fumbling with the camera. "Almost ready. Can you take a seat so that I can check the lighting?"

Alexander did so. He wanted to ask why in heaven's name her apartment was so bare when she had all these lovely things, but he bit his tongue, figuring that it would be tactless at best. Perhaps she liked, or preferred a minimalist space—some people were like that, him included. His work office, if not his home, was fairly minimalist. But no artwork, no posters, no family photos?

This is a business arrangement—it's none of your business.

Alexander stood to help her finish setting up, then sat back where she indicated. She fussed about with the camera for a few minutes, grabbed a remote, and settled next to him, then turned on a monitor she'd placed at their feet. She settled herself next to him.

"*Final* light check. Look up," she said briskly, and Alexander did. Delysia shifted so that she was flush against his side; he was very aware of how near she was, but she seemed undisturbed, for the most part. She'd shifted to that public-facing persona—he could see it in her eyes, in her face, in the set of her slender shoulders. She checked the monitor.

"Oh, your hair—can I?" she asked.

Alexander nodded, then held very still as her small

warm fingers went through his hair, rumpling it up just a bit. With all the *Gilded Express* planning, he hadn't had the time to get a haircut yet, and his curls were thickening, clustering on his head. He did not care for the rumpled look, not at all, but he supposed Delysia knew what she was doing.

He cleared his throat when she pulled back and nodded when she asked if he was ready. "You're not going to get dressed?"

"No, the post caption says we're getting ready to go to an event." She patted her rollers self-consciously.

"Ah."

"Hey, guys," she said, shooting a smile at the camera. "I'm here with my boyfriend Alexander just to check in—people have been asking about how we met, so we figured we'd set your minds at rest!"

"That is true," Alexander said, feeling a bit like a fool while addressing a nonexistent audience. *Pretend it's a virtual lecture*, he told himself, and he did relax a little bit. Besides, Delysia took over most of the conversation. They concocted a tale about her spilling wine at a tasting, and him coming to her rescue with a handkerchief and club soda.

"I spoke," Alexander said, playing up the stodgy professor bit to the max, "about the history of the vineyard, and other—really, idiotic things. Her eyes were glazing over but I couldn't stop talking."

As he was speaking, Delysia was laughing, eyes bright, looking at him as if he were the only one that mattered. It sparked something deep within him that felt warm and bright in his chest, as if someone had lit a gentle flame there. Impulsively he lifted her hand, kissed her knuckles. It was a playful attempt at mock gallantry, but her cheeks reddened. He wondered if he had gone too far and released her hand.

She cleared her throat. "I think that's a take," she said in her normal voice, breaking the spell.

"Yes, of course," he said quickly, masking a disappointment he was sure he had no right to feel. They finished the segment quickly, and packed Delysia's bright bit of a room back into her closet, then stood a little awkwardly in the middle of Delysia's living room.

"Good work," she said, shifting from foot to foot.

"Thank you. It was fun."

"I'm glad you thought so."

He ran his hands over his hair, smoothing the curls that Delysia had arranged so artfully. It seemed odd just to record and be on his way, but he wasn't sure what else to do. It wasn't as if they were *friends*, and even if Alexander wanted to make an overture…he wasn't sure if Delysia would—

As if his mouth was moving of its own volition Alexander found himself talking. "I'll be—looking for some refreshment after this. Would you care to join me for a coffee?" He heard as if he was listening in on someone else how stiff he sounded and clapped his mouth shut against any potential babbling that might escape.

Delysia's honey-brown eyes widened in real surprise. "Now?"

"Yes." He felt heat begin to prickle on the back of his neck.

She looked trapped for a second. "Um…"

Shit. Alexander bit his lower lip. "Actually, it's a terrible imposition. You've got plenty to do here—I didn't know what I was thinking. Rain check?"

"Alexander—"

"Thank you for today." He cut her off by bending to touch her cheek with his, then headed for the door with all possible speed.

"I actually can—"

"Oh, no worry, I've got it," he said, deftly opening her three locks and ducking out the door. "See you soon!"

When he made it to the hallway, he closed his eyes, then shook himself off and began to walk briskly toward the street exit. Since all this began, deep down inside Alexander had wondered if Delysia perhaps wasn't just tolerating his presence during all this. His college students certainly gave him that impression. Why not her?

Not that it matters. It's only business, he reminded himself.

Alexander had experienced similar luck with women. His dating history was limited to one undergrad who found him decidedly boring and had no hesitation in telling him, and a couple of fellow graduate students so engrossed in their own research that he supposed they did not mind, or paid no attention to, his rambling on random subjects that caught his attention.

It was no wonder, considering the way he'd grown up, mostly alone in that big rambling house. He wasn't going to think of that now, though.

In response to this he'd become a much more avid listener, and was content to sit quietly on dates and let the women chatter away. This did not make for particularly satisfying relationships, though, and it was new to find someone who was nearly as quiet as he tried to be. There was something in her silence, though, that made him think that perhaps, just perhaps, this time it might be her actual personality, and not just a lack of interest…?

"For God's sake, you do run on," he said out loud, shoving his hands deep in his pockets.

"Alexander?" Delysia's voice rang out down the hall. He spun around; she was standing in the doorway, unwinding the metal rollers one-by-one. "I'd like to go. If you don't mind waiting? I hesitated because I thought it'd take too long for me to get ready, but—" She paused. "Coffee, right?"

"Coffee," he echoed a little dumbly.

The two ended up not in a coffee shop, but in what Delysia called a cereal bar, a few blocks away from her apartment. The tiny cafeteria served nothing but soft-serve and cereal that lined the walls in bins with their boxes mounted on top. Alexander had never seen so many varieties in his life, and he found himself laughing as he looked around.

"This is madness," he said, squinting at a life-sized cardboard cutout of Count Chocula before accepting a large bowl from Delysia.

"It's the best possible kind of madness. I bring Faye's nieces here when they visit," Delysia said cheerfully. "They ask for it by name now. You can be decadent and do soft-serve with cereal mixed in, or whole milk, if you're a traditionalist. They even have non-dairy options."

"This is hilarious." He looked at the menu with great concentration before deciding on a bowl of Frosted Flakes. "You know, I was Tony the Tiger for Halloween one year."

Delysia laughed out loud. "I could see it." She asked for a sprinkle of Cinnamon Toast Crunch on her vanilla ice cream, and the two took their trays to a quiet table looking out on the busy street.

"Brooklyn feels so different from when I was a kid," he remarked, taking up his spoon.

"Did you live here?"

"No, but my mother worked at the library. Archivist."

"And gave birth to a historian. That makes sense."

Alexander smiled and hesitated before digging in, wondering if Delysia was going to use the opportunity to take a photograph and post it, while their bowls were laid out. After all, this was the sort of kitschy thing that fans seemed to adore. However, she placed her phone face-down on the table, lifted her chin, and licked her spoon.

He was surprised at how much that pleased him, deep down inside.

"I was actually going to offer you something up in my apartment," she said, "but I had nothing on hand except tea and a box of Raisin Bran. That's where I got the idea for cereal."

He laughed out loud. "I wouldn't have minded."

"My mother would have dropped dead from horror if she heard I'd been entertaining with that." She considered the garish characters printed atop the round plastic table, then looked up and smiled. "She'd be horrified with this place too, come to think of it. This is nice, though."

"Unexpected, but definitely nice. How'd you find it?"

"Oh, in the influencer circuit, years ago. It's modeled after a place in Brixton."

"Brixton, in the UK?"

"Yes, have you been?"

"I used to go to the market there a couple weekends a semester when I was at Cambridge. It was a trip, but there's this Nigerian-brand black soap that my aunt uses that I could only find there in those days…"

"Dudu Osun?"

Alexander nearly sprayed the table. "Yes! How did you know?"

"It's pretty popular," Delysia chuckled. "You know, she can get it online."

He snorted, leaning back on his stool. "She was too afraid of getting fake ones. But she was…good to me, after my mother passed. I didn't mind. Don't know what she did after I graduated, though. I bought fifty bars and used half my luggage allowance lugging them back. Perhaps she hasn't yet run out."

Delysia nodded thoughtfully, taking another swirl of cereal-studded ice cream and inhaling it in one go. "Aunts," she said with a chuckle.

"You said it."

The two chatted quietly over their snacks until the sunlight began to fade; easy, inconsequential things. The sugar and milk seemed to open Delysia up a bit, and Alexander found himself captivated by the soft modulated voice she favored when she wasn't recording. She spoke of her childhood in Dubai, attending one of their many American prep schools, visiting countries in the Gulf on weekends, where her cousins had scattered about over the years. Her name actually was Delysia, named after—

"The French singer," Alexander guessed.

"How the hell did you know that?"

"I googled," he said with a chuckle, lifting up the cell phone he'd held out of sight. She slapped his arm.

"Well, you're wrong. I'm named after a character in one of my mother's favorite books. Maybe the author liked your singer."

"Perhaps."

They continued. She had no full siblings, but had several half brothers and sisters, all much older, scattered throughout the Horn and the Gulf with their families. She had one cousin in the Americas, but he lived far away in Montreal, going to school. Her father still lived in Eritrea and hadn't left for years; her mother had been a nanny in Dubai until—

"She's in poor health," Delysia said. A shadow passed over her face. She did not elaborate, and Alexander did not ask, though he felt quite sorry for her. "I'm only here until I…until I've saved up a bit. Then I'm going back to Dubai for good."

Ah. He wondered if that explained the tiny apartment, devoid of any personal touches; perhaps it felt temporary to her. In a way, Alexander could sympathize. He knew what it felt like to be alone.

"You're very strong," he found himself saying, and Delysia flushed. The rose-tinted copper of her skin glowed against the background of the fading light of day, and Alexander was startled into looking down at his watch.

They'd been there for almost two hours.

"Goodness—I've kept you forever," he said, and stood up, hastily stacking their bowls with their dregs of sugary cereal, piling used napkins on top. "I *am* sorry."

"Don't be. It was nice." Delysia's head was resting on her hand, and she lifted her lashes slowly, languidly. "Thank you, Alexander."

"My pleasure." They were silent for another moment, but this one was companionable, rather than awkward. Alexander took a breath. "I should be going."

"Me, too." She stood and collected her handbag. Al-

exander piled the plates neatly in the tray over the bin
reserved for that purpose, and the two headed out into
the crisp fall air.

He turned to her and smiled. "See you at the launch,
then?"

"See you," she parroted. Then, to his shock, she took
a step closer to him, stood on her toes, and pressed her
lips to his in a brief closed-mouthed kiss, hardly a kiss
at all. It was sugary and cinnamony and very gentle.

"Good night," she breathed out, and headed off
quickly, hair fluttering in the wind.

When Delysia got back to her apartment, the sleepi-
ness that had begun in the Cereal Bar weakened her
completely, loosening her limbs, making her feel as if
everything was moving in slow motion. She drew a hot
bath in her apartment's tiny tub, stripped off and folded
her clothes with ritualistic care, and sank into the water
after tipping most of a jar of lavender bath salts into it.

This was overindulgent; she had too much to do tonight. A natural hair company that had just broken into
major retailers had asked her to cover a curl shingling
cream, and a jeweler had sent her a delicate gold necklace with her initials dangling from the gossamer-thin
chain. That she could do, she decided—she was already
wearing it, after all.

She listlessly positioned her phone, allowing one
shoulder, her neck, and just the faintest hint of the swell
at the top of her breasts to show. The delicate piece would
look even lovelier silhouetted against miles of wet skin,
and she could plug the bath salts, too. She captioned the
photo quickly and posted. *Done.*

Were she back in Dubai, after a night at work, she

would probably hit up one of her numerous cousins, or go to an aunt's house for dinner, or catch a movie, or… She sighed, shifting in the water. In her first couple of years in New York, she'd enthusiastically thrown herself into the city's social scene. Then her mother had gotten sick, losing weight and sleeping badly, and it all had culminated in that awful, dreadful day when Mama fainted in the shopping mall.

Delysia sighed and shifted again. She didn't even know what had happened to those early, tenuous friendships in New York. Most of those people had gone to school with her, or were connected to things that didn't really matter anymore. Her one obsession had been with making enough money to pay for her mother's treatment. Stumbling into a relationship with Nicky had been a curse, but she had to admit, it had shown her she could make a living, and not have to wait for a career that would leave her hundreds of thousands of dollars in debt.

She'd quit medical school the day she crossed one hundred thousand followers. And now, three years later, over a million people viewed, commented, watched her every move on a daily basis, consumed the life she created for them. They loved it, hated it, criticized it, shared it. It left no time for hobbies. It left no time for school. It left no time for friendships that weren't based on reciprocal likes. For Delysia, this was no hobby; this wasn't even a business. It was literally her mother's lifeline.

And it wasn't anybody's fault but hers that she was so lonely, she told herself. Plenty of content creators had lives outside the business; in fact, at the events where they met and danced and drank and gossiped and shared sponsorships and built those artificial relationships for the net, most were going home to siblings. Partners. Rela-

tives. People that they were eager to shed the glittery facade for, people they could crawl in bed with and gossip
with and make love to and talk about real things with.

Delysia had hoped Nicky—and Eden, by extension—
would be those people for her, in this place that seemed
all the more alien to her with every year that passed. But
they weren't, and Delysia stopped hoping for anything,
except perhaps an end to all her expenses, so she could
move back home.

Home.

She slowly rinsed off, dried herself, pulled on shorts
and a tank top, and padded out to her living room. Something of Alexander's essence had lingered, in a way;
there was a clean spiciness in the air she had begun to
associate with the smell of his skin.

She had kissed him. With no more heat than she would
any friend, but—still. She'd kissed him. His scent and
serious, thin face had drawn her in again. She'd also seen
a softness in his expression that night, over their bowls
of disgustingly sugary cereal, that was open enough to
worry her. Despite his age and occupation, Alexander
couldn't hide his expressions any more than a kid could,
and she sort of liked him very much for that.

She shook away the thought with so much violence
that her hair swished over her cheeks, and went over to
her desk, where a pile of bone-white envelopes stood.

As she did once a week, she separated them into piles,
opened a black-and-white composition notebook that
acted as her ledger. There were her utility bills, her credit
card bills that represented the first few months where
she'd tried to go to school and take care of her mother's
care at the same time. There were her student loan bills,
for a degree she'd never get to use, a career she'd never

have. And there were the royalty statements from her endorsements, little white slips of paper that Faye mailed her for her records. It was always a thrill, those few minutes or hours the money was hers, before it was distributed to one of her many obligations.

A few years ago the sight of that pile of envelopes made her sick to her stomach. Now she had the means to chip away at it, just a little at a time. When she was tired and didn't want to record, or didn't feel like going to a party, or had no desire to open one of the cardboard boxes that arrived with items for her to review, she looked at how many envelopes there were still in the obligations pile, and it put things right back in perspective.

Now, thinking about Alexander and his soft lips and quiet expressions, she focused hard on her obligations pile. This trip would mean a windfall, both then and after, and was worth, she told herself, a few messy feelings that he probably didn't share.

The sooner this trip was over, the better it would be for both of them.

Chapter Six

The day the *Gilded Express* launched, Alexander found himself quite in awe. He could barely believe it, seeing it all come to life from the pages and diagrams and documents and plans; it felt akin to seeing a fairy story from one of his old picture books come to life.

The Boston train yard they'd selected for the launch was absolutely overrun—with camera crews, photographers, tourists with cameras. Faye, along with the planner (Kim Kardashian's, solicited by Delysia via her account after a week-long competition for the honor) had attached an "Old Hollywood Glitterati" theme to the day. Ten influencers—and their partners—for the trip were milling about, dressed like stars from times past.

Alexander identified Marilyn Monroe, Doris Day, Dorothy Dandridge, and what looked like a generic Hitchcock heroine (which made sense for a train, he supposed). A brandy-fortified Buster Keaton had to be restrained with some effort from posing with rope on the tracks, and cocktails were flowing freely, passed round by white-coated servers in black bow ties, along with steaming canapés. It was giddy, unrestrained madness, and the cameras were recording everywhere. Alexander had to force himself not to flinch.

He recognized Delysia the moment he saw her, despite her costume. She was perched on the stairs leading up to the platform, wearing a stark, tailored wool suit with a long straight skirt and sleek black pumps. A white cloche sat on top of her hair, which was slicked back into a low bun. Her mouth was a full slash of red. She cradled a tiny white terrier in her gloved hands.

He tilted his head, considering for a moment; then he walked over, shoved his hands deep in his pockets. He did not speak; instead, chose to watch her for a moment. She was laughing, looking up at the camera shyly, turning to find the most becoming angle. Her photographer, a woman swathed in a fur coat that reached the floor, saw Alexander before she did and lowered the phone.

"Your Humphrey Bogart's here," she said dryly, and Delysia whirled around. When she saw Alexander, her cheeks crimsoned. She blushed very easily. That was another thing he'd noticed over the past few weeks. It was quite sweet, he thought.

"Sabrina Fairchild?"

"Very good." She sounded a bit short of breath; it was windy, he supposed.

"My mother loved the film. I've seen it several times."

"She had good taste then."

They stared at each other for a moment, a bit awkwardly. Then he gestured at the wriggling puppy in her arms. "Will he be joining us?"

She started, then laughed. "No. Hired for the shoot."

"Shall we get one of you together then?" asked the photographer.

Alexander lifted a brow. Delysia nodded, patting her

cheeks with her free hand. He made his way down to her and took the pup from her, allowing it to baptize him with a silky warm tongue. He could feel tension radiating from her body. When he bent closer, he smelled soap, gardenias, just enough to be warmed by her skin, envelop her in a halo of scent. He was surprised to have to resist an impulse to press his lips to the warm copper skin of her neck. She turned those large brown eyes on him; to his surprise, they were slightly wet. His thumbs went below them to her cheekbones, almost automatically. She blinked hard once, leaned away from him slightly.

"Please," she said softly, and he knew in an instant this had nothing to do with the narrative they were trying to create. It was want, pure and simple. It heralded back to all those times when they'd been close enough to do this but hadn't, and it made something ache deep in his chest. "You can kiss me. Make it good."

It was as if someone else had taken over. He cupped her cheek in his hand before leaning in. The jolt of warm flesh on flesh made them both rigid for a moment, then relaxed. She tasted sweet and rich and fitted against him perfectly. When his tongue teased the seam of her full lips she opened them eagerly; his hands dropped to her waist to draw her close, and she let out a soft exhalation that he felt in the deepest part of him.

"Delysia, sweetheart," he found himself murmuring, and pulled away from her, lifted her chin.

She bit her lip and was about to answer, but they were interrupted by a squawk. "Professor Hill!"

He looked and to his horror recognized a gaggle of girls from the university, waving a sign he had *no* interest in reading. Delysia's low laugh rang out. Her fingers closed over his, and she leaned in to press those full lips to his ear.

"Take me inside," she said softly, and in an instant he knew he was screwed. Undeniably so. He took a moment to let her go ahead of him, keeping his eyes *squarely* on the back of her head and nowhere else, forced rationality back.

This was play-acting, this was for his career, and he had no interest whatsoever in pursuing anything with Delysia Daniels.

We need some ground rules.

Especially me, she thought.

She'd been quite naughty—very naughty, actually. But she hadn't expected the retiring professor from Long Island to take her game and one-up it.

After their searing kiss on the platform, Alexander said little, just reached for her hand and grasped it tight in his. "We're toward the rear," he said, after clearing his throat twice. "Do you think you can recognize my cars?"

"You know I can't," Delysia said flippantly, trying to lighten the mood. Alexander's thumb was passing back and forth over her wrist almost absentmindedly; she wondered if he could feel her pulse beating wildly there.

Alexander introduced himself to a porter, who nodded and gestured that they should follow him. It was a slow trip, with pauses for Alexander to point out condensers, and indicators, and brake frames…

"You are such a geek," Delysia said, and nudged him.

"That is factual." He shot her a smile; his face nearly stole her breath. She hadn't seen him so alive since this whole thing had started. "There she is," he said as they came upon their suite, and he waved the porter away. "You ready?"

"I'm ready." Delysia was also incredibly amused. "Is this what gets you going?"

"I literally have been waiting for this moment all my life. And I'm only about half-serious when I say that. Up you go," he added, indicating the retractable stairs that led to the door, but Delysia shook her head.

"This is your moment, Alexander. You first."

He grinned and cleared the entrance in about two steps, then pushed the door open. Delysia reached his back, then swayed a little dangerously on her heels. He hadn't moved.

"Alexander?" she asked, and touched his shoulder.

Wordlessly, he went forward.

The suite looked completely different, and yet very familiar. They were in the same seating area Alexander had taken her to in Southampton, but it had been completely restored. The wood and gold fixtures gleamed, the carpets and upholstery were bright and vibrant. A fire crackled in a small electric fireplace installed in one wall, and two overstuffed chairs, bolted to the floor, were drawn cozily close.

"Alexander?" Delysia said again, but quieter this time. He was still looking around, an expression of wonder on his face.

"I've been working on it, I've seen it," he said, as if trying to talk himself out of the emotion that had closed his throat when they'd entered. "But I left the setting up to the staff, I wanted to be surprised…"

"Looks like they did that pretty well," Delysia said lightly. She couldn't take her eyes off his face; it was one of the few times she'd seen him looking anything but stoic. He was trying to smile, forcing it, but his eyes were dark with emotion.

"It looks exactly like—" He broke off.

"Exactly like…?"

"Like my father wanted." Alexander took a deep breath, then managed to smile. "I apologize. He wouldn't have believed this. He'd have been so pleased. So pleased," he repeated, and his voice grew a little rough.

Working completely off of impulse, Delysia reached out and took his hand, then squeezed it once and let it go. Alexander coughed and squared his shoulders as if the touch had brought him back to himself, and cleared his throat yet again. "Well! Let me show you around."

Their suite included both a lounge and sleeping car, and he would, he explained in that odd formal way of his, be very comfortable sleeping in the sitting-room area, which had a sofa bed. The car itself was beautiful—modeled after Queen Elizabeth's Victorian suite, featuring the most luxurious of fabrics, of fittings, of design. She barely recognized it. He'd been chattering away about original brass fittings and tubs and fabrics flown in from France and the effects of a swaying train on a four-poster bed, but Delysia was content instead to look at his thin face. It was animated with the excitement of the moment, and she felt warm inside at his happiness, and more disturbingly, at the memory of the kiss they'd shared less than an hour ago.

She had a *problem*.

"… Delysia?"

She blinked and came back down to earth. The din outside the train had quieted, finally; the influencers on board had gone to their suites to check in.

"It's starting to snow," Alexander said, and went to

draw back the heavy velvet curtains shielding their little cocoon of luxury from prying eyes. It was an ideal post to make for their launch, but for once Delysia didn't feel like snapping a photo with her phone.

"Let's sit," she said, indicating the two damask chairs in front of the fire. Alexander looked surprised but pleased, and the two settled themselves into their seats. Delysia eased her feet out of her tight shoes. Alexander stared out the window, a little dreamily. This was a good place to dream, she thought.

After a moment she rummaged in her handbag, pulled out a tiny flask and uncapped it. Alexander lifted his brows.

"Don't judge me, it was sent as a gift," she said with a laugh. "I think…maybe we can have a drink for your dad?"

He looked shocked, then touched. "Delysia—"

"He sort of started this off, didn't he?"

"He did." Alexander smiled, a little tremulously, and Delysia tipped the little bottle back against her lips, then handed it to him. Alexander did the same, and returned it to her. When their fingers touched he held hers fast, for a fraction of a second.

"Thank you," he said, and the words were heavy with things unsaid. Delysia felt that now-familiar surge of emotion that seemed to come whenever he looked at her like that; now it was her turn to clear her throat. She didn't know whether it was the ridiculously romantic setting, or the legacy of the man whose essence almost seemed to linger in this tiny space, the legacy he'd left them, or Alexander himself, but…

"It was nothing," she whispered, and bit her lip.

* * *

The *Gilded Express* pulled off exactly on schedule in a flurry of thick white flakes, its passengers giddy with excitement, ready for a week of play-acting at the highest level. There was something infinitely exciting about wandering from car to car at barely half past two, dressed in evening finery, in surroundings as luxurious as any of the finest hotels. Servers circulated the lounge cars holding trays of canapés obtained from Boston's Plaza Hotel. Brandy, whisky, and mulled wine were passed around in heavy crystal-cut goblets of Romanov glass borrowed from a private collection Alexander had sourced. It was opulence at the highest level (carefully tempered with nods to sustainability, to the environment, of course).

Later that night guests would have towels and soap laid out and have their eiderdown quilts turned down, with chocolates and tea and cherry brandy and whisky offered before bed. They didn't feel like they were in the real world anymore; this felt as if they'd been transported to some faraway land, making the din outside irrelevant. It was audacious. And for the moment, it was a roaring success.

Delysia had spent years building an image of herself online—she knew how to craft a narrative of beauty, of richness, of a life that would inspire envy, or awe, or at the very least spark a curiosity that would keep followers hitting that little heart-shaped "like" button. However, she'd never been the driving force behind something this big.

She hung back a little when she reached the lounge car. She and Alexander had agreed to arrive separately, to mingle a little, and he was already there. She could see Faye across the room as well, her thin shoulders enveloped in black feathers, looking incredibly smug.

Alexander, resplendent in a black tuxedo, a glass of barely touched Hibiki in his left hand, was perched on a high barstool by the south windows, gesturing to three influencers that she recognized immediately. She was pretty sure Alexander didn't, though.

He'd started the night off with a touching acknowledgment of the history of the lands they would pass through on the journey, of their legacy, their beauty, their strength. He then gave a brief overview of the night's activities, and invited them to "laugh, love, and delight" to their heart's content that night.

Delysia waited for a lull in conversation, then snuggled into his side and put her lips to his ear. "Very well done."

His smile was slight. "I'm a professor. Rhetoric is virtually our only useful quality."

"You two are charming," Aya Trent, an influencer who'd made her name hawking lip-plumping gloss, said indulgently. She patted her date on the hand, kissed both of them, then winced. "Dear God, Eden Kim is staring *right* at us. Get me out of here," she hissed to her date, then turned to Delysia as she prepared to flee. "She hasn't stopped grilling me about you since her birthday party." She was gone in an instant.

"Her birthday…" Alexander looked bemused.

"Yes, it was her party at the club we went to that night." That first night, when Alexander had surprised Delysia with a kiss that she still felt down to her toes. Delysia shifted from heel to heel. Her dress this evening, a flapper-inspired, heavily beaded number that she described to her followers as a "really chic lampshade" touched the floor round her feet but left her back completely bare. She should have been uncomfortable at the pressure of Alexander's hand on her skin, but instead she felt warm. Safe. He was touching her more intimately than he had before. It was as if the lull of the swaying train, coupled by the warmth of food and alcohol and pleasantness, had blunted some of the chivalry he wrapped around himself like a shield.

"Ah," Alexander said quietly, then grinned. "The tiara? The *circus*?"

"Yes. In more ways than one. That was pretty understated for her, actually."

"She seemed pleasant enough that night."

"She's a vicious gossip on a good day and she's constantly…" Delysia trailed off. When she was sharing these details with Alexander's serious face, it all just seemed so *sophomoric*. "We live in the same town, have a similar aesthetic. Most of my followers follow her too, so I guess it's a scramble for endorsements."

"And you've just got a bunch of large ones, with this project."

"Yes!" He got it, exactly. "Plus—" She hesitated.

Alexander raised an eyebrow.

"I dated her twin brother for a while," Delysia stammered. "You met him. Nicky."

"Ah." At that, Alexander looked *very* interested, but now Eden was heading deliberately toward them, her dark brown eyes ringed heavily with kohl. She'd completely ignored the theme of the evening, choosing instead a tight sequined green number that made her look exactly, Delysia thought, like Poison Ivy. The supervillain, not the plant. In motion, catching the lights, the sequins made her feel a little nauseous, too. Or maybe that was just her natural reaction to Eden.

"Your window for escape is closing," Alexander muttered.

"Then help me look busy," Delysia said. It was as if some quick-moving alien had taken over her body, acting for her even against her better choices. She half-turned. "There," she said, indicating a little alcove that led to the connecting door between cars; miraculously, it was empty. She took his hand, tugged it so he would move faster.

"Delysia?"

"Don't talk," she said quietly, once they were half-hidden, and still feeling as if she were moving outside her own body, rose on tiptoe and kissed him.

She knew she was in over her head the moment their lips touched—this was nothing like their kisses for the camera up until now, and Alexander wasn't holding back. She realized in one startled moment that Alexander Abbott-Hill was a damned good kisser when he wasn't trying to be as…gentleman-like. He took his time, smelled incredible, and his lips were deliciously warm and slow, flavored by the smoothest, smokiest whisky she'd ever tasted. The inches between them evaporated like smoke.

When they finally parted, both of them were breathing hard, and Alexander's lips dropped to her neck. The touch was like a live wire to all her senses. His hands dropped to her hips, and she gripped his lapels, suddenly feeling a little faint.

Oh, the Krug was a bad idea. Bad, bad, *bad* idea.

"I'm not sure this is the place, Delysia," Alexander said softly against her neck. She clamped her thighs together in response—she couldn't speak—but not tightly enough. Christ.

"Caught you!"

At the sound of Eden's voice the two sprang apart, almost guiltily. Delysia managed to recover first, cleared her throat. "Eden!" she said brightly.

Eden wagged her finger in mock chastisement, then leaned in and air-kissed Delysia on both cheeks, eyes glittering insincerely. "Good to see you both again, and I'm glad Delysia kept you around! How cute you two are—like a couple of *teenagers*, no? What a triumph, Delly. Everyone seems to be blown away. Picture, darling?"

Delysia jabbed a slightly confused—and definitely still dazed—Alexander in the ribs and hissed "Smile" between her teeth before relaxing into her usual, practiced, post-ready pose.

Once Eden was done, she turned back to them, smiling that reptilian smile. "You look absolutely adorable. *Very* in love."

"Oh, that's merely the glow of exhaustion from all this planning," Alexander said lightly.

Eden laughed. "She never looked like this while dating Nicky."

Bitch, Delysia thought, and her stomach lurched violently. She didn't know why she was so angry; after all, Nicky had been a long time ago, and Alexander hadn't even known her then. All she knew was that it was vitally important that she not ever, ever look ridiculous in his eyes. And now, all she felt was shame. *Shame.*

Calm down. He doesn't know. And he'd never know how hard she'd fallen for Nicky—and how utterly devastated she was when he'd cut her loose. Even Eden didn't know. Only Faye did, and Delysia knew the woman would never tell a soul.

Eden was still talking. "I find your work fascinating, Dr. Abbott-Hill. I'm from Seoul, you know, and our travel systems there…"

Eden's voice faded in and out as Delysia peeked over her shoulder at the party. She supposed she should thank Eden for killing her buzz. She'd been this close to dragging Alexander back to their suite and…

Her face heated at the thought. What was *wrong* with her? Alexander's hand was resting on her hip now, making lazy circles on her fabric-covered skin. The only things that seemed to matter right now were warmth, and softness, and a *serious* surge of lust.

She looked at Alexander, and to her surprise, his expression was…amused? Eden finished her speech and headed back to the bar; the two watched her go.

"Interesting young lady," Alexander said dryly, then patted Delysia absentmindedly on the hip he held, released her, and maneuvered round her to head back to the party. "Faye says there's a man here who owns a small fleet of yachts, can you imagine? I wonder if he'd be interested in adding a luxury car to his collection. Oh, did you want me to refresh your drink, Delysia?"

"I—no," she sputtered, feeling as if she'd been hit in the face by a dash of cold water. "No. Nothing at all."

"All right then, I suppose we'll run into each other later. Cheers. I'll do my best to avoid your friend. Oh, and check your phone," he added, pulling his out and typing as he walked away.

Bereft, Delysia stood in the passage for a moment, still feeling a bit stunned and clutching to her bag as if to dear life. When it vibrated, she opened it with all the focus of a sleepwalker. She held the screen up to her face, squinted. What she saw made a lump rise in her throat.

It was them, about an hour before they'd left, on the train platform. He'd sent it to her, with one of those little yellow emojis tipping its lips up into a half-smile. It was shot in the orange-tinted light of late dusk, on the train platform, Alexander in his usual brown tweeds, her in her *Sabrina* drag. They weren't kissing; this must have been before or after that. His forehead was rested on hers, and their body language was unmistakable. His arms were wrapped around her waist, their noses were touching, and the expression on his face—

A text came through then. Faye thinks this is a good one.

Delysia slumped against the wall, welcoming the vibrations of the swaying train. Suddenly, inexplicably, she felt like she wanted to cry.

The launch party aboard the *Gilded Express* was absolutely exhausting, but it was far from their last obligation of the night. They were scheduled to attend an evening Red Sox game along with their fellow passengers. During the planning stages, both Delysia and Alexander had balked at the idea.

"I hate baseball," she'd groused. "Bunch of men in ugly jumpsuits flailing around in the dirt."

Alexander had been quick to agree. "I've only been to a game *once*, and I was hit by a foul ball. Never again. Besides, it's not exactly in keeping with the theme of the trip, is it? There's nothing luxurious about baseball—and isn't baseball over in November?"

Faye had been immovable. "It's a charity game, it's against the Mets, and you have no idea what strings I had to pull to get us seen there at all. It's a coup for all of you, really. You'll go and you'll shut up about it."

She appeared at their suite once the train completed its short journey to Fenway Park, armed with jerseys, pennants, caps. "What side?" she demanded as soon as Alexander opened the door. Then her eyes bugged out of her head. "Why aren't you *ready*?"

"Because we don't want to go," Delysia drawled from the place on the sofa where she'd been lost in a vintage copy of *Life* magazine with Diana Ross on the cover. She'd been quiet since the afternoon party, saying little. Alexander had put aside the concern that nagged at him, choosing to bury his nose in a book of his own. Thinking meant ruminating over their passionate encounter earlier, not to mention the train platform itself, and the fact that the start of this journey seemed to have unleashed something in both of them that neither was ready to admit was there.

It was almost a relief to have Faye burst in on them like that.

"You will go," she said, dumping the lot into Alexander's arms, "and you'll cheer and laugh and eat hot dogs and drink beer and do whatever else they do at baseball games."

"Are *you* coming?" Alexander said, and a bit acidly.

"I wouldn't be caught dead. Twenty minutes," Faye warned, and was gone.

Their eyes met and they both sighed, simultaneously. Then they began to laugh.

"Please tell me you're taking one of those enormous handbags," he said, gesturing to the Balenciaga Delysia had carried aboard. "I'm putting a book in it."

"It'd better be a small one," Delysia said darkly. She

stood and began rooting through the pile of…stuff Faye had brought. "Mets or Red Sox? I think you look better in blue."

"Doesn't matter." Alexander found himself fighting a smile, despite himself; Delysia saw it and raised her brows. "What?"

"I think we finally found something in common," he said with a laugh. "A decided lack of enthusiasm for baseball." Inwardly, he was grateful.

Perhaps a baseball game would be exactly what they needed to get rid of the weirdness that had followed them since that kiss on the platform—and the kisses that had followed during the lounge party, kisses that still lit up something warm and low in his abdomen when he thought of them. He could say categorically that the platform kiss was for the cameras, no matter how good it'd felt. He couldn't say the same for the party, though, and Delysia certainly wasn't keen to clarify anything.

He sneaked a look at her. She was preoccupied with poking one arm, then the other, through the arms of a Mets hoodie rendered in an aggressive shade of orange.

He sighed inwardly.

Once he'd gotten over his initial moans and groans, Alexander had to admit that the outing was kind of fun. He'd never been to Fenway Park, and the energy of the crowds pouring into the stadium was infectious. Faye had arranged for them all to move in a group that night, and all ten couples laughed, passed around a covert bottle of Krug, and posed for photographs on the sidewalk. Nicky and Eden, to his relief, were friendly but kept their distance.

Alexander felt absolutely out of place, although he

tried his best to hide it. He smiled at the jokes whether he got them or not, made himself de facto photographer whenever the group wanted to pose, and was sure to give Delysia plenty of space. When the group finally was in line to enter one of Fenway Park's luxury suites, he hung back a little, closed his eyes, and took a breath. God. The game hadn't even started yet. There would be cheering and jumping and even more posing, with Miller Lite beers and with foot-long hot dogs, and Faye had hinted, terrifyingly, at a stint on the kiss cam.

He jumped a little when he felt Delysia's hand on his arm. "You okay?" Her face was enveloped completely by that massive orange Mets hoodie; it definitely wasn't her color.

"Fine!" His voice sounded a little odd, even to him, and he cleared his throat before continuing. "A little tired."

Delysia smiled, just a little. "You look like you did at Eden's birthday party."

"How was that?"

"Like you wanted to run."

He laughed, just a little, and rubbed his eyes. "It actually wasn't as bad then," he admitted. "Big parties are…" He paused, trying to find the words. "You can kind of melt into the crowd, be an observer. Here—" He gestured, took a breath. "In about a half hour I've taken about a hundred pictures, heard about Aya's wedding, FaceTimed with Elliot and Dean's one-year-old, agreed to be featured in Kaylee's music video, playing a bartender…"

Delysia was covering her mouth, laughing softly.

"I'm exhausted," he admitted. "How do you do this all the time?"

Her face was warm, amused. Despite their early start

and the inevitably late night to come, she looked fresh. Calm. Relaxed, even. "You learn to pace yourself."

The doors to the private box opened, and the group let out a cheer. Alexander didn't do too well at hiding a wince, and Delysia patted him on the back. From where they were he could see an opulently decorated sitting area, leather furniture, a granite bar, a table covered with silver chafing dishes. Another set of doors led out to a balcony that looked out over the diamond. He squared his shoulders and took another breath.

Just a couple more hours. Or however long a baseball match lasted.

He started when Delysia's hand crept into his, stopping him. *Come*, she mouthed, and tilted her head. He followed her wordlessly a few paces back. She glanced around them as if she was afraid of being overheard.

The smile on her face was one he hadn't seen yet. It was amused, and more than a little mischievous. "What do you say we ditch?" she asked.

He lifted his eyebrows. "Ditch?"

"Yes. Ditch." She tucked her hand into the crook of his arm and began walking, swinging her handbag. "Get back on the train, go—somewhere. Anywhere."

"Ditch," he repeated, a bit stupidly. "Won't Faye—"

"Oh, she'll be *furious*," Delysia admitted. "But really, it's better in the end. What could be more romantic than sneaking off with your lover? Besides, I owe you."

"You owe me." Alexander shook his head. "You do realize that I'm making more in the next couple of weeks than I have so far this year, before taxes? And I'm likely going to get publications, speaking engagements… I can stand a Sox game for that."

"You might, but I can't." Delysia swung the bag one

more time, then gave up and handed it to him. "God, that thing's heavy—and it's all your books anyway, so you might as well. Besides," she added, returning to her topic, and ticking off on her fingers as she spoke. "You've come to the SoHo Lounge, a Cirque du Soleil party, the Cereal Bar…"

"All I was happy to do," he interrupted.

She snorted. "All you tolerated."

"It was interesting, from an anthropological point of view."

She hit him in the arm, and he laughed. He was never sure if his humor would land, so with most people he didn't even try, but Delysia was looking up at him with true amusement, not the tolerance he always assumed most people used around him. As a kid who'd spent most of his time in the Southampton History Department or tagging round lectures with his father, he'd given up trying to keep up with his peers ages ago.

"The point is," Delysia said, hugging herself against the evening chill stealing round their bodies, "I owe you. And these games have about a hundred innings, and we'll be back before the end."

"How do you know?"

"Aya promised she'd text me."

"So you've got a conspirator, then!"

Delysia smiled, pulled away from him, and rested her hands on her hips. "Well? Your choice. I'm giving you five minutes to google what there is to do around here. I'm freezing," she ordered.

Alexander stood for a long, long moment. Then, he met her eyes and began to laugh.

"What?" Delysia demanded.

"Come on. I'll tell you in a minute."

* * *

"You did this *professionally*?"

"Hush, he'll hear you," Alexander hissed. "We didn't pay."

For the second time that evening Delysia had to cover her mouth with her hands. The two were standing as discreetly as possible at the corner of Congress Street, hands in their pockets, on the edge of a circle of tourists preparing to go on a walking ghost tour of Boston. They tried to look as inconspicuous as they could, considering she was dressed in Mets gear from head to toe, and he Red Sox.

"We're getting looks," she muttered.

"That's because we don't match."

That observation nearly set her off again, and a couple of people from the group looked back at them. "Fenway Park's that way," yelled a man with a camera around his neck, and the two quickly pretended to consult their phones.

"Thank you," Alexander yelled back, and they ran, laughing, across the street. "I wasn't planning to have us follow them," he assured her. "I just wanted you to see what it looks like."

"So you did this? You were a *tour guide*?"

"Myself and my colleagues were historians and storytellers," Alexander said with dignity. Delysia was still laughing; she couldn't picture anyone as stiff as Alexander donning a three-cornered hat and giving tours to little kids.

"You did this willingly?"

"Oh, I loved it." Alexander spoke so earnestly she stopped laughing, immediately. "I did it first when I was here doing research. I knew a man who works for the company, he knew I was a grad student, and he offered. It was a bit of a joke at first, but I enjoyed it."

"So that's what we're going to do tonight?"

"Yes." There was a gleam in Alexander's eyes she'd never seen before—humor, real humor. "Backward, so we don't run into the group again. Possibly with some food…"

For the next hour or so, still dressed in their baseball gear, Alexander ushered her around the city in fine style, hamming up the tour guide routine to a degree that had her laughing one minute, gawping at him the next. They trailed the steps of the Boston Strangler—slowly, as Alexander told the story, with dramatic pauses for snacks at a food cart: lobster mac and cheese, falafel, baked beans (Delysia wasn't sure how authentic they were, but they were delicious). They had drinks at the Omni Hotel, where Alexander swore he'd seen Charles Dickens one night on tour, peering at his group from the third floor, reflected in a mirror in the hall.

"I don't believe you!"

"He's why a lot of people come to the Omni Hotel," Alexander laughed, taking a sip of the brandy he'd ordered. Under the soft yellow lighting in the bar his face was bright and rested, and inside Delysia felt very glad.

They ended the tour at a graveyard not five minutes from the hotel; Delysia looked at the headstones beneath the trees and shivered.

"I don't want to go in," she said quietly. Graveyards made her think of the dead, and the things that had to happen before someone died, and her mother, and how sick she was.

"You don't have to worry. Ghosts are too busy at night to hang around headstones." Alexander's voice was light, but he drew closer to her. Delysia felt glad for his warm presence. "And we should be getting back anyway."

"Right."

Neither of them moved, however. Alexander looked lost in thought again, and for once she was content not to draw him out. She was surprised to find herself opening her mouth to tell him why she hated graveyards so much, but she closed it instead. She'd dated Nicky for ages and he still didn't know her real reason for being an influencer. No one did, at least not here. It would take a lot more than baked beans in a paper cup and ghost stories to invite those sorts of confidences.

She cleared her throat and licked her lips, ready to suggest they head back. However, her phone buzzed and they both jumped a little. She rummaged in her handbag, peered at the screen.

"Faye," she said after a beat.

"Is she absolutely furious?"

"Not really." Delysia managed a smile. Faye actually hadn't realized her star clients were missing, which was pretty funny, but she didn't feel like explaining the joke. It was as if the chilliness of that Boston night had permeated her skin, stealing the warmth inside, evaporating it into the night air.

She also felt very tired.

Alexander said nothing, but his phone was out in an instant, and when he put it away his face had returned to its usual sobriety; her companion of the past hour and a half was completely gone. "Uber'll be here in five" was all he said, and Delysia felt a rush of gratitude.

"Thank you," she whispered.

He nodded without smiling. "No, thank you," he said,

and it was all she could do not to close her eyes, lean against him, revel in his warmth. "Are you all right?"

"I'm cold," she admitted in a voice that was shakier than she liked. "I don't like cemeteries much." She wasn't looking at him, so she felt rather than saw him shuck off his windbreaker, tuck it around her shoulders. She still didn't look at him then; instead, she closed her eyes. His hands lingered at her shoulders for a fraction of a second, and he pulled away.

"Car's almost here," he said.

"Good." She didn't turn around; she was still staring out over the grounds.

"We can walk up, if you want—"

"No, it's okay." Walking away only meant she was trying to make herself feel better, and that didn't help anything. She needed to stare at it until it didn't bother her anymore. It had no power over her. Her mother was going to get better.

She had to, or none of this would be worth it—and if Delysia wanted to be able to keep going, she had to keep telling herself it was.

Chapter Seven

Going to sleep in Boston and waking up in New York City, even though they'd just come from there, felt surprisingly decadent. Delysia was teased awake by the scent of strong coffee tickling her nostrils. She opened her eyes and poked her nose from beneath the plush eiderdown quilt and thousand-thread-count sheets to see a cheerful round face and two hands bearing a silver tray.

"Your mister's been up for hours. He says you've got an appointment as soon as we stop at Grand Central," said the porter—Rhonda, Delysia remembered.

Delysia sat up. The privacy screen used to shield Alexander's sofa bed was folded neatly and completely tucked away; to all observers, he'd simply gotten up earlier than her. He was seated at a small table by the window, sipping from a steaming mug. When he saw her sit up, he waved. A tantalizing smell of breakfast wafted from that direction, and Delysia wrinkled her nose appreciatively.

"Eggs, sausage, cherry scones, plain scones, cream, lemon curd…" Rhonda began rattling off. "Dr. Abbott-Hill ordered breakfast so you could eat when you wanted.

It's all under those silver serving dishes, and there's tea and coffee besides—"

"Say no more," Delysia said, and sprang from the bed. Rhonda's presence made it decidedly less awkward, even though she definitely wished she were wearing a bra—not that Alexander would look anyway, she thought, and irritably. She grabbed her giant Supreme hoodie from the bedpost, wrapped it around her twice, and headed to the adjoining washroom to brush her teeth and splash water on her face.

When she came back, all traces of Rhonda were gone, and Alexander had pulled open the drapes to reveal the woods on either side of the train flashing by at a fantastic pace. "Rhonda tells me most of our guests took advantage of in-room dining this morning," he said, dryly. "Hangovers, I suppose."

"One shower and Bloody Mary and they'll be ready to go again, trust me."

She checked him out. He wore iron-gray pajamas with a subtle cherry-red check, faded but still more formal than any nightwear she owned, with a dark blue bathrobe she'd bet her latest endorsement was from Brooks Brothers belted neatly over it, and a pair of thick blue slippers. His hair was parted and combed down with water. He looked so like a refugee from the set of a '50s sitcom that she half-expected Lucille Ball to pop out and start squawking.

Alexander caught the look and smiled. "What is it?"

"Nothing." It'd sounded, she was pretty sure, funnier in her head.

"No, indulge me." He shook out the *Guardian* with one crisp shake à la Ricky Ricardo, and that pretty much did it for Delysia. She began to laugh, then explained.

To her surprise his mouth twitched. "Blame my mother. She had some very old-fashioned ideas when it comes to nightwear. Like you do when it comes to sit-coms, apparently."

"I like the oldies," she retorted a little primly. "And you never rebelled?"

"I did so in other ways."

"How?" Curious, Delysia settled herself opposite him, lifted silver lids off the serving dishes. The aromas within were bewitching, and she soon had a large china plate with eggs, scones, bacon, and fruit all vying for valuable space.

"Travel does wonders for the appetite, I see," said Alexander, raising a brow.

She stuck her tongue out at him. So far, she thought with a quick, traitorous beat of her heart, it had been easy to suppress her growing crush in the blind light of day, with them exchanging light pleasantries. "Answer the question, Dr. Abbott-Hill."

He laughed. "Well, I didn't follow my father into the family business, so that was a bit of a disappointment."

"Wine?" she guessed.

He shook his head. "No. Well, not exactly. Mostly doing what it took to keep an estate running without actually having to *work*. I think he thought of himself as an independent historian, but that doesn't pay any bills."

"So you've got the name without the money," Delysia guessed around a mouthful of feather-light eggs and cheese.

"There hasn't been money in the family for at least a century, just rotting property that should have gone ages ago." Alexander paused. That faraway look had entered his eyes again. "Growing up with him was…interesting." He was quiet for a long moment. Delysia was beginning to think he'd decided not to continue when he spoke again.

"You've seen the house—very *Downton Abbey* dramatic, and just as unnecessary. Very cold. Bad wiring. And he was gone a lot, doing research, presenting…" Alexander trailed off. "He was a fellow at the Schomburg, on the board or something like that. It took a lot of his time."

"You were by yourself?"

"For the most part." Alexander smiled, a little ruefully. "There were sitters, mostly students from the university—maybe that's why I became interested in teaching." He chewed on his lower lip as if he were pondering whether or not to say something, then reached down and rolled up his cuff. "See that scar?"

Delysia looked. It was slightly paler than the deep tones of his skin, made a faint indentation. She reached out and touched it with her fingertips, then nodded.

"I managed to spill water on myself, out of an electric boiler. I was ten. Dad was better after that." His voice was matter-of-fact. "He took me along with him then, most of the time, and I guess I absorbed the love of history, if not the house. I've been trying to offload it for years, but houses that big are hard to sell. It is a historic house in that area, though, so I get something for that. I also have rented out most of the acreage to a winery, and that pays the bills. It was a sheep farm before that— wine doesn't smell as bad. And it's easier to keep the kids off the lawn."

At that, Delysia laughed so hard she sprayed a mouthful of crumbs—thankfully, catching them with her napkin. "You realize you're not a Boomer, right? You're not even a Gen X, I'd guess."

"No." His eyes were warm and gentle. "I am ancient compared to your set, though. I'm thirty-six."

"Hardly geriatric."

"I suppose not." He took a sip of coffee.

"And a Cambridge grad," she remembered. "God. That explains everything."

"Oh, shut up."

The rest of breakfast was spent in companionable quiet. Rhonda came once to offer hot water and warm wet napkins to wipe jammy fingers. When she cleared the plates, she left a printed schedule in its place. "We'll be pulling in shortly, ma'am, sir," she said cheerily. "Hope you enjoyed your breakfast."

"Photo shoot," Delysia said, squinting at the schedule, "at Grand Central. For Ralph Lauren…"

"Ah, splendid. Is that a friend of yours?"

Delysia looked up in disbelief. Alexander was grinning.

"Got you," he said, then went back to the *Guardian*.

When the *Gilded Express* disembarked in New York City, its occupants had plenty of options for the day. There was a Broadway matinee, lunch at Tavern on the Green, a lecture on the leisure reading habits of Robert Moses at the Grolier Club (not many sign-ups for this one, much to Alexander's disgust) and various chartered outings to Bloomingdale's, Tiffany's, and other shopping meccas. The crème de la crème of the internet were all tweeting, Instagramming, TikToking, Snapchatting, blogging about their experiences. *#thegildedexpress* was picking up steam online in a small but vocal group of dedicated luxury brand followers, and Faye was confident they'd triple their buzz by that evening.

"It's like Coachella. Put enough famous people in one place, no matter how tacky and disgusting, and people will follow it like it's the Second Coming."

If Alexander had his way, he would have spent the day following up with the enquiries that had flooded his Instagram account, emails, even voicemail. He was eager to filter through and sort the proposals, requests—he'd even seen a couple of research proposals, one from an Ivy League professor!—in the mix, something that filled him with excitement. However, his and Delysia's itinerary today featured a morning-long photo shoot, a little too obviously titled "Midnight Train Going Anywhere," which would be featured in the *New Yorker*, of all places, in a piece on "luxury influencers," which apparently was a sub-genre of influencer?

He'd managed to bite back sarcasm on that—imagine, trying to be published there for years and finally landing in with *this*.

Faye was going to be there, which he dreaded. He could not pull off acting the part of the doting boyfriend, posing for a camera without looking too awkward, *and* dealing with Faye's mouth all in one session. Delysia had been strangely quiet, too, since the night before. He was glad their breakfast had cleared the air—somewhat.

When he dragged his head out of his tweeds, which did happen on occasion, he had to admit two things: he found Delysia Daniels as attractive as he did confusing, and he was enjoying this assignment of theirs far more than he had anticipated. Living in close quarters with her hadn't helped; she was equal parts charming, funny, and surprisingly shy. In between the madcap efforts to create her online persona, he caught glimpses of a gentle, considerate young woman whose layers made it difficult to use his usual analysis, nail down an opinion.

And—well. His proximity to her physically arose other feelings that he'd thought were buried quite effectively in his work for years. He did feel a little guilty, sometimes, for playing his role with her so enthusiastically, but her response—

He shook himself sternly. He wasn't here to get into trouble with any young woman, charming as she was. He didn't even know how to get in trouble with a girl— his dating history was as staid as his career. However, a different part of him seemed to take over whenever she was in close proximity. It was a mixture of want, protectiveness, and a near feeling of fascination that he— he, Alexander Abbott-Hill—could possibly be the one to make a thoroughly modern girl like Delysia, well... melt. There was something in the way she fitted her body to his so trustingly and the soft sounds she didn't realize she made whenever they kissed that he felt down in his bones—among other places.

He'd never taken advantage of a woman, though, whether encumbered by alcohol, infatuation or the romance of the moment, and he wasn't going to start now. He also hadn't been with a woman in years. He wasn't going to count how many.

I suppose I'm a bit out of practice. He was the best person he knew at compartmentalizing things neatly, and he would do just that with any flickers of feeling this closeness to Delysia might arouse.

It was almost a relief to see Faye swaying in her heels and a fur-trimmed trench coat, guarding the section of

Grand Central Station that had been blocked off for the photo shoot as soon as the AM rush hour had ceased (he was sure that despite this, New Yorkers would be cursing him anyway). He recognized the withered, white-haired, world-renowned photographer Tess Samuels immediately. She'd done the last presidential portrait, after all. How the hell did Faye know these people?

When he asked, Faye grinned. Tess's people, she said, had called *them*.

"She's very glad to document a piece of history." Faye sounded so smug that Alexander knew for sure now that she was instrumental in putting this together. "Not to mention excited to photograph—"

"An influencer?"

Faye snorted, and loudly. "Are you kidding me? She wouldn't touch Delysia with a ten-foot pole, not without you."

"I don't understand—"

"You're a member of one of America's first families, darling."

"Yes, but we're not famous or—"

"Your naiveté is charming, really, but I haven't got time for it. Come over here—" and Faye hustled him over to Tess.

"I'm very pleased to meet you," he said earnestly. "I'm a great admirer of your work."

Tess smiled enigmatically. "He's got a fine face for photography. Good bones," she said to Faye as if he weren't there. Faye nodded eagerly, and the tiny woman wandered off to adjust the large white lights and backdrop she'd rigged over a cluster of old wooden benches.

"I thought you said she'd be delighted to meet me," he muttered to Faye.

"Genius is simmering, that's all. Anyway, take a look at this—it's all storyboarded here, don't you see? We're shooting in scenes, four altogether. It'll tell a story, your love story? There's an outfit for each, all tagged and bagged in that dressing area, and a makeup artist is waiting just outside it? Look, there's a chair for you and one for Delysia…"

As she prattled on, he flipped through the storyboard, pausing to read the text carefully, and look over the artists' concept sketches, which were lovely pieces of art in themselves. There would be a shot of the two of them in the waiting room, him in his tweeds, reading the *New Yorker,* and Delysia, flanked by an entourage. There would be a shot of them in the lounge car, noticing each other for the first time. There would be a cozy, candlelit dinner scene with Delysia pouring tea à la Lily Bart, an intimate scene in a sleeper car, and finally, a tender farewell on the platform. It was straightforward and not very original, but it was sweet. And if—

"Diddy did something like this, years ago. In Paris, of course, with Annie Leibovitz, for *Vogue*?" Faye said briskly. "We're hoping someone recognizes the tribute?"

And doesn't sue, Alexander thought, but that was hardly his problem, was it? "I'll go get changed. Is Delysia—"

"Yeah, she's around." Faye waved vaguely.

Alexander shook his head and ducked into the cluster of folding screens that served as walls and instantly had his senses assaulted by loud pop music that played tinnily from speakers on poles, even brighter lights, and a heavy synthetic scent of gardenias mixed with talcum powder. The place was in utter chaos—fabric was draped on every surface, interns with tape measures round their necks were absorbed in various tasks, and Delysia—

When he saw her, he nearly dropped his storyboard. "Dear God, I'm sorry!" he blurted, then turned round quickly—but not quickly enough to avoid registering smooth, copper-hued skin, covered by very little. A woman was holding the outfit that presumably would cover all of it, but she didn't seem in any rush.

"Alexander!" he heard Delysia hiss, and then he remembered that this was supposed to be his girlfriend, whom he shared a suite with, who he presumably saw in a state of undress all the time. "He does this at home too, if you can believe it," she added cheerfully, and then, Delysia was at his elbow, kissing his cheek. "Sorry, Alexander. I should have warned you about walking into an ambush."

"Not a problem," he managed. He still couldn't look right at her, although he saw with some relief she'd donned a bathrobe. A satin one that clung to the soft points of her body in the most distracting way, but he'd take anything at the moment.

Her sweet face looked worried, but he didn't have time to address that. A fellow swooped in and dragged him off to his own corner, divesting him of his jacket, shirt, and trousers and dressing him with all the efficiency of a kindergarten teacher. His attire wasn't too far off from his normal work wear—just ten times more expensive, and fitted to perfection. He had never had the experience of being sewn into clothing, and the difference it made was substantial.

Then there was a chair, and powder on his face, and a great deal of combing and arranging of his hair, and spirited discussion over whether or not a bow tie would be too much, and *then* he was done.

Delysia would be lying outright if she didn't admit that she was just a tiny bit pleased by Alexander nearly passing out when he happened upon her in the dressing room. She'd done many photo shoots in her life, and stripping down backstage felt as natural as breathing. The poor guy had looked so shocked.

Delysia was quite proud of her slim voluptuousness, and the fact that Alexander's eyes had skimmed over her with more than a little heat—alongside the panic— made her stomach tie in knots that weren't going away. She'd caught more than a glimpse of him as well, peeking sideways as he was dressed. The body under those tweeds was lean, more than substantial. Sexy, in a very understated way.

She whispered the story to Faye during their first tea break—she had to tell *someone*. The older woman found it hilarious.

"If you two would just get together it'd make my job easier," Faye said impatiently as she bolted down hot coffee and a buttered roll. "Tiptoeing around your sexual tension is exhausting at best."

"We don't—" Delysia began hotly.

"Are you kidding me? You're always looking like you want to eat him for lunch. Not," Faye added, "that I blame you. He's very attractive in a very headmaster-ish sort of way. I kind of want to see what it would be like to make him snap. I bet he's very intense. He looks like the type that would pin you down in some dark corner and—"

"Faye!" Delysia's face was getting hot.

Her publicist laughed. "Sorry! Just get it out of your system, Delly. Have a good shag. This trip's only a week, and you can ghost him after."

"I am *not* going to—"

Faye put up a finger; her phone had begun to ring. She picked it up and waved Delysia away.

Have a good shag. She wanted to kill Faye. And possibly herself, for entertaining the idea. Still—that insistent, naughty little voice inside was sort of telling her she *could* get him if she tried. He'd been indifferent up to this point, but she knew what she'd seen on his face earlier. And it would be thorough and dirty and wrong and absolutely delicious.

Delysia's wayward thoughts didn't help at all during the shoot. She felt as if her skin was on fire every time he touched her, and their bedroom scene, which took place in their berth, didn't help matters much. Soft yellow lighting, a tousled bed, and her gazing out the window with Alexander sleeping soundly next to her, curled round her protectively. There was a tangle of flannel sheets to protect his modesty, a suggestion of nakedness. She wore a shirt so cottony-soft it felt like luxury on the skin. Her hair was loose, tumbled round her face. Alexander's fingers were tangled gently yet possessively in the ends. There was strength in those fingers, and it felt like every part of her body knew it now.

"Gorgeous," purred Tess, lowering her camera. "That's a wrap. Good job, you two."

"Thanks for putting up with amateur hour," Delysia said breezily.

"Oh, you two didn't need much direction." Tess winked and walked away to pack up.

Delysia shifted from Alexander. He opened his eyes

and sat up. She was aching. Bereft, even. Her body was screaming out for something primal, but it knew it wanted him specifically, too. Tess's assistants began milling around their room, cleaning up.

Alexander smiled at her. "I can't believe I'm saying this, but I'm actually wiped."

"It took longer than I thought," Delysia admitted, looking down at her watch. Alexander was frowning at the gold face of the battered Swiss watch on his wrist (an heirloom, she was willing to bet). Alexander wore these little reflections of his status as casually as he did his skin.

"I wanted to catch that lecture at the Grolier Club, but it's already started." He sighed. "Yourself?"

There was quite a variety of events to choose from, but she felt a little listless. "It's nearly three. I don't know."

Alexander nodded. "And we've got to be back here at five for dinner and for pulling off to Philly. You know," he said in a confidential way, "this has been nice. I wasn't sure we'd be able to pull it off, but it's splendid so far."

"It has been." Delysia swung her legs over the bed, revealing a great deal of soft caramel skin and a flash of dark lace. Alexander's eyes flickered slowly over her legs, then came back and rested on her face. Delysia was surprised to see acknowledgment there now, and a sudden dark smokiness that made a lump threaten her airway.

"I feel," Alexander said, "as if I should return the favor of a quiet afternoon, after Boston. Would you have a late lunch with me, if you haven't much to do? I mean, just us. Without, heaven forbid, Faye. I'm not a very good boyfriend if she's always along."

Delysia found herself stifling a laugh. "Well, I was supposed to meet Eden Kim downtown for a function. She'd be delighted to get rid of me, though. She'll probably hint to the press I'm having a nervous breakdown at Grand Central."

"The release of those pictures will set everyone straight." He paused, then grimaced. "My students are going to have a field day. And you do realize we'll have to move to go anywhere," he added. He was still shirtless, half-swaddled in the flannel blankets with the *Gilded Express* crest on them.

"I know. That's the worst part of it."

"We could just stay in, order something from the dining car..." His voice trailed off, invitingly. "Take a nap."

Yes, they could. There was the small television mounted on the wall, and a full subscription to Netflix, and a queue of movies she never had time to watch. "Have you ever seen *The Avengers*?" she asked, reaching for the remote where it was tucked into its holder on the wall.

He groaned. "Not a superhero film."

"Oh, I suppose you'd want a documentary, then."

"What's wrong with that? There's a particularly fine one on Bobby Kennedy, and—"

"We're going to have to toss a coin for it."

"That seems fair enough."

Alexander won the coin toss, but Delysia found she didn't even mind. The two pilfered sandwiches, cake, and punch from the dining car, along with a bottle of wine (not the Abbott-Hill brand) and one of old-fashioned, over-sweet cordial. Two glasses of the first and one of the second made Bobby Kennedy *much* more interesting, she found out.

"You're a little punchy," Alexander said, amused. He'd limited himself after a sip of Delysia's cordial to a glass of milk, and Delysia had teased him good and hard about it. ("I'll have a whisky tonight, that's enough" was all he'd say in return.)

"Not really. I'm more drowsy than tipsy." Delysia snuggled deep into the flannel sheets, into his side. It was oddly comfortable; she felt as if she belonged here, in a sense.

"Good. You're all right, then," he said, and patted her knee in a fairly brotherly manner. She still hadn't bothered to put bottoms on, choosing instead to believe that her button-down was much longer than it was. She didn't know if that's what made her snap, just a little— for Christ's sake, they were both half-naked in her bed, and all he wanted to talk about was Bobby *Kennedy*?

I bet he's very intense. Faye's voice came back to her, unbidden. But it wasn't…it wasn't about that at all, not really. It was his gentleness, and his intelligence, and the fact that he was here, and he hadn't even tried to— Delysia cleared her throat. Alexander looked up at her and raised his eyebrows. She spoke quickly to cover her embarrassment. She hadn't even realized she'd made the noise out loud. "Tell me," she said, "the most embarrassing thing you've ever done."

It was out of her mouth before she could censor it, and she didn't even know where the question came from. It was dumb, and probably yes, she'd had a little more cordial than was good for her, but their conversation was getting where it should be winding down—and she didn't want it to.

To his credit Alexander didn't even blink; he looked up at the ceiling instead. "Most embarrassing," he said slowly, as if in deep thought. His arm snaked around and took the cordial from her, and he took a long sip.

"It'd better be good," she warned.

He laughed. "Well, I'm trying to pick one. There are so many."

"Okay, maybe—"

"No, no, it's fine. I've got one." He took a deep breath. "I'll tell you about the first time I was so embarrassed I wanted to hide."

"Okay," she said, and moved a little closer. She liked it when Alexander told stories. He did so with a dry self-deprecation that made them funny, even when they weren't.

"Classic setup. Girl, crush, upcoming dance," Alexander said. His mouth was twitching a bit at the corners.

"So far, so good."

"Don't interrupt or I'm not going to be able to tell you."

"That bad, huh?"

"Worse. Okay. So, I decided I wanted to ask her. Tiffany Leonard—"

"You remember her name!"

"Of course I do, it's branded in my mind forever." His mouth tipped up. "Her father taught at school, which made it worse. So I'm the kid who practically grew up on the Southampton Campus, read history books, the classics. Nothing normal. No friends my age really, for similar reasons. So instead of asking Tiffany, I ask her father if I can take her—"

"No!"

"—which he appreciated, but Tiff thought rightfully that it was weird, so she tells her friends—"

"*No!*"

"Come on," Alexander said ruefully. "Did you really think it could have any other outcome?"

At this point Delysia was laughing so loud she could hardly get the words out. "I am so sorry—"

"My ears still get hot when I think about it."

"Poor you," she teased, passing a hand over her eyes. "First loves are hard."

"Nothing to do with love. I was determined to make it out of the year having kissed a girl, and Tiffany was the dream."

"Oh man." Delysia took a deep breath. The story would never not be funny, but part of her felt sorry for the kid version of Alexander, probably small and serious, with such little socialization that he looked at books for answers to questions most people learned with experience. "I'm sorry," she said, and rested a head on his shoulder,

"You don't have to be, it was a long time ago." Laughter rumbled deep in his throat. "I'm glad my heartbreak was the cause of some amusement for you."

Delysia readjusted herself on his shoulder and was gratified to feel Alexander's arm sling around her, closing those final few inches between them. "Are you going to reciprocate?"

"What, by telling you my most embarrassing story?" Delysia smiled. "Not as gut-wrenching as yours, I'm afraid. My mother caught wind of the guy I liked, told his mother about it when she picked me up from school, and they both laughed about it." She paused, then shook her head, smiling. "I wanted to sink into the ground."

She also had remembered her mother without feeling that panic deep in her stomach, the panic born of not knowing the future. Alexander, apparently, had a calming effect on her.

She didn't want to think about it anymore.

She lifted her chin and met Alexander's eyes instead. He blinked once.

"Did you ever get to kiss your girl?" she asked quietly, allowing herself a tiny smile. His eyes had changed, something she was growing to expect from him; it was incredible, how much the browns could vary, could go from soft to stormy to the sweetest she'd ever seen, as they were that moment.

"I don't remember," he said, low, and—oh, hell, why not? She did what she wanted to do, which was kiss him.

He was clearly startled by her move, though not displeased; he stared at her before she reached out, looped her arms round his neck, kissed him again. This one was harder, tinged with a little desperation, teasing at the seam of his mouth.

"Haven't you ever just done something you wanted to?" she asked softly, against his lips.

He pulled back ever-so-slightly, and his hand came up to trace the line of her cheek. "Not really." He cleared his throat and bit his lip. After a second's hesitation, he took a deep breath and responded with a vigor that left her shocked.

He was intense, Faye was quite right in her suspicions, and it was as if they'd picked up where they'd left off in the lounge, the night before. He took his time, exploring the contours of both her mouth and body with lips and hands that were deliciously, frustratingly warm and slow. His thumbs found their way to the base of her spine, alternating with lazy circles on areas of her body that she had no idea were so sensitive. It was a culmination of that strange, easy chemistry they'd had from the start. His lips were on her neck now, and she whimpered despite herself.

"Delysia—"

She shook her head. "Please, don't *talk*." If he did, they'd have to be sensible, and she didn't want that right now.

His eyes had darkened to a muddy shade of brown that seemed to mask his usual expression, and suddenly she felt fear creep in somewhere beneath her ribs, along with the arousal that had her pressing her thighs together. This guy wasn't going to be just a quick shag; he had depths that she wasn't sure she was ready to explore.

Too late for that now, she thought, as his lips began to trace the skin bared as his fingers began undoing her buttons, still at that unhurried pace. She might have been the one to initiate the seduction, but—Jesus. *Jesus*.

"Is this okay?" he murmured into her ear, making her jump. His fingers were teasing the lace barrier covering the most sensitive part of her now, and she clapped a hand over her mouth, hoping that when she climaxed she wouldn't cry out.

It wouldn't be long at this rate, and he was still fully dressed. Hell, she hadn't even attempted to *touch* him— she was way too skittish. Nicky was her only reference when it came to sex, really, and he'd attacked her body like a road map, spending the allotted time needed in the necessary bits before diving in as if he'd earned a prize by making her come, but Alexander was treating this like some kind of—she didn't even know.

Those eyes were calm and steady, concentrating on

the pleasure on her face. It felt so good, being touched so gently and so carefully, and Delysia was squirming in a way that she knew would be incredibly embarrassing, in retrospect.

"Breathe, sweetheart," he said softly, and kissed her behind the ear. That proved the trigger, and Delysia did whimper, finally, spending herself on his warm, blunt fingertips. It wasn't enough, even close to enough, and her hands began moving frantically to tug at his clothes, to kiss him hard, demanding more.

"Delysia," he husked against her lips, dropping a restraining hand to her hip. She squirmed in frustration, changed position so she was half-straddling him. She was gratified to hear him groan when she shifted her hips right where she suspected he wanted her to. Her fingers were fighting with a drawstring that suddenly seemed impossibly knotted when he cleared his throat. She could see his Adam's apple bob.

"Delysia," he said again, this time a little louder. She opened her eyes to look into his; the murkiness was gone, replaced with that clear, calm, light-filled brown. His expression was a lot of things—tense, worried, and more than a little embarrassed. "Stop."

Excuse me? She stared at him, fingers still tangled in the knotted cord at his waist.

He sighed. "I—I don't have a condom, Delysia."

Oh my God. "I—" she sputtered, but he was already gently shifting her back onto the bed, pulling away from her, taking a deep breath. She registered the loss of warmth before she did anything else, then suddenly realized they were now sitting together in semi-darkness. How long had they been here, with him kissing and caressing her so gently?

Alexander reached over and turned on the lamp by the bed, and Delysia felt herself flinch. "Oh, don't," she mumbled, looking down and fumbling to cover her exposed breasts and shoulders.

"Delysia."

She hunched her shoulders and worked a little faster. Goddamn it, buttons had never seemed quite so clumsy before. Her body, embarrassingly, seemed to have no idea their little tête-à-tête was over for the moment; the area between her legs was still throbbing, wet, and her nipples were still so sensitive that she bit back a wince when the fabric skimmed over them.

Alexander had dragged the blanket over his lap, so she didn't even know how he was faring, but he'd moved as far away from her as was humanly possible without falling off the bed. She felt a sudden sick stab of misery.

"Delysia."

"Go away," she muttered. "I need to get dressed."

"Delysia. Please look at me."

She didn't want to do that—she wanted to die. Or disappear, at the very least. She heard him sigh, then felt warm hands on her shoulders. She lifted her chin and forced her eyes open.

"I'm not going to apologize for wanting to have sex with you, and you shouldn't either," she said. Her voice sounded odd and shaky.

"I'd hate it if you did," he said gently. He reached out and thumbed a strand of hair from her face. "And I am sorry, Delysia. If we ever did, you deserve better than a cheap tumble like this."

"Don't try to make me feel better," she said with a snuffle.

"I mean it—" And here, he wrapped his arms around

her. Delysia wanted to pull away, but she felt herself relaxing into the warmth of his grip, despite herself. He was talking into her ear now, still in those same unhurried tones. "It should be dinner, and dancing, or one of those dreadful nightclubs you love so much, and loads of good wine, and candlelight, and then I'd bring you back here, and kiss and touch and undress you properly. And after there'd be a hot bath and television, and…" His voice trailed off. "Something like that."

"That's quite the fantasy," Delysia rasped out, then laughed.

"You deserve no less than someone who can give you that." His voice rang with sincerity.

And you're not that someone. Delysia felt brittle inside, suddenly. It did not help when Alexander bent and kissed her with all of the gentleness and none of the heat of before.

Don't you want me? she wanted to cry out. She wished they'd just stop speaking in generalities. She wished she had the courage to ask him not to. But then again, she didn't want to push for specifics.

She'd pushed for specifics once upon a time, with Nicky, and the answer had crushed her.

Instead, she clung to him just for a moment, burying her nose in that smooth good-smelling place between his neck and shoulder.

She'd take this for now, and be content.

Chapter Eight

Delysia stood half-naked in front of her mirror, shivering and frowning. There was a draft coming from the large window in the sleeper car; she hadn't bothered to close the heavy velvet curtains. The City of Brotherly Love, so far, in her opinion, had little to recommend it. The glorious fall weather they'd left behind in New York had succumbed to a gloomy, rainy gray. It was forty-two degrees, misty, and threatening to freeze—and it matched Delysia's mood perfectly.

If she didn't know better, she'd say she was almost heartsick. Which would be ridiculous, because it was Alexander. The man had worn the same faded, olive-green fisherman's sweater three days running, put his shoes out to be polished every night, and had thrown a fit when the American *Financial Times* was delivered rather than the London edition. He acted as if nothing had happened between them, as if he hadn't had her in his bed two days ago and had her quivering in his arms with barely a touch. She supposed it was him trying to be kind, but Christ.

She shook her head as if to clear it, then concentrated

on her outfit for the evening. It was one she'd been excited about, initially.

"Your first major designer!" Faye had crowed when Versace sent over the glittery lady tux. It featured three pieces: a sleek black blazer with sequins glittering on it like stars in a midnight sky, a waistcoat that was really more of a bustier—it made her breasts look like they were being served up for dinner—and tailored black trousers with a fit that bordered on the obscene. She wore her trusty Louboutins with it—she did want to be comfortable, after all—and washed and conditioned her curls so they tumbled round her face and shoulders, framing the dark red slash of her lips.

It was a lot. Still, tonight was a pretty big deal. An A-list hip-hop artist was debuting an all-female version of *Faust* at the Philadelphia Opera Club, and the influencers were slated to appear there tonight—another triumph for the *Gilded Express*.

Not that Alexander, she thought with some irritation, realized that. "Oh, ah, very well," he said vaguely, when Delysia emphasized it, then went off to his stack of books, where he'd been pounding away at his Mac for hours. He'd skipped the champagne tea and Would You Rather? influencer game. The AMA that Faye had cajoled him into streaming live was absentminded at best, and he'd been back to his damn books afterward within minutes.

Pathetic, Delysia thought, stabbing at a false eyelash viciously. She was jealous. And she didn't even have a person to be jealous of. She was jealous of the fact that he was cool, and calm, and impenetrable, and had managed to have that kind of encounter with her—and had the audacity not to be one bit awkward about it afterward. It was literally as if nothing had happened.

Well, screw him. There were only a few more days of this madness, and then she'd be free of his brown eyes and gentle hands and vague manner forever. Hopefully.

"That's a job done," she said to herself finally, studying her reflection in the mirror. She turned away from it and tripped into the next car, swaying on her heels, to tell Alexander he could have the bathroom.

He was tucked away in his corner, as usual, sipping from his stained white mug and frowning into a large book. When he saw her, his eyes lit up. "Ah."

Slightly mollified by the response, Delysia offered him a smile and opened her mouth. She was interrupted when he thrust two glossy postcard-sized sheets of paper under her nose. "Look!"

She blinked and looked. As far as she could tell they were completely identical photographs of…brocade chairs?

"My antiques dealer sent them over this morning," he explained. "To replace the ones that were originally in this lounge, don't you see? If this is to be a *working* train, we'll need to find some way of protecting the more historic pieces. I never thought I'd consider a reproduction, but these are absolutely flawless…"

She didn't know if she was just overtired from the week's activities so far or what, but Delysia suddenly felt a rush of anger that she suppressed with more effort than she liked.

"I came to see if you wanted the bathroom," she said.

"Oh, is it time already?" He peered nearsightedly at his watch, then stretched, shooting her a contented half-smile. Delysia was discomfited to notice the sliver of skin that showed where that damn sweater separated from his trousers; she was even more discomfited to remember how taut and smooth that skin had felt.

I need to get laid tonight, she thought rebelliously, even though she knew it was complete bullshit. She hadn't been close to being with a guy since Nicky. The picture of her that had started this whole thing with Alexander had been exactly what her relationship with him was now: fake, a flirtatious moment reenacting a movie scene on a set she'd been visiting. Apparently, she attracted fake relationships like pollen attracted bees. "It is."

"Well, you know I only need fifteen minutes, unlike you," he joked, and stood to his feet after inserting a bookmark and closing his text reverently. "When are you getting dressed?"

When am I—Delysia blinked. "I *am* dressed, Alexander. This is what my sponsor sent over."

Alexander looked at her in astonishment. "For *tonight*?"

The irritation was returning. "I said so, didn't I?"

Alexander opened and closed his mouth before speaking again. "Er… I'm not sure if this came across in the details," he said, almost apologetically, "but we'll be in the senator's box tonight, not seated with the general public."

"Yes, I know, Faye told me."

"Er…yes. She may have missed the detail, but… there's a white-tie requirement for opening night."

Faye actually *had* given her the detail, but Delysia had assumed it wasn't super-relevant. After all, she and the influencers were the special guests of honor of the evening—celebrities, right? "Yeah, I know. Charming," she said dryly. "Very quaint."

"It's traditional for guests in that box—not necessarily everyone else, people wear jeans to the opera nowadays," he said, voice raising an incredulous half-octave on the word *jeans*. "I'll be wearing a tux, of course, so you'll probably want to—"

"I'm fine with what I have on," Delysia said snippily. "Really, Alexander. No one pays attention to those sort of things anymore, and—"

"You're probably thinking of the Opera Philadelphia," Alexander cut in. "That's the general opera house. This is different. It's a private opera club, supported by the oldest Philadelphia families, with the cornerstone laid in 1807, after the visit of the Lord George Telburn, who was so impressed by a young woman he saw in a performance of *Faust* that he, after a tumultuous affair with her, built a private club for her use when she was banned from—"

"Alexander." His voice had taken on a decidedly class-lecture lilt. "Listen. I *have* to wear this. *Versace* sent it."

"Very well." Alexander's expression was dubious at best. "I suppose our members will understand that you're a…special sort of guest."

Way to make me feel like the evening's entertainment. Delysia rolled her eyes so hard her false lashes were in danger. "Who do we have the esteemed honor of sitting with?"

Alexander completely missed her sarcasm. "Well, the senator, of course, is traditionally invited to opening night, although he doesn't always come—thank heaven for that," he added under his breath. "Most of the board will be present, of course, as it's their club. A few new inductees will be asked to share the box. Us, of course, and the director's family…"

"Wait. You're a member? Is this why we landed the box?"

He gave her a look of astonishment. "My *father* was from Philadelphia, Delysia. His sister arranged this event."

"Oh." Delysia had been fairly sure he'd mentioned that at some point during the planning process, but oh well.

Alexander stood, ran his hands over his hair. "Well. I'm going to go and get ready. And really, you look lovely," he added with just enough sincerity to soothe, if not eliminate, his initial reaction to her attire.

She grunted.

The weather had done little to dampen the spirits of the *Gilded Express*, and #gildedexpress was officially, finally, impenetrably trending. The Philadelphia opera event would only add icing to the proverbial cake.

The event did its best to evoke old-world glamor. Stretch limos and vintage Rolls-Royces charioted the guests to the opera house (not an SUV in sight), and white-gloved ushers with massive umbrellas stood waiting outside the opera house in order to shepherd the VIPs inside. They hurried over the sodden red carpet into the warm, fragrant front lobby, where Victorian chandeliers, brightly lit candle sconces, and shaded lamps made for lighting so flattering that everyone's phone was out, #filterfree.

Alexander, in full evening dress, had arrived an hour before the influencers, ostensibly to ensure everything was in place. The quiet old opera house had seen nothing like the likes of the musician and his ermine-swathed entourage in its three centuries in Philadelphia, and Alexander felt certain the founders were twirling in their graves that evening.

Alexander was looking forward to the entire spectacle. *Faust* was one of his favorite operas, and he definitely saw a potential for creative interpretation. It was all sure to be very exciting. He reached the lobby just in time to see Delysia emerge from a white Jaguar 1952 roadster (as made famous by Audrey Hepburn in *How to Steal a Million*) as grandly as the Duchess of Cambridge might, waving to the local reporters gathered outside.

His breath caught in his throat when he saw her. She was absolutely radiant. The lights illuminated her face and hair, making her look larger than life, almost like a Hollywood actress. Even that unorthodox costume looked wonderful on her. The trousers hugged her hips and made her legs look miles long, and the sequined jacket did little to hide the curves beneath. Remembering exactly how those curves looked, encased in scented, silky skin, made him bite the inside of his cheek, and hard.

He still wasn't sure how that happened, how a simple conversation had nearly led to him taking her, slowly, sweetly, carefully as he ever had, in the confines of his berth. In retrospect he blamed the sheer romance of the setting, coupled with Delysia's soft vulnerability that evening.

However, this wasn't real, he reminded himself. None of it was real. And the sooner they both faced that fact, the better.

I'll talk to her tonight.

Now, she saw him and shot him the giddily dimpled smile he'd come to recognize as her social media–ready look. He couldn't get to her because of all the cameras, but he was content to watch her in her element, for now.

"We're so excited," she was saying to the assembled throng, and he could see their celebrity guest at her side. They looked good together, Alexander thought morosely. The fellow was tall, broad-chested, with smooth, dark skin and wide-set eyes. She looked up at him, starry-eyed and flirtatious, and he was surprised that jealousy cramped under his ribs.

"She looks fantastic, doesn't she?"

Alexander jumped. Faye, appearing as she normally did with no warning whatsoever, was standing at his elbow swathed in peacock-green sequins from head to toe, gloating. It wasn't her best look (the green, and the gloat).

"I'm hoping to start some rumors tonight," she whisper-shouted to Alexander.

"Isn't he married?" If he wasn't, the artist had done a very good impression of it, arriving with a substantially built young woman and two small children.

Faye huffed. "Barely."

Alexander didn't know what that meant and didn't care. "Well. I should be taking her up to the senator's box—we're already late, and—" He could have gone to get her himself, but that would mean stopping to pose on the red carpet, and he…couldn't. He simply couldn't do something that ludicrous, not when the Philadelphia branch of the family would surely be squinting down at the throng below. "Anyway, she's supposed to be dating *me*."

Faye's eyes opened wide, then narrowed. Then she settled her sharp features into a sweet smile. "Well. Yes. That's right, isn't it? I'll get her for you." She buzzed off, leaving Alexander in a tailwind of synthetic florals, and Delysia was at his side in moments.

"Sorry," she said, then fixed her dark eyes on him. "Did you take a picture?"

"Dear God, no." He'd walked in as fast as possible. "Shall we go up? I'll need to know what to have them announce you as—"

"Announce me?"

"Yes, it's tradition. I assumed Miss Delysia Daniels, but I didn't want to presume…also, would you like Mendelssohn's 'Song Without Words' for when we come in?"

"Mendle-what?"

"It's a classical piece—"

"What is this, a wedding?"

That nearly caused a squabble, but they somehow managed to get themselves upstairs without any bloodshed. He offered Delysia his arm and she smiled, a tiny smile. "What?" he said.

"You're excited. About this—" And she included the Grand Opera House in one sweeping motion of the hand. "It's cute. You haven't been excited about much since this trip started."

Words of defense rose to Alexander's lips, but she looked so good-natured he decided to smile instead. "I'll admit to being a bit out of my element," he confessed.

"But not with Mendelssohn and *La bohème*."

"*Faust!*"

By now they'd reached the top of the stairs, and a black-jacketed usher took them in with one hitched brow. "Sir, madam?"

"Dr. Alexander Abbott-Hill and Miss Delysia Daniels."

"Thank you, sir." The man cleared his throat with one

barely perceptible *harrumph!* and announced them. Alexander pushed the curtain aside, and the two stepped into the senator's box.

The box was really more of a lounge with a seating area attached that overlooked the main theater. Couples dressed in long trailing gowns and white ties and tuxedos, like Alexander, milled about, sipping champagne and nibbling on a variety of fine hors d'oeuvres. Alexander felt rather than saw Delysia take a deep breath and draw her backbone straight. He didn't have time to look at her, though, because he saw his aunt approaching. The woman resembled Eartha Kitt at the height of her fame; she was petite and fashionably bony, with her hair arranged high off her head. She gave them both the once-over before speaking.

"Alexander, how good of you to join us," she said in a dry imitation of a high-society matron. She gave him one cool, Shalimar-scented cheek to kiss. "And you, of course, are Delysia Daniels. How are you, darling?"

"I'm fine, ma'am."

"Please, call me Sylvia, all the children do nowadays. Alexander, your uncle is over there." She nodded in the direction of an iron-gray head hovering in the corner, bobbing indignantly while in conversation with another. "But for God's sake, don't disturb him now. Something about the Giants and a bad trade, from what I could gather."

Laughter spilled out from Delysia's lips—barely a giggle, but his aunt caught it and smiled. "Have fun, children," she said, and was gone, leaving Delysia staring at the place her feet had been.

"She liked you!" Alexander said, lips twisting up. "Well done."

"And you figured that out how?"

"If she hadn't, she'd have ignored you entirely. Now, let me take you round and introduce you to everyone."

"Everyone?" she muttered, eyes scanning the silks and satins and the throng of mostly older, conservatively dressed men and women. She looked trapped.

He frowned. "Are you all right?"

"Fine. I just didn't know they'd be so…" Her voice trailed off.

"Old?" he said, trying to lighten the mood a bit. "I know. The real party is downstairs. I'm sorry you're stuck up here with me. Best seats in the house, though, and an usher was hinting about seafood later."

Delysia barely responded. She was tugging at the neckline of her bustier instead, worrying her lower lip between her teeth.

"What is it?"

"I should have changed before coming up, I think," she muttered.

"Well." He'd told her, hadn't he? "They'll just see you as either very eccentric or very young," he said cheerfully. "Neither is bad in your line of work. Now, to show you round…"

"Oh God," she muttered.

"It's not as bad as all that." He mentally sorted the crowd into categories: his aunt and uncle of course, the patronages of the opera club, their friends, and the two Philadelphia cousins who had shown up. Figuring his cousins to be the easiest of the three, he steered Delysia in their direction. Poppy Abbott-Hill and her brother Bertie were middle-aged, dour, and sour, but they loved the opera—and were kind enough to soothe Delysia's nerves, he was sure.

"Oh, Alexander!" Poppy said brightly. She'd seen him coming across the room, and navigated herself through the crowd with all the skill of a caboose dressed in mustard-yellow silk. "Is this *her*?"

"This is her," Alexander said dryly. "Whatever that means. Delysia, this is my cousin Poppy, and her brother Bertie is over there—" He gestured as Bertie waggled his fat fingers wearily in their direction, mouthing *how do you do* before burying his nose into his program.

"Well, aren't you *something*!" Poppy uttered with a slight scream, then slid her arm around an alarmed-looking Delysia's waist. Alexander stifled a laugh. "I very nearly died when Mother told me you were dating an *internet actress*, Alexander. Still, you seem perfectly respectable, darling," she added quickly. "I hear it's quite the thing these days. My Molly is constantly recording some kind of video to put online."

Delysia murmured something inaudible.

"Perhaps you could give her some tips! Anyway, do come with me, I'll introduce you to everyone—you don't want to be stuck with this old fogey all evening when you'll have him all night! Ha! And you must tell me where you picked up your outfit. So *interesting...*" Poppy solidified her hold on Delysia's waist and steered her away into the throng. The last thing Alexander saw was her shooting him a pleading look over one shoulder.

Being carried off consisted of Delysia being led by Poppy into a group of middle-aged ladies more or less dressed identically to each other, in the sort of evening-wear that would have been at the height of fashion around the time Bill Clinton was in office. They clustered in an area of the box that Sylvia called the ladies' lounge. It was furnished with padded velvet seating and partitioned from the rest of the box by heavy curtains that were looped back tonight by a gold velvet rope. An enormous framed portrait of Marian Anderson loomed over them, a heavy autograph scrawled over one corner.

Delysia had mixed with people with money before, of course. Growing up in Dubai had brought her into contact with locals worth as much as small nations, and attending the swanky parties that were the norm for her as an influencer did the same. Alexander's family was different; this was more about quality. Their straightened hair was invariably either teased into *Dynasty*-style waves or French twists—beauty parlor hair, to be sure, and not a hair extension to be found. Gold diamond rings and wedding bands adorned their knobby fingers. Equally good diamond solitaires shone in saggy ears.

"Ladies, this is Alexander's lady-friend," Sylvia announced, and six pairs of mascaraed, eye-shadowed eyes widened, and heads began to nod, "Delysia Daniels. Delysia, this is Agnes Abbott-Hill, Vivian Abbott-Hill, Beverly Abbott-Hill, Matilda Abbott-Hill…"

Sylvia's voice blurred into a tangle of names, surnames, and family connections that Delysia knew she'd have to have Alexander explain to her later. She nodded, smiled, and restrained herself from checking to see if her bustier was sliding downward.

The ladies migrated rather naturally over to the bar, where there was plush seating in the form of overstuffed, red-velvet booths. Some of the older ladies sat, but most stayed upright so as not to wrinkle their dresses. Delysia was handed a small glass of whisky and water—"Have a taste, darling, it's from our own distillery"—and was allowed a single sip before the bombardment of questions began.

"Now, honey..." This was from Beverly. "What a beautiful name you've got."

"Thank you."

"Is it French?"

"I believe so."

"Enough, Beverly, I've been eager to talk to this young lady," cut in a third woman. "You're going to have to tell me..." *Agnes, maybe?* Delysia thought. Never mind. It wasn't like she was going to call any one of these dowagers anything but Ms. Abbott-Hill. "My husband is the head of Africana studies at Philadelphia County U, and Alexander mentioned you're Eritrean?"

"Yes, ma'am, I am."

"Fascinating," the woman said, and patted the seat next to her as if Delysia was a very small girl, and she obediently lowered herself to sit. "Tigrayan or—?"

"Yes, I am."

"Do you speak it?"

"Yes, but with a deplorable American accent, or so my mother tells me," Delysia laughed, and the woman chuckled.

"Have you visited? My husband made a three-country research tour of that part of Africa, several years ago, before the situation became dire..."

Agnes began to prattle on, and Delysia relaxed. She was used to her nationality becoming a subject of conversation anywhere; this was nothing different, and at least, she thought somewhat sardonically, this bunch wasn't *too* patronizing about it. This kind of conversation required she do little but nod and smile. In a strange way it made her miss her own aunties in Dubai. At least

Agnes didn't ask her "how to say" any items in the room in Tigrinya. Aunties were the same everywhere, Delysia thought with a rueful smile.

The tension began to seep from her body, little by little; she even began to be a little less self-conscious about her outfit. Sylvia declared it virtually identical to a white pantsuit she'd worn to parties at Studio 54 in the very late '70s, and the other women began to tease her about the massive platforms and hair she'd favored during that period of her life. The women were kind to Delysia, and attentive. She gathered from the conversation that Alexander hadn't brought many girls around—"You're quite an unusual occurrence," Agnes said, and the group laughed kindly when Delysia blushed.

Time passed quickly, and the lights flickered; the women groaned audibly.

"If I've seen this damn show once, I've seen it a million times," hissed Sylvia in a stage whisper, taking Delysia companionably by the arm.

"Alexander said that you practically run this place."

"Did he? Well, Alexander was always a flatterer." The older woman laughed. "We do a massive production twice a year. You'll have to come back for Christmas—we'll be launching *Aida*. That was Alexander's father's favorite."

"He seemed quite an extraordinary man."

"That he was," Sylvia agreed. "Alexander's a lot like him. Educated to a fault, but not quite of the real world, I think…oh, there go the men. Last chance for a cocktail before all the caterwauling, honey."

She slipped her arm round Delysia's waist in a motherly sort of manner, and the women began walking slowly toward the main seating area of the box.

Delysia felt her nervousness slip away completely. These people weren't bad at all. Alexander's worries had been groundless.

"Damned good crowd you managed to collect tonight," Bertie said, then gave Alexander a slap on the back.

Alexander smiled. He hadn't seen his cousin regularly since before his parents had died. Bertie was quite a bit older, and busy with a family of four in Mount Airy. "Thank you, Bertie. How are you? Are the children here?"

"Oh, they wouldn't be caught dead." His cousin's small eyes surveyed the room rather piggily, then lit up when he spotted waitstaff carrying a tray of bacon-wrapped scallops. "Bring that here, dear. Ah. Thank you," he said, offloading three for himself.

The woman offered Alexander the tray. "I'm fine, thanks."

Bertie snorted, almost inhaling the toothpick holding the canapé together as a result. "You should have something, Alexander. You're as small as ever you were," he added, patting his own considerable girth.

"Yes. Well."

"Although I suppose you've got to keep yourself trim for the cameras and all. I nearly died when Maisie showed me your social media pages. This is a serious thing, then?"

"Photos don't lie, do they?" Alexander said, a little acidly.

Bertie's guffaw grated on Alexander's ears, and the hearty slap on his back that followed irritated him even more. "Very well. You've been far too serious since Cambridge. I'm glad to see you finally having a little fun.

And she's—" His cousin's left eye drooped in an approximation of a wink.

Alexander immediately felt ill.

"She looks ready for a good time, any time."

"Excuse me?" Alexander laughed, a little nervously. "I'm not sure what you mean by that."

"You need that, cuz. Reminds me of this girl that used to follow my band around when I was in university," Bertie reminisced.

"Oh. Rather. Well, we probably should—"

"Exotic girl, too. All tits and legs. We used to—"

"Alexander?"

Both men pivoted to see Poppy, Aunt Agnes, Sylvia, and Delysia right behind them, holding champagne coupes and wearing noteworthy expressions—sour in Delysia's case, mortified in Poppy and Agnes's.

"The lights blinked," Poppy said a little breathlessly. "We should go in. Lovely seeing you, Delysia. Alexander, we'll catch you after, I suppose," and she grabbed her brother, none too gently, and hauled him off.

Alexander bit the inside of his cheek and peered into Delysia's face. It was completely blank now, save for a muscle jerking in her cheek. The skin was flushed underneath her copper undertones, but he supposed that could be because the room was warm.

"I'm going to go," announced Agnes, and gave Delysia an absentminded smile. "Have a good time, dear."

When she left, silence reigned for a long moment.

"So, you met everyone," he said, a bit idiotically.

"That I did."

"How was it?"

"Oh, everyone was lovely. Very nice," she drawled

without looking at him, and at that moment he knew he was in deep shit.

"Delysia, I—"

She shook her head, and abruptly. "Don't. Listen, let's just say that we move in different circles and call it a night, okay? I've heard worse than what he said."

"Oh." So she had heard after all.

They fell silent. The quiet was broken only by the din of chatter and clanking dishes. Delysia was staring at her feet.

"Delysia, I—"

"You know, I don't mind people thinking I'm some— internet *slut*," she said, almost spitting out the word. "What they think is what they think. The ladies were nice, anyway, God knows what they *really* thought. But every boyfriend I've had—even the shittiest—would have punched him in the face for saying something like that."

The wounded look on her face had Alexander catching his breath even more than her words had. "Delysia, I—please don't take it personally. They're not used to someone like you, that's all, and you do look very conspicuous—"

"What the *hell* is that supposed to mean?"

He saw he had misspoken. "It means you're not in white tie!"

She actually took a step back, as if he'd pushed her, but she recovered so quickly he wondered if he'd actually seen it. She took a deep, shaky breath, and lifted her chin. "Forget it, Alexander. I'm not—God. We're not even dating, what's the point of a fight?" she added, more to herself than to him. "Let's just—get in there, okay?"

* * *

Faust was one of the most uncomfortable experiences of Alexander's life so far, and he knew it was compounded by more than a little guilt.

Delysia sat next to him, large eyes fixed immovably on the stage. She drank sparingly from her glass of champagne, clapped politely after each act, said a few words to her neighbors in the box about how beautiful it all was. She even spent the slower numbers with her small hand tucked in Alexander's arm, her head warm and fragrant on his shoulder. Despite her outrageous dress and the flash of hurt and anger he'd seen earlier, there wasn't a single crack in her act, and that somehow made Alexander feel even worse.

Her face now—it wasn't the Delysia he'd had the pleasure of being with for days, nor the woman he'd nearly taken to his bed. This was the bright, carefully curated Delysia Daniels playing a role, and nothing more.

Damn his cousin and that perverted mind of his.

Otherwise, the night was a success that he knew would be talked about for years to come. The influencers' recommendations had secured, Poppy told him excitedly after the last curtain call, a sold-out season, and the powers that be were contemplating a waiting list. The Philadelphia Opera, smelling competition for the first time in its centurial existence, had already reached out about potential collaborations.

Everything they touched, Alexander thought, turned to gold. It was becoming evident to him why Delysia had chosen this life. If one was young enough, beautiful enough, and charismatic enough—well, why not?

He suddenly felt very tired, and very old. And when

Delysia approached him after midnight, when all the revelers had headed out for the evening, he knew he should apologize, but didn't have the words to somehow. Perhaps when they were back in their suite...

Her brown eyes were calm and steady. "Our car is here," she said, "but I won't be going back with you."

"Why?" he asked, and immediately could have bitten his tongue—she was looking at him like he'd taken leave of his senses.

"I am going out," she said, as if to a small child who was having trouble understanding. "With Eden Kim. No need to wait for me, I'll probably crash in her suite when we get back. I just don't want you to wonder where I am."

"Delysia—"

She cut him off with a smile that was both bright and brittle. "It's fine, Alexander. Two more days, right? We can do this; we're grown-ups. Enjoy the rest of your evening." She turned and walked out with her usual unhurried stride, hips swaying gently. He stood there a long time before he tucked his hands in his pockets and walked away, and slowly.

The Mercedes he'd arrived in idled at the curb; he could see it through the plate-glass windows once he reached the ground floor. The photographers were gone, as were club members. Waitstaff were rolling up the red carpet, sweeping up the glitter that still clung like raindrops to his hair. The energy had left the room, along with the occupants; the very building seemed to sag under the weight of exhaustion.

"Sir?"

Alexander turned slowly. A woman stood behind him; her uniform indicated she was an usher.

"This was on your seat in the box, sir," she said, and

held it out. It was a slim, glittery wallet with a gold chain as a wristband.

Alexander opened it. The first thing he saw was a driver's license with Delysia's smiling face on it. "It must have slid out of her handbag—thank you, I'll get it to her," he said to the woman, who nodded and walked off.

How he'd get it to her was the real question. He knew she'd need it; her credit cards were inside, and she'd surely be buying drinks or food at some point, or hiring a taxi to take her back to the train station. Plus, he didn't want her to panic about losing it either.

He picked up his phone, called her. It went straight to voicemail. He called again—same thing.

"Oh, boy," he muttered, and shot a text instead, waited. It hovered tantalizingly in cyberspace for a moment, then showed as delivered but not read.

"For goodness' sake." She was a social media guru, for crying out loud. Unless she was trying to avoid him—

Don't give yourself that much credit.

He opened his account, scrolled his contacts until he found Eden Kim's handle, and looked. Sure enough, there was a live video streaming. Eden was pouting glossily into the camera through a curtain of shiny dark hair, surrounded by a throng of dancing women in a dim room.

"I'm live," she said breathily into the camera, "at the Lyon's Den in North Philly, and fresh off of the *Gilded Express*. Just saw *La bohème*—"

"*Faust*!" he exclaimed.

"…while it was gorgeous, it was also soooooooooooo long! Just trying to get that energy level back up, y'know? Anyway, what do you guys want to see, us doing shots, or see what everyone's wearing?"

Oh dear God. Was this what Delysia did regularly? A quick look at the folks she'd tagged confirmed that yes, indeed, Delysia was with her. He hurried out to the street, called an Uber, and was on the way to the club within minutes.

Chapter Nine

It wasn't difficult to find a distraction from the dumpster fire that had been the evening. When Delysia left the opera house she spotted a white Bentley with two long, slim, creamy-skinned legs dangling lazily over the pavement out of the open rear door.

The legs were subject to anyone's guess, but Delysia would recognize those shoes anywhere—a gorgeous satin-lined, open-toed, rhinestone-buckled pair of stilettos, gift from the House of Valentina. She trotted over to the car.

"Hi, Eden," she said coolly, placing her hands on her hips. "Nice shoes." There was no sign of Nicky, thank God—she'd have smelled his cologne this close.

The legs uncrossed and drew back, and Eden's head emerged from the dark interior. She gave Delysia a slow, serpentine blink, her garnet-red lips curved up into a smile.

"They're House of Valentina, but a girl like you knows that already. You're not still mad at me for getting their endorsement, are you, darling?" she said to Delysia, then air-kissed in her general direction. "Do come in. I'm just waiting on the driver—he's getting me an espresso."

Delysia slid in the back seat gratefully—it was getting rather crisp outside. "Of course I'm not mad." Although she had been. *She* was supposed to be the one to promote the shoes, after meeting a buyer at a party, but Eden had managed to score them first.

In retrospect, her method had been genius. She'd posted a review of Essie jewel-tone nail polishes that had racked up twenty-seven thousand views in a day—and had not-so-coyly mentioned that they might be a great match for the House of Valentina's Kiss Me Tender open-toed stilettos. Delysia had grudgingly accepted the loss. Eden Kim might be shady as hell, but no one could question that she was stylishly shady. (Plus, Delysia had landed a pair of Jimmy Choo rhinestone-studded flats a week later, so it was all water under the proverbial bridge.)

They air-kissed, twice on each side.

"No Abbott-Hill tonight?" Eden asked, lifting a whisper-thin eyebrow that she'd shellacked on earlier. The fashion dictated thick brows now, but not for Eden Kim, never!

"God, don't call him that." Delysia grimaced and shook her head at Eden's offer of a cigarette. The latter lit up and took a long drag with every indication of enjoyment.

"If the shoe fits…" Eden giggled at her own cleverness. "He *is* cute. How the hell did you find him?"

"I was doing an event in Southampton and he was there." Delysia launched breezily into the cover story she and Alexander had prepared weeks ago. "I spilled wine and he was there to rescue me with a handkerchief and a club soda."

"Interesting." Eden's eyes seemed to penetrate Delysia's face.

The driver arrived, thank goodness, passing Eden cof-

fee in a tiny cup, and then they headed out. "If it weren't
for this there'd be no way in hell I'd be able to stay
awake," muttered Eden, downing her espresso in a gulp.

"What, partying isn't enough to keep your eyes
open?" Delysia said, amused. "Face it, Eden. This trip
is the merching opportunity of a lifetime."

"I know." Eden was grudging, but agreed. "I've doubled my numbers for this month. I suppose I should thank
you for not leaving me off your list."

"What, and deny the *Gilded Express* the pleasure of
hosting Eden Kim?" Delysia threw out her arms in a
grand gesture and sank back into the plush car seat, suddenly tired. She'd have to conserve her energy for that
night. Unbidden, her mind flashed to her suite, the soft
bed, the flat-screen television…and Alexander, reading. Or writing. Or making her watch some stupid documentary…

"Frankly, I'm surprised that you're hanging out with
me at all," Eden said, fixing Delysia with an inscru-
table look. "If I had a boyfriend like yours, I'd be out
with him. Unless," she said, as if the answer were very
obvious, "you're trying to get people to speculate about
why you're not together. A little much considering you
two are the face of the damn thing, but I could see how
that would work…"

Delysia closed her eyes, then opened them. "We had
a disagreement," she said shortly. She really didn't want
to start explaining herself to Eden, and was surprised
she was even bothering, but…well. She was tired. She
might regret this later, but whatever. "I just need some
fresh air tonight, and there's none on that damn train."

Eden's penciled brows rose to their limit, but to her
credit, she didn't pry. Instead she patted Delysia's arm

with a hand that was as ice-cold as it was soft, even through the material of her sequined blazer.

"Well, I'm glad you came here then," she said sweetly. "I'm going to make *sure* you have a good time tonight. One second—" and Eden pulled out her phone, speed-dialing someone and beginning to chatter on about VIP rooms and bottle service.

Delysia sank back in the seat again, relieved. This was exactly what she needed, she told herself. Drinks, dancing, and Eden's vapidity, enough to remind her that there was a world out there beyond Alexander Abbott-Hill, his stupid estate, his stupid university, his stupid tweeds, and his stupid, stupid trains.

Eden was as good as her word. When they arrived they were met at the door by a group of gorgeously dressed young men and women—local celebrities, influencers, and the like—who seemed determined to showcase themselves to the best advantage in the City of Brotherly Love.

Eden pinched Delysia's arm to get her attention. "Selfie!" she shouted over the din leaking from inside, and she and Delysia paused in the grimy doorway of the nightclub to take a video. "I'm here with my girl Delyyyyyyyyyysia," Eden drawled. "She's managed to drag herself away from true love long enough to keep me company tonight."

"Hello, y'all," Delysia said brightly. She could feel her voice automatically rise into the appropriate register for recording—sexy, flirtatious, a little husky. "What's on the table for tonight?"

"Us, when we're dancing later," Eden said, then guffawed. "Anyway, my loves, what will it be? Shots? Dancing? Or should we go see who's at the bar?"

She clicked off the video and posted a quick quiz for their followers to answer, then pursed her lips. "I hope to God they don't say dance. I'm not in the mood to mosh in these shoes, and that's what I've heard this dance floor is like."

"Neither am I." Delysia wasn't much of a drinker, she was more of the type who would have one of something and sip over several hours, but tonight she definitely wanted a buzz. "Let's give them fifteen minutes and get a quick drink anyway, shall we?"

Eden's eyes glittered for a moment, then she smiled. "Sounds like a plan."

The two women drifted over to the bar; Eden ordered a dry martini and Delysia, after some hesitation, ordered a vodka soda, then changed her order to a vodka rocks.

"Oh my," Eden said, obviously amused. "You're a Moët girl, if I remember correctly."

"I'm not too old to change."

"No, that's true. Well, let's get you good vodka, if you're going to insist on drinking it." Eden ordered a bottle of Grey Goose and asked that it be sent to a table. The place was secured in moments, and Eden draped herself carefully on a chair, crossing one long leg over the other. She kept looking over her shoulder.

"Expecting anyone?"

"You might say that," Eden replied, and then grinned. "And what do you know, there he is."

Delysia turned—and her glass slipped out of her hand, clattering to the floor.

It was Nicky.

Delysia could barely hear Eden's chattering in the

background; she stood up, jaw tense. She felt Eden's hand on her arm, and the girl made a whiny noise. "Oh, Dells, don't run off because of Nicky. It's been what, a year? It's time for the two of you to make nice…"

Delysia's heart was hammering so hard that she could hear it in her ears. Nicky had reached them by then, and tilted his head, smiled. "Hey, honey," he said, simply.

"Don't call me that," Delysia croaked.

Nicky's dark brown eyes gleamed in his chiseled face. He was more handsome than last year, if that was possible. His black shirt and trousers fit him to perfection, and as he grew closer she caught a familiar whiff of designer cologne, nothing like the comforting mix of pleasant scents on Alexander's skin. She shrank back from him, and he frowned.

"You look good." His eyes skimmed possessively over her body, lingering at the swell of her breasts, her hips. Delysia knew exactly what he was remembering, and immediately felt more naked than she ever had in her life.

"Don't."

Nicky lifted his hands in a gesture of surrender. "Look, Eden thought it was a good idea for me to come out, yeah? So you'll know I have no hard feelings about what you did to me—"

"I did to *you*?" Delysia's head snapped up. "You ditched me, Nicky. In more ways than one."

"It was only business, and you know it," Nicky said dismissively. He waved off Delysia's sputtering. "We wouldn't have been together in the first place if it wasn't for all this, let's be real. You packed out of our place before I came back. That wasn't cool, Dells."

Delysia couldn't answer for a long moment, because she was choked with rage. Faye had warned her about

Nicky. *You don't give a guy like that an emotional advantage*, she'd said.

But Delysia had been blown away by his humor, his good looks, his charisma. She became almost obsessive in her quest to be the perfect girlfriend. At first going to his gigs and posing with him at parties and playing house in his Williamsburg loft had been fun, but it got old really fast—once she realized his concept of dating hadn't included exclusivity—and she realized that in his head, they weren't really dating at all, not for anything but the likes.

This time, she was sure both parties knew what was involved.

"Eden says you're dating that *schoolteacher*," he said as if it were a foreign word. Delysia thought she saw a hint of something malevolent in those dark eyes, and for the millionth time since he'd come over, she wanted to get up and run. Pride kept her sitting, and she raised her chin.

"He's a professor," Delysia snapped. Alexander, who'd treated her like shit tonight.

"You all are making quite a stir so far."

She grunted.

"What, trouble in paradise?"

Delysia flinched. She couldn't help it, and she immediately shrank, waiting for Nicky to move in for the kill. When he didn't say anything for a long time, she risked looking up; he was staring down at her, an odd expression on his narrow face.

"Babe," he said. "Look. It was a long time ago, and we're not going to agree on what was what. Truce?" He held out a hand.

Every bone in her body was screaming at her not

to trust a word he said, but she felt too beaten down to fight it. She watched as her hand disappeared into his and suddenly felt drained of all strength. Alexander… he'd never be for her.

Men like Nicky were on her level.

"Drink, honey?" Nicky was saying, waving over a waiter.

Slowly, deliberately, she let her body relax, angle toward Nicky's massive chest. He chuckled low in his throat, and she fought back another bout of revulsion.

"Pour me a glass then," she said huskily, and bit the inside of her cheek hard when Nicky's lips grazed the side of her neck as he poured. The vodka, however, had blunted the edges of her reality rather nicely already, and she was fine not caring, for the moment.

"Hey, you two." Eden had returned. Delysia blinked, trying to get her bearings.

She saw Eden looking at her intently. When she locked eyes with the other girl, she was startled at the venom she saw there. Then Eden flashed her a smile and a small wink and thumbs-up. *All yours*, she mouthed, and Delysia wondered if she'd imagined it.

She blinked and shook herself off, then looked up in time to see Nicky discreetly produce a packet from his inner pocket, shake out two tiny blue pills, and regard them with great interest before popping them onto his tongue and swallowing them dry. Yet another aspect of Nicky Kim she'd managed to forget. She had to give it to him, though—his microdosing had never made him sloppy. If one didn't look at his pupils when he was far-gone, no one would ever know.

She licked her lips. "Give me one."

Nicky looked at her, surprised. "I thought you didn't—"

"I don't. Hand it over."

His look of surprise changed to one that was slightly diabolical; Delysia didn't even care. If she couldn't drive Alexander out of her head from sheer will, partying tonight like she never had before would take care of it.

She took one of the tiny pills from Nicky, reached for his drink, and washed it down. He laughed out loud, tilted his head. "Go easy, Delly."

Delysia shook her head and drained the foul-tasting liquor. "This is terrible," she announced. "I'd like another."

"Your wish is my command." Nicky leaned in to signal the bartender, still chuckling under his breath.

The Lyon's Den turned out to be the type of place that Alexander had only seen in films. Concrete floors and walls, shadowy corners, music that seemed to make the very foundations of the building shake. Attractive women in very short skirts added to the party atmosphere, pouring drinks and flirting with customers. The place smelled of alcohol, perfume, sweat, and hair products, and was stiflingly hot. He felt overwhelmed as soon as he got past the doorman—he didn't even know where to start.

"Excuse me," he said to one of the waitstaff.

She stopped, saw his tux, and did a double take. "Yes?"

"I'm trying to find someone, please."

She gave him an aggravated look, but pulled a mini-tablet out of the large kangaroo pocket in the front of her miniskirt. "Name of party?"

"Oh, it's not—" He paused. Party? She had left angry at him; he doubted she'd had a reservation. "Her name is Delysia Daniels."

The woman stuck her tongue in her cheek and rapidly studied her tablet. "No one by that name here."

Alexander consulted his Instagram feed—no, they were there all right. Eden had posted *shots, shots, shots!* alongside the picture of a drink that appeared to be on fire. "She's with Eden Kim?"

"Eden Kim?" The woman checked again. "Oh. Yeah. They took a private room about a half hour ago...room five," she finished.

"Private room?" Great. She was already angry enough without him crashing her private space. "I've got her wallet, you see, and I need to give it to her—"

"Well, I'm not going to do that." The woman looked aggravated. "You're going to have to either do the lost and found or go find her."

"I—yes. Very well."

The woman rattled off fast directions, then disappeared into the crowd. Alexander sighed and squared his shoulders, then navigated his way across the dance floor. He was bumped and jostled—and, disturbingly, grinded on—but made it to the back of the club, where black doors with gilt doorknobs indicated the VIP spaces. He tapped once at room five's door. He could hear movement inside. Laughter, actually. Giggles, feminine ones, and a crash, as if someone hit a wall. Then even more hysterical laughter.

He was about to push the door open when it swung open of its own accord. A tall, broad-shouldered man barreled through, raking a hand over his dark hair and mumbling under his breath. He barely looked at Alexander before melting into the dance floor.

Alexander contemplated leaving—he was obviously not Delysia, nor Eden Kim—but decided to have at least a quick peek before looking elsewhere. He pushed the door open just enough to put his eye up to it, poised to make a quick getaway if the room was empty or contained more strangers.

The room was so dim it took him a moment to see what was going on. The soupy light revealed two figures—a woman bent over someone lying prostrate on the floor, holding a phone up at eye level. The woman with the phone tilted it at a few different angles, then she knelt.

Alexander had no idea what made him keep watching, but he did—at least long enough to recognize the woman when she half-turned and the weak light fell on her face. It was Eden. She squatted to get a closer shot of the woman on the floor, who he didn't recognize at first, at least not until he saw those unmistakable black curls.

"Dear God," he muttered, and pushed open the door completely. Eden started like a frightened cat. Her eyes widened with shock, then fear. She straightened so quickly that she dropped her phone. It bounced off Delysia's shoulder, but she didn't move.

By this time he was beside them. He didn't know what his face looked like, but he guessed it must be pretty formidable, because Eden took a full step back.

"What the hell happened?" he said, and looked down. Delysia's shirt was stained with what looked like red wine. He could see her chest rising and falling, though. Thank God for that. "What *happened* to her?"

"She's fine." Eden's voice was high. Shaky, even. "She had too much to drink, is all, and she just—toppled over—"

"And you took *pictures* of that?"

Eden blanched.

"I saw you, Eden. Through the door," Alexander

snapped. Panic was rising in his chest. He knelt on the floor and cupped Delysia's cheek; the skin felt cool, but not unnaturally so, thank God. He stroked it lightly. She lifted her chin, murmured something inaudible.

"She hasn't been here long enough to drink herself into a stupor. We're going to have to take her to the hospital." Alexander sat on the floor and gently lifted Delysia's head into his lap. That did make her stir a bit; she focused blearily on him, opened her mouth, but nothing came out. He ran a hand over her head, tenderly. "Sweetheart, you're fine."

Her breathing was good and her hands were damp but warm. He looked over at Eden, who was twisting the ends of her hair so tightly round her fingers they were turning white. "Alexander, I swear to God I have no idea—"

"You were *filming* her on the floor," Alexander said. He felt sick to his stomach. "What the hell, Eden."

"I wasn't—"

"I saw you. And that's what I'm going to tell security."

At that, Eden went white. "You've got no proof."

She was right, he didn't, but that wasn't his main concern. "Get me a bottle of water. And call 911."

"Alexander—" Real fear crossed her face.

"Do it now!"

Eden skittered off to the booth seating at the other end of the room and produced a bottle of Perrier. Alexander spilled some onto a handkerchief and used it to dab at Delysia's lips, her cheeks, her neck. Eden was hovering over them, still gripping her phone in her hands. Delysia moaned a little and began to stir. Her eyelids fluttered.

"Call 911, Eden," Alexander said without looking up.

Delysia apparently processed that enough to lift her head and try to answer. "No…no ambulance."

"It'd be the kiss of death if it got out," Eden whispered.

"Are you people *kidding* me?"

"You don't get it. If the police came, they'd ask questions, and it'd be on the public record, and—"

"Damage your brand," Alexander said, thoroughly disgusted.

Eden bit her lip.

Alexander felt Delysia stir in his lap again; she was trying to sit up. He helped her, and she sighed deep, leaned her head on his chest.

"Sleepy," she said softly, then closed her eyes. "No police."

He was about to open his mouth when Eden cleared her throat. "Alexander?"

He looked up.

"What if I could… I would guarantee that…" Eden paused. "She'll be sleepy for a while, but she didn't take anything that will do anything…permanent. I swear. She'll just have a bad hangover."

"And you know this because…?"

Eden didn't say anything.

"You're disgusting." Alexander cradled Delysia close to him. Even through alcohol and his own nervous sweat, he could smell the subtly sweet fragrance that was her hallmark. She felt slight in his arms, so unlike her usual presence.

"Sweetheart?" he said quietly. It wasn't for show this time.

She turned her head slowly, as if it hurt. "Don't worry," she whispered, and closed her eyes again.

Alexander swore. Then, he looked up at Eden. The look in his eyes must have held some malevolence, because the young woman backed up, bit her lip.

"I will wait," he said with deadly calm, "exactly thirty minutes. If she isn't better, I'm calling an ambulance, and you're telling them exactly what fucking happened to her."

"Alexander, I swear to God, whatever she's on, she took it herself—"

"And while you're at it, you can delete those pictures." His voice was strange to him, cold, almost detached. "You're a foul little—" He bit back the word he wanted to use, and swallowed instead. He'd think of something, deal with Eden later.

Now, all that mattered was the woman in his arms.

Delysia had never been much of a drinker, and the experience she'd just had pretty much guaranteed she'd never be one. By the time they left the club, she was lucid enough to be able to walk, supported by Alexander's strong arm around her waist. She could speak, albeit from a throat that felt like it'd been attacked by whisky-flavored cotton balls. What hadn't improved, though, was the pounding at her temples.

"You're going to feel terrible for quite some time," Alexander told her with his usual gentleness.

He called a car for them, hoisted her in, watched her intently as they drove. She was sitting at an awkward angle, trying desperately not to touch any part of his body, or to throw up (embarrassingly enough, he'd produced a paper bag that she knew was for that purpose, no matter how he tried to hide it). He asked her questions every couple minutes or so—probably to ensure that she was still conscious—and she answered woodenly, without meeting his eyes. Eden had been there when she'd come to, but she'd left. Too bad. Delysia would have welcomed her company, if only because she would have been distracted from the embarrassment.

"Delysia," Alexander was saying. He took her hand and rubbed it between both of his; they were comfortingly large and warm, and Delysia suddenly wanted to cry, from humiliation and tiredness and from the fact that she still wasn't sure she wouldn't manage not to throw up before they reached the train. She bit the inside of her cheek so hard she tasted blood, but she welcomed it. Anything to keep her conscious and keep the contents of her stomach where they belonged...

"Delysia," he said again.

She made a sound without turning to look at his face.

"How are you feeling?"

In response, Delysia turned her head away completely, resting it on the cool glass of the back seat window. "You're gonna have to get out if she's gonna be sick" was the last thing she heard before drifting off into an uncomfortable and dreamless sleep.

When she came to again, it was Alexander gently shaking her shoulder. "Delysia, sweetheart. We're here."

His voice was gentle and warm. It crept through her icy skin to her very bones, heating her from the inside. She lifted her head and fumbled with the door. The cabbie, eager to be rid of her, opened it with a click, and she pushed it open and instantly almost fell out. Her legs simply weren't working correctly.

"I'm here, Delysia." Alexander again, and she found herself cradled, lifted in his arms. He steadied her on her feet and the two walked painstakingly to the elevators on the platform that would take them up to where the train was stationed for the night. Luckily there were few passengers at this time, and none she recognized. It was too late for most day-to-day customers to be out, and too early for the revelers on the train to have arrived back to their staterooms.

She enjoyed the two extremes, the icy air cut into her nausea a bit, and the warmth of Alexander's body was equally soothing. She was still drowsy enough not to push him away, although everything in her brain was screaming at her to do so. She wasn't stupid. She'd clean the floor with her ass if she let go of him.

When they reached their suite, Delysia was still unable to walk by herself, although she was completely lucid, no longer fading in and out. A throbbing had begun behind her eyes and at her temples. The moment Alexander lowered her to the couch, she felt her stomach lurch.

"Alexander—" was all she managed to rasp out, but she guessed that the look on her face was enough to tip him off. There wasn't any time to get to the washroom. She barely saw the porcelain basin before emptying the contents of her stomach into it.

"I knew you were going to do that," he murmured, and she felt his fingers slide over her head, holding her hair back. He was saying quiet, encouraging things, pausing occasionally to rub her back. She gagged, did it again.

"Just get it all out," he said quietly.

She managed to inhale, a shaky, wet sound that was supremely unattractive. When she sagged back into the sofa cushions tears were running down her cheeks—tears of humiliation, mostly. She'd never done something so disgusting in front of another person, not since she'd turned twenty-one and had her first glass of wine.

"Are you okay?"

"Of course I'm not," she snapped, but it came out as a whisper. The tears were coming faster now. Alexander pulled back a little, looked hurt, but he didn't answer, just got up and disappeared with the basin. When he came back it was with a towel that he'd soaked in hot water.

"Here," he said, and Delysia pressed the soft white cloth to her face. She smelled lavender and vanilla; the heat was wonderfully soothing and she felt the tension behind her eyes loosen, just a bit. She couldn't manage to stop the water streaming out of her eyes, though. She'd graduated to actual sobs, and when Alexander sat beside her and placed a large warm hand on her back, she cried all the harder.

"Don't do that, I smell awful—" and the thought of that set her off again. Alexander made soothing clicking noises with his tongue. He attempted to pull her close, but she shook her head violently. "Stop it."

"Delysia."

"Just go!"

He shook his head. "I can't. Not until I know you're fine. I'll stay on the other side of the room if you want, but I won't leave you."

I won't leave you. Somehow the simply spoken words set her off again.

"Delysia, please stop crying, sweetheart. Your head is going to ache."

"Don't call me that, there aren't—any—cameras here," she spit out reproachfully. "You don't—have—to—"

"Delysia—"

"This is so goddamn embarrassing," she whispered, and turned her back.

He hesitated before speaking. "Delysia. I owe you an apology. I know this isn't the time for it, but—I should have defended you. I'm *sorry*."

Delysia's lips were beginning to feel very dry; she also wasn't sure that she wasn't going to be sick again. She picked up the cooling towel from where it was soaking into the fine upholstery of the sofa, and pressed it to her cheeks.

"Delysia—"

"Please don't say my name like that." She suddenly felt very weary, and very sad. "Why would you defend me? Your cousin was right."

"Delysia—"

"Do you know that my mother thinks I'm still in medical school, Alexander? And that I work part-time in a laboratory, and that's how I support her?" She laughed raggedly. "I lie to her, every single day, because if she knew what I did she'd be ashamed of me. And you think what I do is stupid, too."

"Delysia, I don't—"

"You do. You and your books and your doctorate. You've looked down on me since the beginning. And you know what? I don't give a shit, because I've earned every penny honestly, and it's keeping my mother alive. And I'm not going to apologize for it, not to you or to your vile cousin."

The declaration took quite a bit out of her, and Delysia leaned back, feeling as if someone was drilling through her skull.

"Delysia, I'm sorry," Alexander said quietly. "And you're right, except for one thing—I've never looked down on you. Rather, I think you're one of the most extraordinary women I've ever met. And I'm going to regret not defending you for a very long time."

She didn't say anything, just turned her head to the side.

Alexander was silent for a long moment. Then he stood and left. Delysia didn't move; she was afraid she'd hurl again.

When Alexander came back, he was carrying a tray with a carafe of ice water, a bottle of mouthwash, ibuprofen, and three hot, damp hand towels, rolled up and smelling of lavender and lemon. Delysia eyed him, and his mouth tilted, not in a smile, but a bit remorsefully.

"Don't speak to me if you want, but please let me stay with you," he said simply. "I feel responsible."

"You're not responsible for me."

"No. But if we hadn't quarreled, you wouldn't have gone off with Eden."

At the mention of her name, Delysia's eyes welled up again. Jesus, when would she stop crying? "I'd like some water and medicine, please," she said roughly, and in an instant Alexander had tucked two pills in her hand and supported her head up to sip. The pills went down. For one terrifying moment she wondered if they would stay down, but they did. She took another sip.

"I probably should have called into poison control to ask if pain relief was okay," muttered Alexander. "How are you feeling?"

"Like I've got a hangover from the pits of hell." Delysia took another deep breath and tried two tiny sips this time.

Alexander's lips thinned. "When I came into the room, I saw Eden on the ground with you, and she was…

she had her phone with her. I think she was trying to take pictures."

"What?" Delysia whispered. She suddenly felt very cold and very hot at the same time. She was fully aware of their rivalry, but she hadn't any idea Eden hated her that much. And Alexander was still talking.

"I don't think she posted them anywhere—I threatened her. But, Delysia…" He trailed off. "I wanted to call the police, but you—"

"I said no." She swallowed down a new wave of nausea with some effort, and groped for the mouthwash. When she spit it out, she managed through very dry lips, "If the police had come and it'd gotten out, it would have ruined everything. For this trip, I mean."

Alexander said nothing, and Delysia figured he wasn't at all impressed with her explanation. She could see how weak it was in retrospect. She'd never met someone who she was so attracted to, yet who managed to make her feel like an idiot all at once. "Alexander," she began, and stopped to wince.

"Please don't feel like you have to talk if you feel ill," he said, softly.

Well, she wouldn't then. Delysia meekly submitted to having her face and hands wiped, almost as if she were a child. Alexander brought a large, clean-smelling flannel dressing gown and helped her out of her clothing (Delysia was too miserable to feel embarrassed) and into it. He turned up the heat, brought her a small blanket, more water, and offered to make her ginger tea. Delysia was oddly touched by all his fussing, although a myriad of opposing emotions were coursing through her at that moment.

Alexander would not go to bed, though she asked him

to more than once. Instead he sat in one of the antique armchairs close to the sofa, watching her with those intense dark eyes that turned her insides to jelly as well as made her feel defensive, in a way. She was starting to feel sleepy, surrounded by warmth. Her headache faded a bit, and she asked Alexander for that cup of tea, just to get rid of him.

He came back in moments with two large mugs that smelled of ginger and honey, plus a small package of Club Crackers. She took a sip. "Oh that is *good*," she breathed out with some surprise. The brew was bracingly spicy and sweet, and she could feel it running down her throat, warming her stomach, her limbs, her fingertips even. "Where did you—"

"Rhonda let me into the kitchen."

"What time is it?" She pushed back the sleeve of his dressing gown and peered at the face of her watch. "Oh God, it's nearly four in the morning, and we're hosting an English tea tomorrow, Alexander."

"Aren't the British novelist podcast girls doing all the heavy lifting for that one?"

"Yes, but you're supposed to introduce them."

"Oh. Yes. Yes, that's right."

They fell silent for a moment.

"You really should go to bed, Alexander."

He shook his head.

"Why not?"

"I'm not going to leave you," he said simply. "Also, the sofa is my bed."

Goodness, that was right. Delysia felt her face flush, not only at realizing how much she had inconvenienced him but also being presented with a sudden image of them tucked together in her bed, that sleepy afternoon when they'd crossed the line. Alexander shifted; she wondered if he remembered it, too.

"Alexander—"

"I'm sorry," he said, and his voice was nervous, uncertain. He was picking nervously at a thread on his cuff. "Delysia—I never—what happened the other day. I never talked about it, but—"

Delysia felt her heart leap into her throat.

"I knew it was inappropriate, but it happened because I wanted it to. I've wanted to for quite a long time. And I wanted you to know that because—I don't want you to think—I don't look down on you, Delysia, I admire you incredibly. And I'm a moron who isn't at all right for you, but—" His words were all rushing into each other, and he cleared his throat.

"Alexander—"

He shook his head. "Tonight isn't about me looking down on you. It's quite the opposite."

The words hung in the air as words sometimes do, and there were patches of color on Alexander's tan cheeks. Her face was burning, too, she could feel it. Apparently all it took was a few sweet words to drag them both back to junior high.

Delysia licked her lips and was about to speak when her phone rang, loud and angry. They both jumped, and she pulled it out.

Her mother.

"It's my mum," she said abruptly.

"Oh." Alexander looked surprised. "It's rather late, isn't it? Early," he corrected himself, looking down at his watch.

"She's in Abu Dhabi," Delysia said, simply. "It's afternoon there."

"Ah. Well. I'd be happy to step into the library while you take your call…"

"No, I'd like for her to meet you. If that's okay?"

Alexander looked startled, but agreed.

When Delysia answered, the screen flashed and a woman's face came into shadowy view. "My darling, is that you?"

"Yes, Mama."

Delysia's mother launched into her familiar, musical cadence that immediately made her relax. All Alexander and Delysia could see was a small shrunken woman in a sweater, with a scarf draped loosely around her head and shoulders.

"Who is the man next to you, darling?" her mother asked immediately. Her eyes narrowed, even on camera.

"He's a friend, Mama. Dr. Alexander Abbott-Hill—" Here, she paused and switched to English. "He teaches at a university here and he's helping me with a project. He wanted to say hello."

"So you're my daughter's friend?" she said with emphasis on the last word.

"Ah—yes, ma'am, quite good friends."

"You are a professor."

"Yes, I am."

"They didn't much look like you when I was in school."

"Mama!" Delysia laughed, but shot Alexander a mortified look.

"She seems to have done very well for herself, ma'am."

"Traipsing around the internet when she should be in class, you mean." The older woman snorted. Delysia knew her mother wasn't as upset as she sounded, but she'd been irritated when Delysia had taken up her social media activities. *When do you plan on going to class?* she'd complained then.

Now she shifted her headscarf, revealing a soft nest of graying curls, cropped short last year during the course of her treatment. She sagged against the pillows and Delysia knew she was tired, despite how brief their conversation had been.

"Mama, you should rest," Delysia spoke softly into the silence, switching back to Tigrinya.

"You are right. Bless you both. It was nice to meet your professor."

"Sleep well, Mama."

The screen went black, and she and Alexander were left alone, looking at each other.

Delysia spoke first. "She's sick," she said quietly. "It's her kidneys, they don't work, not properly. I wasn't able to get a visa for her here, but I grew up in Dubai, so…" Her voice trailed off. "Healthcare is great there, but it isn't free. I'd used most of my loan money to pay for the first few months of treatment, but I can't pay for both school and that with my internet work."

"Oh, Delysia." His voice was heavy with feeling, and she suddenly felt dampness press heavy behind her lids. There was something about Alexander that simply radiated kindness; she was drawn to that like a moth to light. "I'm so very sorry," he added, and his hand was on her knee, warm and firm through the thin dressing gown. She blinked rapidly and felt Alexander push something soft into her hand. She looked down, saw a clean square of white and immediately began to laugh instead of cry.

"What—what did I do?"

"A handkerchief?" She dabbed at her eyes carefully—mascara! "Dear God, is it a prop for the trip?" she managed through her snickers.

"Why, no." He actually looked bemused. "I usually travel with a couple, they're much more durable than Kleenex, and—"

"Oh, never mind." She folded it and he gestured that she should keep it. She swallowed hard, steadied her voice. "What now?"

"Well, we should get some sleep, and we'll see about tomorrow." His eyes were still resting on her, intense in a way they hadn't been before this. "Delysia, are you all right to—"

"Of course I am. She's sick, Alexander, and she's getting treated. She isn't *dying*." The last word came out sharper than she intended.

He cleared his throat and offered a smile of his own. "I am sorry."

"I didn't introduce you so you'd feel sorry for me," she said quickly. "I just—I guess I wanted you to know why. Are my eyes red?" She tipped her chin up so he could see.

"You look beautiful," he said so sincerely that her eyes threatened to well up again. "You are a remarkable woman, Delysia Daniels."

God damn it.

Alexander reached out and touched her cheek; she closed her eyes. *I like you*, he'd said. A warmth that had nothing to do with the tea, or the hot towels, was making her body tingle.

"So what happens now?" she said.

She could not see his face, but she felt rather than saw his smile. "I'd like to take you to dinner tomorrow, in DC," he said simply. "If you'll let me."

"Okay," she whispered.

Alexander peered at her as if gauging the sincerity of her words. What he saw must have satisfied him, because when he spoke again, his voice was steady. Calm.

"Do you want to go to bed?" he asked, simply.

She shook her head. "Can we stay up awhile?" If they went to bed, her mind would race, and she didn't think she had the strength for that right now.

The two settled back into the sofa, staring at the square of window framed by gold velvet curtains. Dawn was coming; the sky had been black when they arrived, but now the square of glass was a gray that smudged around the edges. Delysia's head felt oddly clear now as the effects of the pill wore off; Alexander made them another round of tea, and they sipped in companionable silence.

"Thank you," she said after a moment.

His only answer to that was a slight lifting of the corners of his mouth. He took a long sip before speaking. "I liked meeting your mother."

"She liked you, too."

"You could tell just from that short conversation?"

"Oh, you would have known if she didn't." A smile, wide and reluctant, was tugging the edges of Delysia's mouth. "She hated Nicky, and she never even spoke to him, only saw a picture of him that I'd accidentally tagged myself in on Facebook. She called him 'that boy.'"

Alexander winced, and Delysia half-turned to face him. "I grew up in Dubai," she said.

"Yes, I remember."

She was speaking to him, but she was thinking of somewhere far away, somewhere beyond him. "I didn't come here till med school."

"Were you born there?"

She shook her head. "New York. My mother wanted to make sure I had an American passport. She never got approved to come back, though. This was never meant to be permanent."

"You must miss her."

Delysia nodded and shifted. "Everyone is over there, really, scattered all over the Gulf. My father is still in Eritrea, but my cousins, my aunts, uncles, even my father's family…"

"I remember." She'd spoken of them, that day in the Cereal Bar.

"I'm not quite sure if I belong in Dubai, but I know I don't belong here."

Alexander nodded gravely.

"What are you thinking?"

"I was thinking about your apartment," he replied after the briefest of moments. "The bare white walls, except for your filming corner. It doesn't look much like you. You're very—" He gestured vaguely.

"Very what?"

Alexander took a deep breath. "Vibrant."

Were she less tired, Delysia would have blushed, but instead she allowed her body to relax, and rested her head on his shoulder. When his fingers sought hers in the semi-darkness, she laced hers through them.

"I met Nicky the year I left med school," Delysia said after a moment. She spoke abruptly, as if in answer to something that had been asked silently, and rapidly thereafter. "He was my first boyfriend. I was kind of sheltered in Dubai, and I guess I've got him to thank for all this, in a way. He got me my first couple thousand followers…" She trailed off. "I never would have gotten this far if it wasn't for him."

Alexander's eyebrows lifted just a fraction. "You don't have to be grateful to him, Delysia. He *drugged* you."

"He didn't. I took them." Delysia swallowed hard. She must still be high; nothing else could explain why she was still babbling at this rate. "I was so very stupid."

"Please don't tell me you're blaming yourself for this." Alexander's voice grew harsh, and he straightened up on the sofa, and for the first time that evening Delysia saw the carefully tempered anger he must have been curbing all evening. It darkened his eyes, made his body rigid with tension. Even through her nausea and exhaustion, she felt a sudden thrill that shocked her. She'd never seen Alexander angry, or this intense.

"I've always made it easy for him to make an idiot out of me."

"Jesus *Christ*, Delysia—" Alexander made a sharp noise deep in his throat, and closed his eyes.

Delysia gulped her cooling tea. The motion was, thank God, preventing her eyes from welling up. "There is nothing worse," she finally said, "there's nothing more futile than trying to make it work with someone you know is desperately wrong for you. I knew, and I tried anyway."

"Delysia—"

"You don't understand. Nicky and me—started out as a fake relationship, too."

It was as if all the light went out of the room. Alexander simply stared at her. Feeling wretched, Delysia took another, long sip of tea. "We kept up the ruse for a while. When we started sleeping together—" She paused. "Things got complicated. We broke up, we lost endorsements, Eden blamed me. This entire business is based on being likeable, Alexander. If those pictures had gotten out I'd have been done."

When Alexander finally spoke, it was through his teeth. "You," he said, "were not responsible for tonight. You weren't responsible for choosing a shitty boyfriend, and—" He took a deep breath, cut himself off. "I know it isn't any of my business, but—"

In reply, Delysia felt for a place to put her tea on the floor, then inched forward, wrapped her arms around him silently. It might be reckless and stupid, but she wanted that warmth desperately, and she knew she could trust Alexander for that, if nothing else. She also felt an odd desire to comfort him, although she was the one who'd been hurt.

"No one can protect anyone," she said softly. "Thank you for trying."

Chapter Ten

"So how much are you willing to spend?"

Alexander blinked. "Excuse me?"

Faye sighed, then repeated herself. The two were seated in a secluded corner of the main lounge car, with large white mugs in front of them—strong Yorkshire tea for Alexander, black coffee for Faye—and a tray of assorted pastries he'd ordered to charm her with. She hadn't touched a single one, but she *had* been typing busily on her phone the entire time.

"Spend?"

"You," Faye said very patiently, as if talking to a small child, "asked me here, on a very busy day for us, to tell me you wanted to arrange something nice for Delysia when we stop in DC. If our definitions of nice match—which I'm not sure they do at the moment—you're going to have to be willing to spend. Much more than is worth it for a fake relationship," she added.

Alexander supposed she couldn't help it, but he colored anyway. Faye actually looked up from her phone to peer into his face, and she smiled—grimly, but still.

"Are you going to tell me what's what? Are you sleeping with her?" She held up a hand when Alexander began to splutter. "I'm not asking because I'm nosy—I'm her publicist, Alexander. And whatever you want to say about me, you know I've only her best interests in mind."

"You certainly didn't last night, when she was practically drugged by those—"

Faye looked at him sharply. "So it was the Kims? Delysia told me she'd taken some shit from Nicky and got in trouble, but she was vague on the rest."

"Hardly accurate," Alexander mumbled, tugging at the lapel of his blazer and trying hard to calm himself. He didn't want to expand on what had happened without Delysia there, but he supposed Faye knew enough to guess most of it.

"That woman hates her," Faye said more to herself than to Alexander.

"She dated her brother and it ended badly. I think there was some resentment there."

Faye shook her head as if forbidding that line of conversation. "She's an adult, Alexander. I can't stop her from going out with reprehensible people any more than I can stop her from flying." Her face softened a little—just a little. "She told me about how you helped her, though, and how you kept it quiet."

Silence fell between them again as Alexander looked down at his hands. "I don't understand."

"What don't you understand?"

"She wouldn't even talk about Eden." Alexander took a breath. "If that indeed is her friend, then—"

Faye was shaking her head in short, staccato beats. "Delysia doesn't have friends, Alexander. Not really. You're the closest I've seen in a really long time."

"Oh." Alexander had sensed it, of course, but to hear it from the lips of the woman who acted as her surrogate parent made it hit harder, for some reason. Perhaps he and the young woman he'd fallen for so hard had more in common than he'd thought.

At length Faye spoke again, and actually placed her phone down on the table. "Is this going to be a friendly gesture to show your appreciation, Alexander? Or is this a date? It's obvious that you two have been…close this trip." She raised a hand against his protests. "That photo shoot, for one. And the fact that Delysia seems to care so much about what you think. And the fact that—" She hesitated, then forged ahead. "Oh, fuck it. She likes you. It's obvious."

Alexander was discomfited to feel his heart thrumming somewhere low in his chest. He desperately wanted to say "she does?" but knew that would likely sound more idiotic than anything else. Besides, Faye was still speaking.

"Delysia…" She hesitated again. "We've known each other for quite a few years, and let me tell you—Delysia loves hard, Alexander. Very hard. It isn't difficult for her to fall for someone, and when she does she means it wholeheartedly. Nicky Kim devastated her. So if this is because you like her and want to make a…gesture, I'll help you. But if this is about just business, I'll send her a thank-you card and a succulent for her apartment in your name. Don't muddy the waters."

For a long moment all they could hear was the rocking of the train and clicking of the wheels on the tracks, along with the quiet murmurs of the two or so couples that were seated in the lounge.

Alexander bit the inside of his cheek, hard. It was stupid, but for a moment he felt as he had in that awful story he'd told Delysia, approaching the parent of a girl he liked. Still, this wasn't freshman year, and when he spoke his voice was steady and clear. "I want to make a gesture. And…thank you for telling me that, Faye."

She smiled her small, brittle smile, then reached out to grab her phone. She still wasn't typing, though. "So. Tell me what you're envisioning, then."

Alexander took a deep breath. "I want her to be comfortable. I want her to have fun. I want her to know that I'm…honored to be with her."

A glimmer of respect came into Faye's eyes. "Budget?"

"Well…do let's be reasonable. I am a professor, after all."

"And an Abbott-Hill."

"The name didn't come with an endowment."

Faye laughed, a short, barking sound.

"I do know quite a few people in DC…" His voice trailed off. "What does she like, Faye? I know she loves food, and parties, and that Audrey Hepburn film…"

"You've learned quite a lot about her in the past few weeks," Faye said dryly.

Alexander reddened, but then he sat up abruptly.

"What?" demanded Faye.

"I've got it," Alexander said, almost in wonder. "You'll just have to get her to show up, if you can. At the harbor. She'll need warm clothes and sturdy shoes, nonslip ones. I'll look at her shoes in our room, get her size—"

"I can get you that."

"Thank you, Faye. And here's what we'll need, also…"

It was afternoon when the *Gilded Express* pulled into DC, twenty minutes ahead of schedule, and Alexander, Delysia thought, had been uncommonly jittery all morning. He kept looking at his watch, rushing off to make mysterious calls behind doors, jumped practically a foot whenever she spoke to him. It was amusing and irritating at the same time, and she was grateful for it, in a way. It prevented her from having to be anxious about…well, whatever it was he had planned.

Their date.

Even the thought of it produced a tingle of anticipation that went from her heart to the very tips of her toes. She couldn't look at him without her heart hammering in that odd manner that was both new and familiar, and she kept finding excuses to talk to him, as casually as possible of course, or to touch him just as casually, on his arm, his shoulder, his back. When she did he would give her one of those small smiles that were almost breathtaking in their intensity.

"Will you still have time for me in DC?" was all he'd said about their date, and when she nodded, somewhat dumbly: "Okay, we'll go together at one. Dress warmly and bring an evening gown and shoes."

At that, she managed a smile. "Not white tie?"

He winced. "I deserved that. No, bring whatever you'd like."

That, of course, had resulted in Delysia's emptying out her entire wardrobe onto the bed and picking, dissatisfied, at her clothing. Too bad she couldn't get a delivery to a moving train! She called Faye, barking reproachfully about men who wanted to drive her crazy by trying to be mysterious, and where the hell did they get those ideas?

Faye, in rare form, actually showed up in person ten minutes later. She looked at the piles of fabric draped over chairs, bed, and sofa.

"Some of them are gifts," Delysia said defensively. "I haven't endorsed some of them yet."

"No, no, tonight isn't a night for endorsements." Faye shifted gingerly through the mess on the bed, then pulled out a wad of pale fabric, a soft color that was something between a blush and a rose. Delysia had bought it on a whim while on a trip to Paris, in a no-name boutique on the Rue Saint-Honoré. She'd been drawn in by the delicacy of the design and the fineness of the fabric, but hadn't worn it since. She was gifted so many clothes on a regular basis that she barely had time to wear the pieces she bought herself anymore.

"Your most delicate jewelry, soft makeup," Faye said briskly.

"Oh Faye. It's perfect," she murmured.

"Well. You may not be thanking me later. It's got a ton of buttons and straps, not too easy to get off."

"Faye!"

The older woman smiled at Delysia's blushing, then patted her on the shoulder. "I'm going to go. Have fun."

"Faye…"

"Have you got condoms, though?"

"Faye!"

Faye gave a slow and rusty laugh. "He's nervous, too."

At that, Delysia's jaw dropped. "So you—"

"Just call me your fairy godmother," Faye said briskly. "Now get your bag packed. We pull into DC in twenty minutes."

Miraculously, Delysia was ready at one, bag in hand, dressed in flannel-lined jeans, a windbreaker over a turtleneck, with gloves and boots firmly in place and an enormous, Cossack-guard-style fur hat angled on her curls. Alexander met her by the door as the influencers queued to get off. He looked her over once, very carefully.

"What?" Delysia said defensively. "You said to dress warmly. I don't want to be *cold*."

"No, indeed," Alexander agreed, and placed a hand on her lower back, steering her along. She couldn't feel it through her reasonably heavy clothing, but she was more than aware of every finger. "Actually, I rather like it."

"You wouldn't dare not to, not after the other night." Delysia tossed her head and yanked her hat down over her ears to protect them from the wind as Alexander took her bag. "Is that the Williamsburg sweater?"

"Yes, it is." He wore it under a fisherman's vest, with a pair of tailored black jeans and boots. Delysia couldn't recall when she'd ever seen him that casual, even when he'd been working on the train. The look suited him, but she wasn't going to say *that*.

"Where are we going?"

Alexander's eyes lit up, and he gave her one of his quiet smiles. "It's a two-part date," he said. "First one starts in this Uber—"

And he gestured to the black Mercedes waiting as they left the platform. The driver whisked away their bags and when they were settled in the cushy black leather seat, Alexander still refused to tell her where they were going. "It wouldn't be much of a surprise if I did now, would it?"

"Oh, dear Christ," Delysia muttered, then sat back. She tried to maintain her exasperated expression, but her heart was actually beating in anticipation. Alexander peered into her face, and then laughed aloud.

"You look like you want to kill me," he said, amused.

"That's because I do," she groused.

"Well, it's not a secret. We're going to the harbor."

"The harbor." Water, she presumed. Ships. Sailboats. Swimming? Surely not in *winter*? Did Alexander even like to swim? All the man cared about was trains and history.

They reached the boatyard and left the car. The driver handed Alexander a large insulated bag that she hadn't noticed before; he must have brought it himself. Alexander slung the strap across his shoulder, picked up the duffel that presumably held his evening clothes.

"Let's go," he said mildly, and set off in the direction of the boatyard.

They followed the water down a strip of concrete to get to the docks; there was some activity there, but not much. The cool weather had most boats already covered and locked tight for the cooler months. Some were up on racks; one was being lifted from the water by a groaning crane. Many, many boats, too many to count, were moored at short docks. There were a few people, dressed as warmly as Alexander and Delysia were, furling sails and locking hulls. A few boats were in view of the docks, bobbing in the misty gray water.

Alexander was scanning the lay of the land with purpose. Then his face cleared. "There it is," he said, and set off quickly in the direction of one of the docks. A boat, as neatly locked down as the others, floated a few feet off the dock; Alexander grabbed her hand, went toward it almost at a run. He looked down at Delysia and grinned.

"Can you jump on board?" he asked. "I can definitely pull it in closer if you need."

Delysia was dumbfounded. "We're going out on a boat?"

"That's how we're getting where we're going for dinner." Alexander laughed at the look on her face. "Don't give me that. I've seen you on boats on your Instagram page, and Faye says you love the water."

"That was in *August*! In Dubai!" Delysia sputtered. "And you own a *boat*?"

"No, but I've got a friend who does. One of the benefits of going to prep school. C'mon—" he said, and jumped first, then held out his hand.

"You'll catch me if I fall?" Delysia said, half-jokingly.

"That, or we'll go down together."

Delysia landed safely and by the time she did, the exercise had eliminated much of the cold. The boat—"she" as Alexander insisted on calling her—wasn't big at all.

"But she's got everything," Alexander said excitedly. "God, I'd completely forgotten. We used to practically live on this thing in the summer. Ridiculously efficient," he bragged. He showed Delysia a mini-fridge that ran on solar power, and a table that swung down on heavy hinges in front of a sofa that could double as a sleeping space once it was tugged out from the wall.

"So you sail, too," Delysia said softly, after he had settled her on the couch and poured her a cup of hot chocolate. The cooler, it turned out, was packed with food and drink—coffee, hot chocolate, sandwiches, chips, deviled eggs, half of a chocolate cake.

Alexander lifted his shoulders in a shrug. "I guess I've always been sort of fascinated with the way people travel. Not airplanes, though," he said quickly. "Flying tin cans. I would rather take a train any day, even if it takes twice as long. And boats can be just as nice."

The two sat side by side for a long moment, drinking.

The rich, creamy blend was made from real chocolate, sugar, and hot milk; Delysia found it absolutely decadent.

"It's about a forty-minute trip across the bay," he said. "We'll continue on the other side."

"And you're going to sail this?"

"Her," he corrected. "The *Maureen*, to be exact. After a grandmother, or an ex-lover. I can't remember which." He launched into a long and detailed explanation about jibs and masts and sails and tacking and keels and riding flat. When he finished, he took a deep breath. "Got all that?"

Delysia grinned. "I know that the boat will rotate, and I'm supposed to look out for the boom when it does. And I suspect that's all I need to know. And now I also have an idea of what your students go through in your lectures."

Offended, Alexander opened his mouth to retort, but was cut off when a man—presumably one who came with the boat—stomped on board, gnawing on half of a ham sandwich. He selected a beer from the stuffed cooler and greeted them briefly.

"Tiller or sails?" he barked.

"Tiller is fine." Alexander motioned to Delysia to come near him, where he was guiding the tiller. Their nameless captain was fidgeting with the sails; after several minutes he shouted that he was going below deck. When his head disappeared below the ladder, Alexander smiled at her. "He's supposed to be the one to sail us over, but I wanted to show off."

"Don't capsize us," Delysia teased, and he laughed.

"Not much danger of that, which is why I decided I'd risk showing off. It isn't a very windy day."

"The *Maureen* seems pretty laid-back, yes." She offered him a little smile. Alexander's lean body moved easily, at one with the ship; his hands looked strong and capable. "So you learned this in school?"

"There are a lot of little rich boys who learn how to sail," he said dryly. "It was over two summers, mostly. I would come out here and spend at least a month with Tim and his family. It was nice." He hesitated. "I was pretty short on close friends in high school. Tim was a notable exception."

Delysia could imagine how nice it was. She was tense at first, afraid she would lose her footing because of the choppy water, but it wasn't so. It took only a bit of time before she was accustomed to the rocking of the boat, her body adjusting to the rhythm, becoming a part of it. She drank her hot chocolate, watched Alexander, and peered up at the brilliant blue sky.

"Freeing, isn't it?" Alexander said.

"It is. My mother would love this. She loves the water." Delysia lowered herself to the deck, crossed her legs beneath her. It was cold, but she was so warmly dressed it didn't matter. Plus, the way Alexander was looking at her—well. It warmed her from somewhere deep inside, made her think of roaring fires and soft couches and the heat of bare skin on hers.

"How is she?"

"The same." Delysia tugged off a glove and chewed nervously at her thumbnail. "But when someone's that sick, no news is actually good news, I suppose."

"I'm sorry."

"You don't have to be," Delysia said, simply. "She'll get better. Maybe not soon, but eventually. And I have the means to take care of her."

Alexander nodded, and for once, Delysia didn't feel

like he was making fun of what she did. "It's given a lot of people an opportunity they wouldn't have, otherwise."

"Yes."

They were quiet for a few minutes; Alexander offered to let her sail, but she shook her head. She was content to watch him, to look at the gradually disappearing shore, to daydream.

"Are you enjoying yourself?"

"I am."

"I'm glad." He hesitated, then smiled one of those quick bashful smiles of his. "I'm surprised you haven't made the connection yet."

"What connection?"

Alexander laughed out loud. "One point for Faye. She said you wouldn't."

"Wouldn't get what?"

"*Sabrina*." Alexander was still smiling. "The sailing scene. Oh, it's so far off, it's a disaster. This boat's bigger, and it's not summer, and I'm certainly no Bogart. But when I asked what you might like, Faye said, 'Anything from that damned movie,' and I knew Tim kept his boat here, starting in the fall, and—oh, stop laughing," he said impatiently. Delysia was shaking at this point. "I know. I know."

"Would you like me to sing 'We Have No Bananas'?"

"Oh, dear God no. No. Certainly not," but he was smiling. Delysia managed to wipe her eyes and took a deep breath, finally escaping her giggles.

"You're so incredibly sweet," she said softly. Then she navigated around the tiller, enough to bend and kiss him full on the mouth. Alexander was so startled he nearly let go, and when she skittered back, he looked quite awkwardly pleased.

"No, you're not Bogie, but you're terribly nice," Delysia said, and laughed again. "I'm never going to forget this."

"Good—that's the idea." He smiled, then frowned. "Why *Sabrina*? I've always meant to ask that."

She looked surprised, then she laughed. "It's the ultimate love story. Plus, my mother loved it. Same as yours."

"I see."

She raised her hand to shield her eyes, peered out over the water. "I've never actually sailed before. I've been on yachts or rowboats, but never a proper boat like this one."

"Enjoy it. We make land in about an hour."

Delysia extended her legs, gazed out over the water.

"You should probably get your phone out," he suggested. "I mean..."

He was right; this would make an epically funny post. She could hear it already in her head: a gripe about her boyfriend dragging her out in the cold, perhaps followed by an admission that yes, the water was beautiful, perhaps followed by a picture of the two of them, snuggled close beside the till. She didn't want to do that, though; this felt private somehow, like a memory she wanted to share with only him in months to come.

The thought made her shift uncomfortably, made her cheeks warm a little. She was surprised at the feeling it gave her, of a happiness that crept up with warm fingers to her heart. It would be easy to fall in love with Alexander, even easier than it had been in the past. He was just—he was nowhere near perfect, but he just felt so absolutely *right* sometimes.

She wished with a sudden burst of longing that surprised even her that he wasn't on the tiller, so she could press herself to his side. Kiss him, maybe.

"Delysia," he said gently.

She looked up.

"We'll be there soon. And then we have all night."

The words hung in the air like words sometimes do, and Delysia forced a smile against the sudden flip her stomach made. "All night? What are you hinting at, Alexander?"

"What—no. No," he said forcefully, and actually let go of the till for a moment. The look on his face—"Oh. Very funny, Delysia Daniels."

She laughed out loud, throwing her head back to the sky. Suddenly, she felt more lighthearted, more joyful than she had in ages.

When they reached the other side of the harbor, they chucked greasy sandwich wrappers and Styrofoam cups into the bins on the dock, and Delysia repacked the cooler as Alexander tied things down. The driver disappeared into the mists surrounding the dock, and Alexander led Delysia up a winding path where a short, stocky man in a pea-green coat and brown gloves stood waving frantically once he spotted the boat.

"That's Tim," Alexander said, amused, and Delysia soon found her hand being pumped by one of the poshest fellows she'd ever seen in her life. His round cheeks and curly brown beard made him look like an early-career Santa Claus. He followed up his handshake with two kisses to each of her cheeks.

"Welcome, welcome," he boomed effusively. "Alexander, old man, how are you?"

"We were at Exeter and Cambridge together," Alexander explained. "He's one of my oldest friends."

"You flatter me." Tim slapped Alexander on the back with an enthusiasm that sent him reeling. "Anyway, I hope you enjoyed the sailing over…do, do come this way. I've got everything ready for you."

"This way" turned out to be a brisk fifteen-minute walk to a lavishly furnished cottage, right on the water, featuring plate-glass windows that stretched from ceiling to floor, a massive fireplace, and a view that rendered all of the other comforts in the cottage virtually forgettable.

"Enjoy yourselves. Alexander, I've wine downstairs, you remember. None of your family's awful stuff, thank God. There's a little snack in the kitchen. Delysia, I'll just pop your bag in the master suite, shall I? I'll be out of your hair in a moment."

Alexander protested, "Really, Tim, you must stay! Have a glass with us. I'd really like you to get to know Delysia."

"Oh no, no, no, I'm not one to be a third wheel."

"Even in your own house?" Alexander said with a laugh.

"Stop it." Tim gave Alexander another of his spine-shattering pounds on the back and hustled his bulk toward the door. As Alexander turned back to take Delysia's things to the master suite, he leaned in and said in a stage whisper, "It's *so* nice to meet you, really. Alexander is absolutely smitten and your work is simply fascinating."

"He told you what I do?"

"Oh, he couldn't shut up about it. I was reading your blog until quite late into the night, I'm afraid. You're an incredibly vivid and witty writer—you must excuse me, I teach English at Columbia. It's hard to snap out of teaching mode."

"I quite understand," Delysia said with a laugh.

"We've got a texting group, the boys from school. I'm afraid we think him quite a braggart—he won't shut up about you. I can see he's exaggerated absolutely nothing."

Delysia was touched despite his bluster. "Thank you."

"Well." He harrumphed a bit, clearing his throat. "Have a good time—my home is your home. My apartment is just in Georgetown, so I can get here quickly if you need anything. Alexander's got my contact, of course. Just let him know."

Delysia thanked him again. He doffed his hat, then disappeared down the walk, somehow squeezed himself into a red MINI Cooper, and drove off.

When she closed the door and locked it, Alexander was standing in the entryway, smiling at her. "What did you think of Tim?"

"He's lovely." She paused. "I also heard about your texting group. Bragging point, am I?"

Alexander turned crimson and began to stutter. Delysia smirked a little. "It's okay. You're very lucky I think it's sweet."

"He shouldn't have told you that," Alexander mumbled. His ears were still red. "It was nothing disrespectful, I swear. I just—"

He was quiet then. Delysia closed the distance between them in a couple of steps and kissed him, soft at first, then full on the lips. When she pulled back they were both out of breath.

"Thank you," she managed, then raked her fingers through her curls. Despite his earlier discomfort, Alexander looked just a tiny bit pleased with himself. He shoved his hands in his pockets; silence fell around them.

"So…?" Delysia said after a moment.

"Well. Yes. We'll have lunch, and then dress to go out, and—" Alexander hesitated. "Tim said we could stay here tonight, and there is an extra room. I thought it might be nice, the change. Then we could go back tomorrow, and well, take it from there."

Here. Tonight. Alone with him, after a date. She didn't know… She bit her lip, then realized she hadn't actually responded. "Yes! I mean, that sounds lovely!"

Her voice sounded a little high, unnatural, even to her, and she cleared her throat. She wasn't sure why she was suddenly so emotional at the thought of a bunch of history and classics professors hearing Alexander fawn over her, or his being embarrassed that she found out, or at the thought of being alone with Alexander, in this deliciously romantic setting.

Well—she'd find out and soon, if the look in his eyes was anything to go by. And she suddenly felt a deliciously tense pull of anticipation between her legs.

"Come," Alexander said quietly, breaking into her reverie. "Let's get some food into you."

She looked tired, Alexander thought with a sudden stab of sympathy. He was watching Delysia where she was lying on the sofa, absentmindedly thumbing through a book bound in maroon leather, the other hand playing with her hair. She had retreated into a little shell despite his best efforts at keeping up conversation. He knew that he probably wasn't the best at engaging her—hell, he didn't know anything for sure except that he liked being with her. But if she was having a terrible time—

He busied himself by attending to the food. Tim's "little snack" consisted of creamy tomato soup, very hot grilled cheese paninis, roasted root vegetables, and of course, a cellar full of wine. An angel food cake so delicate it trembled in its box and fresh strawberries with cream completed the meal.

Alexander set out the bounty on a couple of trays, then brought them out to the sitting room. Delysia sat up quickly when he came, tucking her feet beneath her. He caught a glimpse of small cherry-tipped toes before she did. She cleared her throat.

"What's there to eat?" she asked, and her voice was a little too bright, too cheerful. A knot began to twist in his stomach; what if she wasn't having a good time?

"A winter night's feast," he said grandly, then immediately chastised himself for how fucking stupid that sounded. He placed the trays down on the table.

Delysia's eyes widened. "Bless your Tim. I am starving," she declared, still in that over-bright voice he'd heard her use while streaming.

"He really did well." He paused. "What were you reading?"

She held up the book so he could see, and he smiled.

"*The Decline and Fall of the Roman Empire*? A little heavy, isn't it?"

"Oh, it's one of my mother's favorites. I first read it when I was ten."

"That's impressive. It's listed on my thesis, and I never actually finished it," Alexander said, and laughed. When he sat down beside her she shifted—nervously, he thought.

Dear Christ.

Now that he thought about it, bringing her here like

this, well, it could be misconstrued as creepy, couldn't it? Especially since he'd dragged her out in the middle of nowhere, where she'd never been before, with him virtually still a stranger, and—

Oh God. He'd really screwed up, hadn't he?

"...Alexander?"

He blinked, looked at Delysia. She was peering at him a little curiously. "I'm sorry—I was lost in my thoughts for a moment. What did you say?"

"I was asking if you needed pepper," Delysia repeated, lifting her brows. "I'm going in the kitchen to get some."

"I—" He opened his mouth to answer her, but the other words tumbled out instead, running into each other with all the grace and subtlety of—well, a runaway train. "Listen, Delysia," he said a bit breathlessly. "I don't want you to think—this isn't me trying to get you to do anything, at all. I just—well, I thought it would be nice if you had somewhere low-key where you could rest for the afternoon. That's all. We're supposed to be going out, I've got tickets to *Noises Off* for us to use, and we're coming back here to sleep. Not together!" he quickly amended. "Just sleep, and we'll be back to the *Gilded Express* in the morning, unless you want to go back tonight, which I can definitely arrange—"

She was staring at him as if he'd grown another head. "Alexander—"

"I'm sorry," he blurted out again, raking his hands over his head. "I really am. It's just that—you look so tired sometimes. And worried, especially after what happened the other night, and with what's going on with your mom. I just wanted to help. This isn't—if you're not comfortable, let's go back now—"

Through the haze of his dreadful word-explosion—
which he felt as if he was watching from very, very far
away—he could see Delysia set her plate down, sit up,
bite her lip. And the next thing he knew—

She kissed him.

This was different, too, from all the kisses they'd
shared over the past week, both real and fake. She slanted
her mouth over his with a bit of desperation, as if she
were trying to get across a message she wasn't sure he'd
understand. When they came up for air she pulled back
slightly and he opened his mouth.

"No," she muttered, tapped his lips with her fingers,
and she slid forward, half-straddled his lap. "No more
talking. You're incredibly sweet, but right now you're
not making sense to me."

All Alexander could register, at that moment, was the
smell of her hair, the softness of her skin. Memories of
that afternoon in their berth came rushing back with a
speed that made his breath catch harshly in his throat,
and when her lips grazed his neck his whole body tensed
involuntarily.

"Don't you want me?" she murmured, a little soft and
a little sad. His response was to let his hands slide precisely where they wanted to, beneath her fleece-lined
shirt to the heated skin of her back. He was gratified to
hear her sharp intake of breath.

"Alexander, please don't stop this time," she whispered, and when he kissed her again it was with little
reservation.

"I have to, I don't have—" he started.

"I do. In my bag. Just don't *stop*, for God's sake."

The thought that yes, she might actually have come
today with this in mind, that she'd been thinking about it,

anticipating it, made him gulp—and made a flash of heat run through his body that he hadn't felt in so very long.

Delysia was still kissing him, a little tentatively, but suddenly soft and tender wasn't enough. He drew her tight against his lap, hands anchoring her hips; he felt rather than heard her gasp of surprise. He twisted and then she was on the sofa, beneath him. She looked up at him in shock, then laughed breathlessly. Alexander felt the last of his reserve melt away into their next fiery kiss.

Time seemed to blur for Alexander then; it had been so long since he'd done this, with anyone, and Delysia's lush, soft skin seemed made for exploring, for kissing, for touching. He took his time, breathing words against her skin that made her shiver in the best possible way. Almost lazily, he began undoing the tiny buttons on her shirt as he threaded his fingers through the silk of her hair. Delysia was kissing him back hungrily, almost frantically, fisting his shirt and squirming in a way that was proving to be delightful. She wrapped her legs around his waist and rocked forward, bringing him in direct contact with the most sensitive part of her. They both exhaled, and hard.

After a moment Alexander pulled back. He didn't think he could, but he managed. Delysia stared up at him, dazed. He licked his lips and spoke with a voice that was low and raspy. "Delysia, sweetheart. Eat."

"I…" She half sat up, and he had to avert his eyes, as the soft bounty of her breasts, barely encased in pale blush lace, was doing nothing for his reserve.

"Please, sweetheart. *Eat*."

"But why—"

Alexander pulled himself away from her with some effort, picked up the bowl of tomato soup, handed it to her. "We've got all night," he said, still quite low. "There—" and he pushed a spoon into her hand, helped her sit up. He watched her take the first, second, third bites, holding her clothing together with one hand, staring at him as if he'd lost his mind completely.

When their bowls were nearly empty, she licked her lips and turned so she was facing him. "*Why?*" she demanded.

Alexander reached out, slid an arm around her waist, tugged her close. He felt her body soften, melt against him; he marveled at how quickly his arousal surged again after the interruption. She was intoxicating. Her essence permeated the air around him, something that he breathed, that stuck to his skin.

"Because," he said slowly, deliberately, pushing the soft flannel from her shoulders, which gave him much better access to the parts of her he found most interesting at the moment. A twist of his fingers and the bra was open, spilling her warm and soft into his hands. His thumb grazed the hardening skin of her nipple, and she jumped a little.

"Be-because?" she managed, as Alexander had gotten a bit distracted.

"Because aside from a sandwich on the boat, you haven't had anything to eat all day. And it's early still and it's—" He kissed her, soft and sure on the shell of her ear, her neck, and she whimpered.

"Alexander—"

"Eat," he said against her skin. There was laughter in his voice now, and Delysia's cheeks and chest became suffused by a blaze of color. She threw out her hands as if to ward him off, a little too hard, and hit the bowl, which skittered across the table and landed on the floor, narrowly missing the rug. She clapped her hands to her mouth, and they both stared at it in horror. Then, Alexander began to laugh, and Delysia was laughing too, and climbing on top of him, shedding clothes until all that was left were the flimsiest lace panties he'd ever seen. She pinned him with one hand and started taking care of his clothes with the other, kissing a trail down his neck to his chest. When he groaned, it was almost involuntary, and he knew for sure he'd be needing the contents of Delysia's bag that night.

"Wait," he found himself gasping out again, and Delysia shot him a look that could possibly melt glass.

"*What?*"

"I won't," he said, then bit back another groan as her small warm hand dipped to wander to a very sensitive place. "First, you have to promise. I want to date you. Properly."

She froze. "Alexander—"

Two could play that game. He shoved a hand inside her panties and almost lost his resolve; the silken heat was too much. He found the little nub between her folds, circled it slowly. She actually bucked in his arms, but he held her steady.

"Promise me," he whispered stubbornly, and stopped stroking her.

"I don't want to date anyone right now," she managed, and the last word came out on a whimper. She shifted her hips, grinding down on his fingertips, and moaned out the next two words. "Not really."

"Delysia—" Suddenly a thought came to him. "The trip," he whispered. "Just till we're back in New York. I'll leave you alone then, if you want me to."

"Alexander..."

"Just till the end of the trip."

She took a deep breath; he took the opportunity to slide one finger inside her, biting his own lip hard when she cried out, clamping round his fingers. God, she felt so absolutely tight and sweet and *ready*.

"Okay," she gritted out, and he straightened up to draw her in in a searing kiss.

Chapter Eleven

One of Delysia's favorite features on the *Gilded Express* was the claw-foot tub in the bathroom she and Alexander shared. There was something delightfully excessive about sitting in a tub with lavender-scented hot water up to one's breasts while the world raced by outside. Alexander always made himself scarce during her bath times, as if he knew instinctively that she chose that time to think, to rest.

The two had stumbled out of Tim's cottage early that morning, bleary-eyed and yawning, in search of breakfast and a ride back to the train. They'd been bleary-eyed for a good reason: Alexander had woken her at some point that night with a series of soft kisses down her shoulder and spine, and the memory of the slow, sweaty tangle that resulted still had her body throbbing.

She had not been wrong about their chemistry in bed. Alexander handled her body with a quiet confidence that surprised her; was as observant of her body's cues as he was his research. Pleasure came slow and sure with him. After, there was quiet conversation, and long lingering cups of tea, and it just felt *right*.

Delysia supposed she had a boyfriend now, or if not

quite that, someone who planned on pursuing her with the same quiet determination as he did everything else.

Just till we're back... I'll leave you alone then, if you want me to...

"*If* I want him to," Delysia muttered, rubbing her aching head. It was a big if, a very big if indeed. Despite his stoicism, Alexander was excellent at grand gestures. Yesterday had proven that, and to be honest, it fit in perfectly with the little fantasy world that the *Gilded Express* had created for them. Real life wasn't as tidy, though, and the emotions that went with it would make things messier than either of them were ready for.

When she shared these thoughts with him, huddled close in a car on the way back to the station, he'd looked thoughtful.

"It's okay to not know what's going to happen," he said finally. "Just—if it makes you happy, Delysia, let it. It's all right."

In the place of happiness, though, was deep anxiety, and digging to the source of it would take more energy than she was willing to commit. So she swallowed her misgivings, smiled at him, did her best to keep her promise.

Just till the end of the trip, she thought, and closed her eyes. Didn't she deserve some joy, however short-lived it might be?

Delysia waited with a mixture of excitement and dread for another grand gesture from Alexander, but she needn't have worried. None was forthcoming. The night before, Alexander had slept on his sofa bed, same as he always did. They breakfasted together in front of the window, traded sections of the paper, lingered over strong cups of tea. If it wasn't for the intensity burning in his dark eyes, she'd have sworn nothing had changed between them.

Still, that intensity was there, and that tender, vulnerable bit of herself she'd kept locked down since Nicky was a palpable ache now, struggling to surface. She'd felt it the first time they'd kissed, just a flicker that she'd ignored. It came back again with each encounter, each touch, each conversation, reaching up with warm fingers to encircle her throat, push emotions she'd buried back to the surface. And now that she'd finally submitted to her growing feelings, it threatened to break through, envelop her with a want she wasn't sure he'd be able to satisfy. Sleeping with him was one thing, but giving him the opportunity to disappoint her was another. If he did, after all his kindness...

Let it. It's all right.

Startled, Delysia looked up. Alexander's voice was so vivid in her head that she was surprised to see his head still buried in the arts section. She played with a piece of toast until he lowered it, looked at her.

"Are you all right?" he said simply.

She took a breath. "No," she said.

To her surprise, he laughed out loud. "I'm not either. This is very strange."

His admission eased a little of her anxiety, but only a little. There were so many things he didn't know—that he was only the second guy she'd been with, that she'd never actually dated anyone without the lens of artifice behind it. She didn't have words for that, not now, so she inhaled instead, and said the one thing she was sure about sharing.

"I'd like to try."

His face lit up then, though all he did was smile.

Delysia smiled back, inhaled a bit shakily. "So what happens today?"

"Well—" Alexander picked up his phone, scrolled. "Faye's got us visiting a model UN meeting, but after that we've got a rest day, provided we 'post suitable content,'" he said in a dead-on imitation of Delysia's publicist. "Any ideas?"

She shook her head, still toying with that same piece of bread. "None."

"We'll figure it out."

As the day went on, things felt a little easier. Outside the walls of the *Gilded Express*, away from the weight of their obligations, they could concentrate on each other, let the realities melt away. It was unhurried, calm, languid, unstructured; they ate, drank, talked, were silent. They took their laptops to a coffee shop and worked on their various projects: Delysia on content creation, Alexander on one of the research articles that were a constant part of his life. They went to a natural foods grocery, bought some of the little luxuries they didn't have on the train—mixed nuts in a brand that Delysia loved, Alexander's coffee, a package of toffees. It felt very domestic; they argued over who would pay, shared a cup of steaming soup that reminded Delysia of that first night in Southampton.

She felt drawn to him by some indescribable force. Any awkwardness was surpassed by a need for touch, and she spent most of the afternoon nestled into his side as they walked or where they sat, kissing him when she could, feeling as if she'd never be sated. She'd been that way with Nicky, and he'd accommodated her, but he'd always been looking for the next photo angle, or to see if other people were checking them out.

Alexander *did* look back at her, though, and he did so with a tenderness that she felt in her core. It was good that they were outside, she thought, with that familiar heat prickling over her skin. When they did kiss—in dark, quiet corners, shielded from view on the street—it only stoked the flame. It was startling to see that time had passed, later on, when it was time to return to the train, where they would be back at their duties.

"What are you thinking?" he asked her, once they were walking back.

She was thinking about how wonderfully solid his body felt against hers, and other much more sensual things that she didn't want to say out loud.

"This was nice," was all she said, and she felt his hand seek hers out, squeeze once.

"Two more days," he reminded her, and she laughed, a short, ragged sound.

"What?" he asked.

"Putting a deadline on it just seems so cynical," she said, softly.

"Don't think about that."

"How can I not?"

"You'll just have to try." He looked so at peace that for just a second, Delysia wondered if this might be all right after all. "And," he added teasingly, "keep an open mind, no matter how dumb my ideas seem."

"Why, what are you planning?"

"Oh, everything." His grin was terrifying, but it was also pretty funny. "Don't worry, it's all been vetted by Faye. Even if we—" He paused, bit his lip. "Listen. I want you to enjoy it, okay? This means nothing beyond the next couple of days, unless you want it to."

You'll want it to. The warning bubbled up, quick and urgent, but Delysia lifted her chin, tamped it down.

"Do your best," she said, light and sweet for the first time that day, and Alexander chuckled.

This was a problem. A major problem. A one-night problem that had turned into a two-day problem, that had turned into a three-day problem. She'd told him to do his best. Alexander had been true to his word, and planned something special for every night they'd been there. There had been lavish meals both on and off the train, a delivery of hothouse flowers that filled their entire suite in every shade of purple found in nature, dancing and drinking and awkward-as-hell videos that Alexander insisted on posting (she'd doubled her viewership in two days; she supposed Faye was right about the public loving a love story).

Still, they were close to the end of their journey, and as the skyline loomed in the imaginary distance, so did the obligations she was going back to. Her bills. Her mother. The fact that she'd planned this so that she could eventually go back home, leave no ties behind. And she was terrified that Alexander would make a declaration, because she wasn't sure that she would be able to do what she had to do when she did it.

Falling in love would be absolutely irresponsible; she hadn't been kidding when she said she didn't want a relationship, even if Alexander hadn't been a snobby Long Islander with delusions of academic grandeur.

"Jesus, Delly, that's cold even for you."

Delysia blinked. She hadn't realized she'd said *that* bit

out loud. She was holed up with Faye in the observation car, ostensibly to go over her post–*Gilded Express* calendar. Alexander had waved her off good-naturedly for the meeting. They'd been inseparable for the past couple of days and even worse at nights, when they retreated to their suite and he fixed those calm eyes on her in a way only meant that her resolve shattered, lost somewhere in a hazy desire to have his dark head between her legs…

"You're drifting again," Faye snapped, and Delysia snapped back to attention.

"Sorry, Faye."

"Not a problem. But if you want to reschedule, we can? Alexander has some events a couple weeks out from this, and I wondered if we would coordinate on—"

"Alexander has events?" If she was distracted before, she sure wasn't anymore.

"Well, yes. Your little professor has amassed quite a following." Faye pulled a calendar up. "He's got a couple of appearances at lectures, the New York Public Library, the Smithsonian's exhibition on nineteenth-century travel…"

Delysia skimmed the list. "Excuse me—the SoHo Lounge?"

"Oh, yes. They've been looking for him nonstop since the first night. They've got me down as his de facto agent." And here, Faye practically simpered. It wasn't her best look. "I've got him booked up until next March."

"God."

"He's actually rather good at it," Faye admitted. "Handsome, self-deprecating, decent sense of style, if a little stereotypical. He's awkward but well-spoken— something that actors try to do all the time but can't quite pull off. It must be that English education." She paused for a second before deciding to say what she wanted to say. "So, are you and he…?"

"No—no," Delysia said, then cursed inwardly as Faye's eyes narrowed.

The older woman pursed her lips. "Are you or aren't you?"

"We're not, but we—" She fumbled for words for a moment, and Faye's eyes lit up in understanding.

"Oh dear God, you're sleeping with him. Well, I should have known. You two were reeking of it in DC when you came back."

Delysia didn't bother to deny it. She just sank down in her chair, closed her eyes, covered them with her hands.

"Oh, dear. Was it that bad?"

"No." Delysia rubbed her eyes and stood up. "I have to go."

Faye's eyes registered more compassion than Delysia had ever seen in her. "Delysia, it wouldn't be the worst thing in the world."

Yes, it would. Delysia stood up, and abruptly. "Are we done yet?"

"Sure, honey."

She squared her shoulders and left. She had to find Alexander.

She found Alexander in the train galley, yukking it up with the train staff, phone set up on Delysia's tripod. They were deep in discussion on how to make the New York–style cheesecake pudding that would be served with coffee and brandy that evening. He was at his most animated, wearing a tight black turtleneck and jeans, hair artfully arranged. A pair of tortoiseshells she hadn't seen before were sliding down his nose.

"—and that's how you do it, without setting the whole car afire," he said dryly, directly to the camera, then motioned her over. "Delysia, honey!"

She mouthed *not now*, and he gave a little shrug, re-addressing the camera. "She's here, folks, just a little camera-shy…"

Oh, for God's sake. "Hi, everyone," she said cheerfully, then popped into frame. Alexander tugged her close and kissed her on the nose tenderly.

"Have one," he invited, offering a plump strawberry, and Delysia took it from his hand, which was covered with powdered sugar.

"Delicious!" she said brightly, and took a spoon dipped in chocolate next. "I had no idea you were so talented," she teased. "I thought all you do is teach."

"She thinks I'm useless," he said dryly, to their imaginary audience, and when Delysia peered at the screen, she blanched. Goodness. Alexander had as many attendees as she might for a clip of this length.

She dialed it up a notch then, hating herself a little for it. After all, she was planning to dump him right after. Could you dump someone you've only agreed to be in a relationship with for the next two days? Well, she'd find out. For the moment, she enjoyed Alexander's closeness, despite herself, and his dry, droll voice narrating their actions. They stopped streaming when the gong rang for the dinner crew to start their preparations. Alexander collected his phone, and the two left the car.

The second they were alone, he stopped to look down at her, eyes sparkling. "I've been waiting all day to kiss you," he said with his usual warmth, and to her horror Delysia let him. She even allowed her arms to lift to encircle his neck, taking the scents of clean linen, tweed, bay rum—all scents that seemed to cling to his skin even when he wasn't wearing those stodgy blazers. She allowed him to explore her mouth with the leisure that was his trademark, and when he finally pulled back she felt a little dizzy.

"I'm sorry," he said sheepishly, "that's not really me. I'll try not to jump on you like that again."

"No, it was fine," she whispered, and touched her lips with a finger. They were soft and smooth to the touch, but to her they felt swollen, bruised, as they had been last night. "You…recorded a live video?"

"Yeah, I've been uploading them all day," he said, and laughed. "Faye was right, the public seems to love them. Although I can't imagine who had the time to sit and watch them all day." He slipped an arm around her; she couldn't hear a word he was saying, not anymore, but she felt the warmth of him through her clothes. She felt sleepy and safe and just…home.

Two days.

She'd never been so tempted in her life. But it wouldn't be honest, not when she knew he was trying his best to persuade her into a relationship. He wouldn't say, but he was hoping. She could see it in his eyes, in his voice, in the way he touched her. And something, despite herself, made her want, desperately, to respond.

No.

She cleared her throat, breaking the spell. Alexander paused himself, and she was able to see that they were almost to the sleeper cars, in a quiet lounge car meant for yoga, or meditating. "What is it, Delysia?"

She took a deep breath. "Alexander, you knew this was coming. I can't do this."

"Do what?" He was maintaining his composure, but

she could already tell he knew what she was referring to. She immediately recognized the posture—the stiff shoulders, the carefully blank expression. "Delysia—"

"I didn't want to. You knew I didn't want to, and you used that against me in DC."

Alexander reeled as if she'd punched him in the gut. She knew it wasn't fair, but it also was the only way she'd get him to shut up, to not talk, not contradict her, not talk her into what she wanted more than anything else right now, so she forged ahead. "You knew I wanted you, and you used that against me to make that dumb promise. But we've got two more days on this thing, and we're not going to be together, Alexander. Not ever. We're just not, and it wasn't fair for me to make you feel like maybe we could."

She was making less sense with every word she said, she knew. Alexander opened his mouth as if he wanted to say something, but she didn't allow him to. "Don't feel bad. I know this is about you making good after the opera night, and—look. You don't have to make it up to me. We're just different, okay?"

At that, Alexander's face darkened. He stepped toward her and Delysia flinched—not because she was afraid he would hurt her, but because he was close, so close, and her body remembered just how much she'd wanted him, almost since the beginning. However, the look of horror on his face now told her that he interpreted her shrinking back as something quite the opposite.

"Delysia. I never intended—" He swallowed hard, held his hands out as if beseeching her. "I'm so very, very sorry."

Again, not his fault—and he was apologizing for it. God. She felt like a murderess, at best.

"I didn't intend—I don't intend to hurt you, Delysia. Never. I simply can't fathom how stupid I—"

"You weren't stupid." She felt it leak out of her, felt her body sag with the exhaustion of all that mental fighting. *It was me*, she wanted to say, *and I'm terrified of any good thing.* But she couldn't tell him that, could she? Not when she was trying to get rid of him.

He took a full step back, and Delysia felt the chasm between them as acutely as if the ground had opened. But she'd told herself then, and she would now—she'd never give a man an opportunity to treat her as second best. Not ever again. Not even if he'd said what Alexander said, done what he'd done...

She could love him, if she let him in. And she simply hadn't the mental capacity for that. Not anymore. Not to mention that this wasn't her home. Everything she'd built here was temporary, and that included relationships.

They were interrupted by a buzz; both of them reached for their phones. It was a gesture that had become almost automatic to Alexander now, Delysia thought a little sadly.

"It's for me," he said, almost apologetically. Then, he looked down. "Channel 12 New York. They want us to do *Good Morning America* the day we get back." His Adam's apple bobbed as he swallowed nervously.

Delysia smiled a little sadly. "They're calling you instead of me now."

Alexander did not smile back; he looked grave and unhappy. He slid his phone in his pocket, then lowered his head. "I never meant to manipulate you." His face was definitely closed off now. "I see now how wrong it was. I hope you can forgive my behavior."

Overwhelmed, Delysia pressed her hands to her face.

She wouldn't cry, she thought. Not now, not ever. Even when she felt water trickling down her face, she refused to acknowledge it. She refused to acknowledge the fact that she wanted nothing more than to have him tug her into his chest, hold her, kiss her, let their bodies melt into each other—

A shrill ring shattered the silence. Delysia's phone, this time. She pulled it out of her pocket, gasped, held it up to her ear. She knew her face must look absolutely ravaged—all flushed and tear-streaked—but she didn't care. It was the number of the head doctor on her mother's case, the one who never called unless something serious happened.

"Mama?" she gasped out.

Alexander must have immediately grasped the gravity of the situation, because his eyes narrowed immediately, and he didn't move.

"I—yes. Yes. Yes." As the doctor spoke, Delysia let the words wash over her, taking them in, understanding but not really comprehending. When she ended the call, Alexander reached out and touched her arm. She jumped as if he'd prodded her with something hot.

"Is everything all right?" he asked.

"They've cleared her for surgery," Delysia blurted out, then immediately burst into a flood of noisy tears. She managed to get out the rest, gasping and choking in the most undignified manner as she did so.

"She's got a kidney—finally strong enough for them to operate—need to go to Dubai, now—my passport isn't here—"

"We leave for New York later tonight," said Alexander, glancing at his watch. "Check if there's a flight. Early afternoon's probably best."

"Okay," Delysia gasped. Tears were falling faster than she could wipe them away. "The flight's twelve hours direct, I won't get there till tomorrow. They have to do the surgery quickly. I might not make it. God, I want to be there," she managed, and burst into a round of fresh tears. "I'm just so scared and so *happy*."

She felt the warmth of Alexander's arms creeping round her shoulders and she clung to him, grateful that he was there.

"Listen," he said, "get online. Book your ticket, get packed. I'll take care of everything else."

"Okay," she croaked.

"And Delysia?"

She looked up; his face was uncharacteristically soft.

"This is good, okay? This is very good. Keep the faith, your mum is going to be fine."

Tears were still running down her chin, meeting the moisture coming from her nose, but she was smiling, now. God, she must look like a mess. "I know."

When Alexander produced another one of those absurdly giant handkerchiefs, she was even able to laugh.

The grandfather clock in the corner of their suite chimed twice before Delysia admitted to herself that sleep was likely not to happen, not this night. Her mother was taking her final hours of rest before going in for surgery, and Delysia didn't want to bother her. She switched off her phone to prevent any temptation, and told herself she'd wait for updates in the morning.

Alexander, with his usual tact, had retreated back to their usual sleeping arrangements, without a word of reproach to her. She'd seen his face when she'd told him she couldn't start anything with him; it was something deeper than disappointment, something she could not explore, not at this time. She was set to go home, and the thought of engaging her heart fully with anyone, no matter how right it felt, and at a time like this…it was simply terrifying.

Still, she could not sleep. She could hear Alexander's steady breathing from the sofa bed, only a few feet away. The clacking of the wheels on the tracks should have soothed her to sleep as it did him, but her body was taut with tension. She ached. It was as if every cell that made her up was aware that Alexander wasn't sleeping next to her, and was arching, reaching out for him.

Impatiently she kicked off the covers; the satin-lined eiderdown and Egyptian cotton seemed more stifling than anything at the moment. She stood to her feet, marveling for a moment that the swaying of the train no longer disturbed her balance, and looked over at where Alexander was sprawled on the sofa bed, a vague shape beneath his blankets.

Desire coiled low in her stomach, a not-so-unpleasant shock of heat. She stood helplessly, arms dangling at her sides. This was hopeless. She'd come into this with no intention to do anything but grow her platform, but she'd met someone so far out of her usual scope that every encounter with him felt like a new segment of an episodic, very hallucinatory dream.

Quickly, Delysia shucked off the threadbare sweatshirt she wore, stood shivering in thin lace underwear, crossing her arms over her breasts. In a moment she'd hooked her thumbs in the waistband and shucked them too, and before she could think about it, could talk herself out of it, she pulled back the covers, slid into bed with him.

Her first thought was that the sofa bed mattress was atrociously thin. The second was that she'd absolutely die if he rejected her. She did not press her body to his, not yet. Instead she let her lips hover over his ear.

"Alexander?" she said quietly.

He stirred, turned over on his side, murmured something, and to her relief she felt his arm slide beneath her to draw her close. "Are you all—"

"I'm fine," she said, and swallowed hard. "Can I sleep here?"

"Of course." His voice was rough; he cleared his throat. She could not quite make out his actual features, just a vague outline of his nose and the curls atop his head, rumpled from sleep. He wasn't wearing a shirt, and she hissed a little as her nipples brushed the bare skin of his back. She felt him stiffen. "Delysia—"

"I know," she said, and bit her lip. How the hell was she supposed to explain her presence, especially after their disaster of a conversation earlier? She didn't know what it was, except for the indisputable fact that this was more about closeness than sex. She'd still meant what she said earlier, but now—

"Do you want me to go?" she asked a little hesitantly.

His answer was to run his fingers along the grooves of her ribs in a caress that felt all too familiar. She felt liquid warmth at the base of her spine. She squirmed, and her breathing began to quicken. Then he brought his lips to hers, found them in the dark. Delysia could have pulled away, pretended that this wasn't what she wanted, but instead she kissed him back, sliding her tongue against his almost desperately, taking control. As usual he was trying to steady her, trying to slow her down.

No. That wasn't going to do it for her, not tonight.

Gathering her wits, she broke the kiss and shifted a little so that she was half-straddling him, and rotated her hips to grind against the warm skin of his thigh. It seemed almost impossible that she could want this so badly *already*, but there it was, stealing air from her, smearing telltale wetness on his skin.

"Can I?" she asked quietly, then tipped forward and kissed him again, dropping a hand to his abdomen, brushing the skin she found with the backs of her fingers.

"Please," he responded, barely more than a whisper.

She didn't know whether it was the rhythmic clacking of the train, but Delysia was suddenly possessed by a near-eerie calm, paired with a tenderness she hadn't known she was capable of feeling until Alexander. She began with a hazy, languid exploration of the skin of his neck, fingers trailing down to stroke where he was only half-hard, still sleepy. She descended his chest and stomach, exploring the smooth saltiness of his skin and dips of muscle with lips and tongue, slowly, cautiously leaving soft wet trails where she went. She felt tremors in her own body when his muscles tightened, tremors she fought at first, then allowed to wash over her, protected by the darkness that shielded both of them. She'd never really explored a guy's body like this, not really. There had only ever been Nicky Kim, and with him there had never been time.

When she reached his abdomen and tugged away the clothing she found she paused for a moment, cupped the heat of him in her hand before softly touching her lips to warm skin. With Nicky she had hated this more than anything—his teasing voice, the way he shoved her head down—but this, this was different. She felt no disgust, only curiosity, and a slight sense of apprehension that was dulled considerably by lust.

"Delysia—" He sounded very awake now, and very hoarse.

She was as deliberate with this as she had been on the way down, flicking her tongue almost lazily, before enveloping him completely with her mouth, almost but not quite toying with him, gauging her movements by his sounds, by the way his muscle-taut thigh tightened underneath her hand. She didn't quite know where all this self-possession was coming from—only that she felt like she was the one in control, for once. There was no constricting grip on the back of her neck, no twisting, no yanking, no grunted orders, and Alexander's fingers were gentle, just a whisper of contact in her hair. The position was an incredibly vulnerable one in some ways, but she didn't feel uncomfortable. Not this time.

She heard him grunt deep in his throat. The sound tightened that feeling between her legs, pulled so taut she nearly whimpered, herself. His hands came down to cup the sides of her head, stilling her movement. "Delysia—"

Delysia hollowed her cheeks before pulling away slowly; she'd tasted salt, knew he was close. She looked up through a curtain of tangled hair, a little anxiously. Had he not liked...?

She straightened up slowly, using his thighs for leverage, and then his arms were around her, holding her close, wordlessly. She buried her face into the curve of his neck and shoulder, shifted her hips forward. "Alexander, *please.*"

He fumbled in the dark for something. As if from far away, she heard cardboard rip, and a low curse. And then he was there again, that warm lean body in the dark, and he was shifting her back, angling her, sliding into her with ease. When he stopped she knew he was trying to get a hold on himself; she deliberately shifted her hips back so that he'd slide in deeper, clenched her walls around him.

"Yes," she hissed, low, in a voice that wasn't quite hers. It was too husky, too raw. All the nerve endings in her body seemed to be gathered in that one spot that Alexander was thrusting into, sparking something within her that was growing with every movement.

"Harder, please," she gritted out instead, bracing herself. This was—oh, *God*. She whimpered, dug her nails into his arm. Her little affectations were completely gone—any dignity was an afterthought at this point. She was just this close to climaxing, clamped so tight around him; she could feel it, and if he'd just—

He dropped a hand between them. Whether it was from skill or sheer luck, she had no idea, but his touch was like a switch being flicked, and she couldn't remember any more a few tense seconds after that. She tightened around him involuntarily and a sound broke from her that she knew would probably absolutely mortify her if she thought of it later. She muffled the tail end of it in the warm skin of Alexander's shoulder. He rocked against her once, twice, a third time, then let go with audible relief, steadying himself through heavy breaths.

He did not make a sound, only dropped down to the bed, tugging her with him. His heart was racing; she could hear it thudding through the warm wall of his chest.

Somewhere during those heated tangled moments the train had stopped, likely to fuel or change engines, and the silence was oddly eerie now. Alexander did not speak, and Delysia was grateful. He was an indulgence, she told herself sternly. He was something she could not afford, something that was appropriate for this gloriously surreal cocoon of luxury these few weeks had been. But ultimately, this happiness wasn't for real life. She could not risk spoiling what they'd created by giving him an opportunity to disappoint her.

"We should move to the bed," Alexander finally said.

Delysia shook her head. Moving would break the spell, would introduce the awkwardness of washing and getting dressed and possibly having to recall the words of dismissal she'd spoken to him only hours ago.

I didn't want to. You knew I didn't want to, and you used that against me in DC...

Christ, she really had no shame, did she?

"It's so cold, outside the blankets," she said finally by way of excuse, although she was anything but. Her body was still tingling, all the way to her toes.

"Right," Alexander said after a pause.

She wanted to speak more than anything, to say the words her heart was pushing up to her throat. But she swallowed them down, instead, and closed her eyes tightly.

"Thank you, Alexander," she said after a moment, into the darkness. He sighed a little and said nothing, only drew her a bit closer, as if he were trying to use their bodies to bridge the gap she'd created.

"Get some sleep" was all he said, and Delysia sighed and closed her eyes, giving up her body to light and fitful sleep.

Chapter Twelve

New York, New York

Under the guise of working on an article he was publishing about the train restoration he'd completed for this trip, Alexander managed to avoid everyone completely, taking a pile of books to the cafe car, sitting up with a pot of coffee, and trying not to worry when Delysia didn't text. She would when she wanted to, he thought. And she was still in the air anyway, hurtling toward the UAE on a supersonic jet.

He could not deny that her words had hurt him deeply; he felt a connection between them that he thought it was impossible not to share. But still…

She made herself clear. Don't think about it.

And he wouldn't either. Not about how hard it was to forget the softness of her skin, her laugh, how he'd tucked her body close to him both in private and in public. Her sweetness and her compassion for others, the way she made him laugh—and made him realize how lonely he actually was sometimes. She'd hugged him so tight at the airport he'd been absolutely breathless.

"I don't know how to thank you," she'd said, sniffing back another round of tears. He had never wanted to kiss her more, but instead he'd pressed his lips to her cheek. Platonically.

"Text me," he'd whispered, and if something in her face had closed off a little, she didn't articulate it. She'd nodded, shouldered her hand luggage, and disappeared through the gates into security. And now he was sitting here, in the dining car, writing about the science of luxury, when his heart was on a plane to Dubai.

He supposed he should focus on wrapping up the trip. New York was the farewell stop, and they'd be there in a few hours, culminating with a gala at the Schwarzman Building of the New York Public Library. Alexander's tux had been delivered to him that morning when he returned, bleary-eyed, to the train after dropping Delysia off at the airport. He'd have to do the event solo. He'd be terrified if Delysia weren't so heavy on his mind.

Faye appeared in the dining car just then as if he'd conjured her up by thinking about the event. Her tablet and keyboard were tucked under her arm; she wore her usual steely expression. She marched over to Alexander and settled herself opposite him on the table. "We need to prep for tonight," she said without ceremony.

Alexander nodded. Silence fell between the two of them.

"Have you heard from her?" he blurted out.

Faye's sharp blue eyes flickered carefully over his face before she replied. "I haven't."

"No, I've been tracking her flight, they've got a few more hours, but there's Wi-Fi up there, and so I thought…" He trailed off. He'd definitely crossed the line from concerned to pathetic.

Faye said nothing. All he could hear for several moments was the ticking of the antique grandfather clock he'd had installed in the corner of the dining car.

God, that felt so long ago.

"I haven't heard from her," Faye said.

"All right." He wondered just how much Faye knew, but he certainly wasn't going to be the one to ask. Faye cleared her throat, then began walking him step-by-step through the itinerary. It had been a pretty straightforward bit previously, with he and Delysia acting as host and hostess of the event ("Think Jackie and Jack Kennedy!" Faye had said brightly during their first run-through) but now, with Delysia gone, the event took on a decidedly less domestic turn. Faye arranged that he be joined by a different influencer every hour, and record a short video with each to post to his Instagram account. Not Eden or Nicky Kim, for which he was grateful. The twins had disembarked in Boston and hadn't been seen since.

"Delysia is going to post a short note explaining she's got a family emergency. Since you're supposed to be pretending to be pining for her"—and here Faye shot him a very significant look, at which he blushed—"you might mention her once or twice during the night. The official line if anyone asks is that she's got a family emergency abroad."

"All right."

Going through the itinerary did not take long. Alexander found his eyes wandering to his phone every few moments, but there was nothing from Delysia. *Stop looking*, he told himself, and turned it facedown.

Faye was staring at him thoughtfully, twisting her glasses chain round her fingers. "So, Alexander," she said, "what's your next move after the trip is over?"

"Well..." Alexander had to think for a moment. "Back

to Southampton, I suppose. Delysia and I will release a statement announcing our separation after the semester closes. I'd rather not have my students asking about it."

"And after that?" She didn't wait for a reply, but leaned forward. "I ask because I wanted to know if you'd ever consider engaging an agent."

For a second, Alexander didn't know what she meant. "I'm sorry?"

"An agent," Faye said. "For these new opportunities you've attracted with this trip. I have to say, I've fielded as many calls for you as I have for Delysia lately. I think people assume I represent both of you."

"Oh," Alexander said, not too brightly. He was too startled to do otherwise.

"The latest call was from Brooks Brothers, asking if you wanted one of their corduroy blazers…"

"They want to give me clothes?" Alexander was very well aware he sounded like an idiot, but he honestly wasn't making the connection.

Faye's eyes bulged ever-so-slightly. "They want you to *endorse* the jacket, Alexander. Be seen wearing it, by the forty thousand followers you've managed to amass in less than two months. And they're not the only ones. Not even close. I've had J.Crew approach me, Timberland, and various other people…nothing as high-level as Delysia, of course, but you could make a pretty penny if you wanted…"

"Oh, dear." Alexander did understand now. "Well. No. Thank you, but I hardly think—"

"Don't underestimate yourself. You translate well to the web medium. Sleep on it. In the meantime, here's some copies of the rundown for tonight. Call me if you've got any questions."

"Will do. Thank you, Faye."

She hesitated as if she wanted to say something else. She stood up instead, swaying a bit on her heels. "I'll see you later, then," she said, and was gone.

Dubai, United Arab Emirates

It had been nearly a year and a half since Delysia had set foot in Dubai, and because of that, most of the details were fuzzy. However, after stepping off of the plane into a wall of heat that slammed into her with a force that made her gasp, it all came back to her in a rush— the vague smell of dust that pervaded the great city, the luxury cars and taxis racing about, the metro whooshing overhead, the variety of faces and national dress on the streets.

She headed straight to the hospital without even pausing to see her hotel. She'd go to her uncle's after a day or two, but for now, she wanted to be as close to the hospital as possible. Faye was taking care of that, and it was sure to be one of the hottest places in town. Her agent hadn't been quite so vulgar as to suggest that Delysia take advantage of her impromptu trip to shoot some footage for her blog and account, but if things went well with her mother, she knew Faye would broach the topic eventually.

If.

One tiny word, and Delysia broke out into a cold sweat.

When Delysia reached the hospital, she called her mother's doctor and instead got a nurse, who instructed her to come to a ward and wait. "Dr. Ahmed gave me instructions to take your call. Your mother is in surgery, and has been for a few hours. We couldn't delay," the nurse explained, briskly but not unkindly. "These things have a time limit, and your mother agreed this course was best."

"I understand."

"She should be out in a couple of hours. I'll let you know if there is news."

Delysia found the room assigned to her mother, drank an ice-cold Coke without tasting it, washed her face and hands multiple times. She couldn't concentrate enough to read, music and podcasts grated, the thought of eating anything made her want to hurl, and she certainly didn't want to engage with anyone on social media, not tonight. Alexander's worried face loomed in her memory now and again, and she nearly almost texted him, to tell him she'd arrived, she was waiting, and how damned scary it all was. But she couldn't—not when she was so determined to cut him off. It wouldn't be fair.

She finally texted Faye. Arrived safely, will update.

She hesitated for a moment, then her fingers flew over the keypad again. Please let Alexander know, and thank him for everything.

"Why are you so skinny?" was the first thing Delysia's mother wailed when she saw her daughter, upon the nurses wheeling her in from recovery, nearly a day later. Delysia, who was practically about to snap into two from the nervous tension, began to laugh—then, burst into tears.

Her nurses patted Delysia good-naturedly on the back, offered tea, told her her mother would be fine. Her new kidney was working splendidly, and she'd be able to go home in a few days.

"I'll stay for as long as you need me, Mama," Delysia whispered, sitting as close to her mother as she dared. The older woman already looked better than she had in years—real color was in her cheeks, and her voice sounded stronger. She reached out and squeezed Delysia's hand, and she felt close to tears again. She felt for the first time since her mother had gotten sick that she finally had her back.

Her mother adjusted her new headscarf—a soft, filmy, embroidered piece that Delysia had brought as a gift—and spoke firmly. "No need, Delysia. You have your own life to live, and I will be very strong, very soon."

"Well, I'll just wait until that day then," Delysia said stubbornly, and her mother sighed, but conceded.

"It will be nice to spend some time with you," she admitted. "Now, tell your old mother about your life. How is school?"

The same lie she'd always told was at the tip of Delysia's tongue, but she suddenly didn't want to. Not anymore. She didn't have to be ashamed of what she did.

"Mama," she said carefully. "I have a confession to make. I'm not in school anymore."

Her mother's mouth twitched. "I know, Delysia."

What? The shock must have shown on her face, because her mother reached out and patted her hand as if to calm her.

"Do you think your old mother can't operate a smartphone, darling? I've been following all your shenanigans for years," she said, and snorted. "Two years ago I called that woman who represents you. Faye, is it? She told me why you did it, promised to keep you out of trouble. And I can see she has."

Delysia felt her eyes well up.

"Don't cry, child." Her mother sighed. "I'm your mother. It feels like a failing, being unable to take care of you. I should be supporting you, so you can be the doctor you've always wanted to be. But—Delysia. Thank you. I don't know what I would have done if you hadn't—"

Her voice broke then, and Delysia pulled her chair as close as it would come to the bed, resting her head on her mother's shoulder.

After a moment, the older woman cleared her throat. "Tell me about this trip you're on now."

Glad to engage her mother, Delysia began relaying the story of the *Gilded Express*, showing her (carefully selected) photographs, and doing her best to select the funniest, most interesting bits of the trip. Her mother laughed at some, shook her head at others, but her eyes grew softer as she looked, as Delysia went on.

"I'm very proud of you," she said simply, and Delysia had to struggle not to cry again.

"Now, tell me," her mother said, sitting back and folding her hands, "about your professor, and why you haven't mentioned him until now."

"Mama…"

"Well?"

Delysia bit her lip. "We aren't together anymore, Mama."

"Why? Is it because you had to come out here?"

"I…" Delysia couldn't very well explain that it was because he'd started falling for her and she'd run like a scared chicken. No, that wouldn't do at all. "We…it wasn't…we were just having fun, Mama. Not too serious."

Her mother fixed her with an impenetrable gaze. "Not too serious? He is the first man you have *ever* introduced me to, Delysia. And I know there have *been* others."

At that, Delysia actually blushed. Her mother was right.

The older woman looked at her hard, then, miraculously, left it alone. "Well, tell me where you're staying. And do you plan on doing something with your hair while you're here? I haven't been to a salon in ages, but one of the nurses tells me there is a miracle worker, practically, in Deira, who works out of her house. Get my handbag for me, I've got her number there…good heavens, child, why are you crying?"

"You're going to be all right, Mama," Delysia whispered, wiping her cheeks.

"Well, of course I'm going to be, especially after all your care." Her mother's face turned grave for a second. "I know you sacrificed so much, Delysia, to help me. I appreciate it. I'm also praying that now you have the leave to live your life the way you want it, without the added burden of an ailing mother."

"You're not a burden, Mama."

"No, not anymore," her mother agreed. "Now, enough of that. Let us order lunch, and we can talk about that hair…"

Chapter Thirteen

Three months later

"Welcome," Alexander said grandly, "to the history of luxury."

Twenty-two pairs of undergraduate eyes stared at Alexander, wide, focused, ready to absorb whatever he had to give. They sat, not in one of the hot, dusty little classrooms they often assigned him on campus, but in one of the three private dining rooms at the SoHo Lounge, where he'd officially become a member at Faye's prodding a month ago. Then, in a burst of inspiration quite unlike him, he'd booked the venue for the first day of class, and talked the *Gilded Express*'s sponsors into attaching his private cars to the seven thirty into Manhattan.

Now they sat around white-linened tables with fruit-infused water in gleaming crystal glasses, along with hors d'oeuvres being passed around by waitstaff.

"Sadly, we're not going to be able to have class here every week," he said, and here he got a few chuckles, "but I thought I'd start the semester with an experience that we all can agree is a bit more…luxurious than the average college classroom. We'll be talking a bit this se-

mester about the evolution of luxury and how what we
see as luxurious has evolved over the years, and how
modern technology interacts with it.

"I'd like you," he finished, "to start at your tables by
introducing yourselves, and identifying what elements
of your experience so far this morning have felt luxurious, or would feel luxurious to someone."

Alexander took a moment to check his phone as his
students began chatting back and forth. As usual, his cell
was riddled with notifications, even though he'd checked
them a mere hour before. He could completely see why
someone might quit a day job to do this full-time. Between his social media interactions and his endorsements, he had to force himself to create time to work.

His exposure had paid off at work, though—requests
for him as an advisor in the history graduate school had
doubled, and he suspected at least a few of the new ap-
plicants had at least heard of him.

Heartbreak—or something very like it, he couldn't
have had his heart broken in only a couple of months,
could he?—had upped his productivity, as well. After
the trip, Christmas and the crossover into 2019 had been
spent in *quiet* solitude on the Abbott-Hill estate, with
him taking the time to catch up on all the work he'd
fallen behind on during the trip. Two academic articles
were set to be published, the *New Yorker* had contacted
him for a piece on his experience, and a British company
that had gotten wind of his penchant for tweed had sent
him enough blazers to last him till retirement.

He had no idea what Delysia thought of his newly
minted success, though. She had firmly disappeared off
the map, posting no content aside from a brief post on
all her platforms about "taking a hiatus for family rea-

sons." He tried calling and texting a couple of times, but they all went unanswered.

He'd truly, thoroughly been ghosted.

The fact that he was now working with Faye—he'd broken down at last, taken her on as an agent—made Delysia's ignoring him even more palpable. He could not separate the two in his mind, and it was strange meeting and strategizing with Faye without a single mention of Delysia.

"Just tell me she's all right," he said abruptly to Faye, one of the last times they'd spoken of her.

The older woman hesitated, then opened her mouth and closed it.

"Faye, please."

Faye, for the first and, he was fairly sure, the last time, spoke rapidly. "Her mother is recovering and they both are fine."

"Thank God," he muttered. He had a million other questions, but kept his word and didn't push Faye any further. At least she was fine, physically. So was he. But mentally—that was another story.

He could almost say he was pining. But that was impossible, he told himself resolutely. He'd only known her for two months. And perhaps someday, if he tried hard enough, he'd be able to forget those sweet, slow, kiss-and touch-filled nights they'd shared.

He wasn't rash enough to say he'd fallen in love. For someone as pragmatic as Alexander, he doubted he could in as short a period of time as they'd had together. However, there was no doubt that his heart had gotten involved, and deeply so.

She might never speak to him again, but he knew he'd care for her for the rest of his life.

The beeping of his stopwatch brought him back to the present, and he began the class. Afterward, students who wanted one were given a tour of the Sky Bar, and many took advantage of the view to take pictures with New York City looming behind like a well-positioned backdrop. Alexander was asked to pose for a couple of photographs himself—another thing that only used to happen with Delysia.

He'd also given up on trying not to think about her. Maybe if he allowed thoughts of her to run rampant, he'd finally be able to forget.

When class was over, Alexander made his way over to the main lounge, selecting a seat in front of the fireplace. They'd lighted what he supposed would be one of the last fires of the season, which made him sadder than it should. He didn't have much time to reflect, though—his phone rang at exactly eleven thirty, and he picked up.

"So. Are you ready?"

He rolled his eyes. "It's lovely to hear from you too, Faye."

She snorted, as if to eliminate pleasantries altogether. "You've got an AMA scheduled for noon. Are you ready?"

"Yes." It was his first solo Ask Me Anything, and he supposed he was as ready as one could be for the possibility of thousands of people firing random questions at him through cyberspace. He'd done this with Delysia once or twice, but she'd been the one fielding the questions.

"Good." She rattled off what they'd already discussed at their last meeting. He could pick any questions he wanted, skip any he wanted. Obnoxious people would ask invasive things. He should take every opportunity possible to mention an endorsement, and...

"What about questions regarding Delysia?" he asked flatly. She'd kept her promise to leave him alone, but hadn't announced they were separating, not on social media. Secretly he'd held a hope that this was significant, but her silence over the past several weeks had dashed that hope.

"Don't answer any questions about her."

"Faye," he said.

"All right, that might be a little...difficult. Choose one or two easy ones that have to do with the *Gilded Express*, maybe? It's only an hour. You can fend off the shippers for that period of time."

"The shippers?"

"Yeah, short for relationship?"

Silence.

Faye sighed loudly. "It's a term that means they're a fan of the relationship—"

"Never mind." Alexander had no interest in trying to master yet another internet abbreviation.

"Very well. Take your time, and text me if you get stuck anywhere." He heard Faye exhale through her nose. "People are sort of curious since you're so private compared to Delysia, so this should be interesting."

Twenty minutes later, Alexander discovered that "interesting" didn't begin to cut it. He introduced himself in two or three brief lines, dutifully sipped his brandy alexander (the chef had thought himself very clever, at that) and peered a little nearsightedly at the questions popping up on his screen.

Are ur glasses real

"Well, yes," he said with some surprise. "I'm quite nearsighted."

Where's your jacket from??? I Love it!!!

"Why, thank you! It's an old jacket of my father's. Brooks Brothers, probably purchased sometime in the '70s. The fabric is absolutely wonderful. A Prince Charles tartan check rendered in tweed—"

Outside the app, a panicked text from Faye popped up. What r u doing?! Shut up about the friggin tweed and take another question!

Alexander got the hang of it as he went on, and he actually found himself enjoying himself. Questions about Delysia were far and few between. Their fans, for the most part, seemed to believe her statement and respected her request for privacy, and after one or two "thank you so much for your concerns," he relaxed even more, began to enjoy it, even.

We r in your class this semester, the first session was amazing. thanks prof Hill!

"You're welcome." He smiled, sat back in the butter-soft leather chair that had been reserved for him. Then—

Tell us about Delysia. We wanna know everything!!!

It took all of Alexander's willpower not to react on camera. By the time he was able to focus enough to consider ignoring the question, others had jumped on the bandwagon.

Oh, yes!

awwwwww yes y'all are so romantic

i love the way you kiss her, it's so sweet and old fash-
ioned

Alexander felt a lump rise to his throat. He could see
notifications piling up in his text app, rather frantically—
Faye must be trying to detour the conversation back to
safe waters. He considered it for a moment, then bit his
lip. He could sound flip and faux-cheerful for a number
of other things, but not Delysia. And not tonight.

"Oh, a lot of questions about Delysia," he said slowly,
and he bit his bottom lip hard before releasing it. "Well. We
met…here, actually. A mutual friend introduced us—" And
here he thought of Faye, her sharp lines and quick tongue,
and the way she'd quietly championed Delysia loyally, un-
failingly. "We didn't hit it off at first, but I showed her one
of my restoration projects, and she took me to a nightclub—my first, actually. We found some mutual interests."

There were other questions pouring in: did they live
together, were they going to get married, how much
older was he than her? Alexander, though, took a deep
breath and barged ahead, ignoring them. This might
be—probably was—the stupidest thing he'd ever done,
but he was going to do it anyway. What the hell did he
have to lose? It wasn't like she'd stop talking to him a
second time because of this.

"I miss her," he said simply. "So much I can feel it physically, sometimes. We haven't been dating for very long, but
she's become an enormous part of my life in a very short
time. Maybe it's because I'm such a reclusive fellow, but I

haven't dated much, and there are very few people who've gotten as close to me as Delysia has managed to. I can't be selfish; she's a dedicated and loving daughter, and her mother needs her right now, much more than I can claim to. But Delysia is an extraordinary woman, and I can't wait to see her again, in whatever capacity she wants me."

He was quite out of breath when he finished his little speech, but his timing was good, for the clock showed that the end of the AMA was only a couple minutes away. He quickly thanked everyone for coming, wished them all a wonderful afternoon, and hoped they enjoyed their lunches. People were still flooding the video with hearts and smiley faces and hug emojis when he logged out, and took the deepest breath he'd taken all day.

When he stood, it was on shaky legs, but he felt surprisingly calm. Maybe it was because he'd finally said, out loud, the things that had been making his chest hurt, his stomach churn, since Delysia had left him standing alone in that airport. At least, he thought, he could never say that he hadn't said it. And that, in itself, was freeing.

Alexander headed to the bathroom, splashed cold water on his face slowly, methodically, then dried his face and hands with the rough paper towels in the bathrooms. He felt flushed; perhaps it was the brandy. Out of a habit he'd only recently cultivated, he turned on his phone; comments were pouring in to the posted video, still, but one notification in particular made his heart leap into his throat.

Delysia's handle, a single heart emoji. And only a few words, but ones that made the blood rush from his head so rapidly he had to lean against the counter.

Mum's better. Talk soon.

* * *

When Delysia was a child, her mother had gifted her a series of books about children who took a magical journey through a mirror, wandering through a land of monsters and lions and queens and fantastical elements. When they found the mirror and returned home, no time had passed; it was they who were greatly changed.

Coming home made Delysia think of this story. Dubai had changed, yes. It had grown bigger and more sprawling, and there were new stores and clubs and franchises and things to do. The years were written on the faces of her uncles and aunts, and her little cousins, some barely walking when she left, were tweens and teens. However, Dubai felt the same—warm and safe and all-encompassing, placing her in a cocoon of feeling that everyone who loved her deeply was well within reach.

Her mother had been living with her uncle Abraham for months; after a week in her hotel Delysia was installed in a large airy bedroom with twin fourteen-year-old cousins, both of whom were determined to be the next YouTube celebrities, and quite in awe of her. They chatted night and day, cajoled Delysia into participating in hair and makeup tutorials, accompanied her on trips to the grocery and the *suq* and the salon, and kept her so busy in general that she had no time to think of New York, or Faye, or the million-plus followers held in limbo with a message that she was taking time off to "care for a sick parent."

She wouldn't have even seen Alexander's video if her cousins, who had followed every moment of their carefully curated romance with enough breathless attention to thrill Faye for life, hadn't brought her the phone after dinner the night it had gone live, screaming with teenage, fan-girl ecstasy when he'd shared his feelings with the whole world.

"You gotta answer, of course," said Amani, the eldest of the twins. Her sister Iman agreed, and the two of them pressed round faces over each of Delysia's shoulders, peering down at the hailstorm of comments dropping into the little screen with Alexander's talking face on it.

"Girls…"

"Say something!" Amani stared at her accusingly. "Wait. Are you still together?"

"We—" Delysia could feel her cheeks warming, and her teenage cousins stared at her, mouths agape. Then she collected herself long enough to order them out of the room, vowing inwardly to look for a villa for her and her mother the next day.

She did think of Alexander, though. The thoughts came in during quieter moments when she could hear her own thoughts, gently insistent, drawing from vivid memories of their time together. New York had faded to a pleasant, general recollection of noise and smell and speed and energy and productivity, but Alexander stood out in her mind's eye, sharp and specific, and popped up at the oddest times. She remembered him spouting obscure facts while thumbing through a trivia book while in line at Kinokuniya. She remembered his coffee-stained Southampton University mug while standing behind a group of NYU Abu Dhabi students at Starbucks, gossiping about classes and how they were late to catch the shuttle. She even thought she'd seen him once, standing in a group of Sudanese men chatting and laughing on the walkway by the Sharjah Corniche; the man's short dark curls and dark brown blazer had been what caught her eye.

At night, it was harder. The twins loved sleeping under a blast of AC that rivaled Arctic winds, and Delysia lay in her bed, huddled in the warmth of the threadbare sweatshirt she'd worn so much on the *Gilded Express*. Her mind raced with thoughts of her mother and her recovery and where they would live afterward and what her life here would look like…

Sometimes she actually had to get up those nights, creep silently over cold tiles into the villa's enormous kitchen, and brew herself a cup of tea, wanting something else to blame for the way her skin bloomed with heat. She remembered his touch as palpably as if she'd just left his bed, and those memories—she closed her eyes. She could still feel his hands, warm on her skin, his lips on her hair and neck.

It wasn't even about the sex, though that had been amazing. It had been a feeling of nearness, of peace. For the first time since she'd moved overseas, she'd felt like she was in the right place at the right time. Cherished. Loved.

Being with Alexander felt like being at home, and the thought of what that might imply—

She hadn't been ready to deal with her feelings then, and she certainly wasn't now. Still, it wasn't fair to leave him hanging. She'd be devastated if she had told someone she loved them and they'd headed off to another country to stay indefinitely without saying anything concrete back. Hell, that had happened to her. But Alexander hadn't demanded it from her. He didn't demand anything from her, except that she do exactly what she wanted.

So what the hell are you going to do about him, Delysia?

Delysia picked up the phone, scrolled to Alexander's

page, to the recording that had streamed live only hours ago. Her fingers flew as of their own volition; the message was short.

Mum's better. Talk soon.

As it stood, she could not offer more than this—her life was here. And in the deepest part of her heart, she wasn't sure it could ever be more. She'd retreated so far back into herself that she wasn't sure she'd be able to find her way out, even if she wanted to.

Delysia turned off her phone, then headed back to her room for yet another night of restless sleep.

She had to call him. She wasn't sure what she could possibly say, but she had to call him.

She owed him that, at least.

Chapter Fourteen

Dubai, United Arab Emirates

When Alexander stepped off the flight and onto the tarmac at Dubai International, the wall of heat that hit him ejected a surprised breath from his body. He had expected it to be warm, of course—a summer in the Gulf should produce nothing less—but this felt as if he'd walked right into the jet's engine wind. He hurried onto the bus waiting for the passengers, weary from their nonstop flight from JFK.

Alexander had spent the fifteen hours in the air in more comfort than he'd ever had at home. Faye, when hearing he was to travel to meet Delysia in Dubai, sent out a call to "a few friends," and secured Alexander a first-class ticket in exchange for a "fun, unbiased narrative." Once he'd arrived at JFK, Alexander was subjected to an absolutely bewildering experience featuring champagne, concierges, and a ridiculous variety of food. He was relieved when he was ensconced in the little cocoon of luxury that was his first-class suite, and could breathe, wrap himself in the softness of cashmere wraps and his own thoughts, and muse.

Delysia. She'd called him after the AMA, on video,

looking very tan, very rested, more than he had ever seen her. Dubai looked good on her.

"I'm so sorry," she said, and quietly, "I'd come if I could, really I would, Alexander. But—I'll be in Dubai with my mother, until she doesn't need me, now that she's out of hospital. We don't have anything worth risking, not yet."

Nothing worth risking? The look on his face must have been telling, for she bit her lip hard—and then spoke again.

"I do like you," she said softly, "very much. The *Gilded Express* was an absolute dream. But I have to be realistic, Alexander. And so do you."

"I do love you, Delysia," he said then, quietly, the words nearly lost against the chasm of cyberspace. It was not a grand or dramatic declaration; it was what was in his heart. He hadn't known Delysia for long, but he did recognize her look: she was unsure. Conflicted. He supposed it wasn't fair to do so, but he did want to tip the scales in his favor if he could.

Surprise crossed the face that had become so dear to him over those past few months—and she smiled. It was quick, bright, and completely unrehearsed. She looked like he'd just given her a present, and the joy on her face made something ache deep in his chest. Her face lit up to such a degree of radiance that he held his breath, but then it was gone as she caught herself, and she stepped back.

"You—you've got no idea how much that means to me," she said, and there was a husk in her voice that hadn't been there before.

"I think I might," he said gently. He wanted nothing more than to take her in his arms, but that of course was impossible here, and he took a breath instead. "You once said you weren't going to feel ashamed for—wanting me. I feel the same way about this. I meant it, Delysia. And that holds true whatever we end up as, or don't."

Her chin wobbled, just a little. "I'm not going to lie," she said. "I don't think I'm planning on coming back anytime soon. I broke my lease. But I promise"—and her voice here was almost fierce—"that I won't disappear on you. I *promise*."

"I'm not worried." This was not entirely true, though, and she knew it. She opened her mouth, closed it.

"It really is all right, Delysia." He smiled, just a little. "That's—a gift, I guess. Not a request. Stay safe."

She'd smiled, raised her hand, cut off the call. And now, he was on a flight to Dubai at Delysia's request.

It wasn't something that had happened immediately, this reconnection. Delysia, true to her word, had not disappeared—she'd popped up on his page, liked a few images, left a few comments. Comments had led to DMs; DMs had led to text messages, text messages had led to phone conversations, phone conversations had led to video chats. It had felt as if they were navigating the shaky waters of a new relationship, only on real terms this time.

"I know," she'd said, voice so soft over the phone he could barely hear her, "that this is a dreadful imposition, but I just want you to see what my life here is. That is, if you want to. And that is anytime. No rush."

His heart had been pounding at the other end. "So this means—"

She paused. "Can you come?"

He did allow himself to feel foolish at the thought of flying halfway across the world to meet a woman who'd rejected him.

Love is a gift. Freely given, freely received. And it went beyond whatever their relationship was, or would be. He would do anything for her, and going against that would be going against himself.

When he agreed, she asked hesitantly if he wanted to do any events with her while she was there.

"No. You're enough of a reason to come, Delysia. Don't think you need to make it up to me if I don't get the answer I want."

There was an inhalation of breath at the other end, and then—

"All right then, I'll see you soon." Soon was longer than he would have liked; there was his class to consider, a TA to prep, virtual work for the last few weeks. Luckily his department head was almost thrilled to see him go. Was this how it was, being a celebrity? he wondered. People willing to waive behavior no one else would get away with?

The old Alexander never even would have tried, but he felt an urgency about this that overcame his usual reticence, his usual sense of responsibility. He wasn't sure whether this was good or bad. All he knew was that he wanted to see Delysia, and badly.

When Alexander exited immigration into the chrome, glass, and palm tree–lined splendor of the airport, it was hard not to wander about and goggle, but his eagerness to see Delysia eliminated any tangents.

"Don't call me, it's sinfully expensive," she said the night before they left, as they were hammering out logistics. "Just meet me at the pink taxicabs. You'll know them when you see them."

He saw Delysia before he even noticed the taxis, which were indeed, very pink. She was waving from a distance, her dark hair forming a halo around her head. He hurried over. Much to his relief, she laughed her old laugh, lifting her arms to wind round his neck.

"You look like such a tourist," she said, and kissed him on the cheek.

"I *am* a tourist. Faye dressed me anyway, so if anything is amiss you have to blame her."

"I think she did a good job." Delysia's dark eyes flickered over his blue linen trousers, cuffed carefully at the ankle, soft driving loafers, white linen button-up. "You look," she said with a laugh, "like a very well-off English academic on his yearly holiday."

"She missed all but the nationality, then. And the taxis *are* pink," he said with some surprise, peering at them.

"Yes, but they're for ladies only, so sorry, no ride."

A housewife in a rhinestone-studded *abaya* shot them a scandalized look, then disappeared into one. Delysia laughed and extracted a pair of Ray-Bans from her handbag, handed them to him. "Consider this a welcome to Dubai. You'll actually need them, here. How's the weather back in New York?"

"Warming up," Alexander answered, slipping them on and tugging the handle of his luggage. His hand was already slick with sweat. "Nothing like this, though."

"It's like stepping into Satan's mouth."

"Oh, but it's *splendid*." Alexander peered over her shoulder into the dusty haze, from which a magnificent skyline loomed, while Delysia knocked on the window of the nearest non-pink taxi, giving the driver an address. The man eased himself out of his car and deftly began navigating Alexander's battered leather duffel into the boot.

"It's one of the oldest places in the world, Delysia,"

Alexander added, excitement bleeding into his voice. "Incredible landscape, the sea right there, and you know, the existence of this place spanned the Neolithic period. David Miller published a paper about it a few years ago. I think that it's one of the earliest proven civilizations outside of Africa, and—"

He stopped when he saw the driver and Delysia staring at him. The driver muttered something, shook his head, and scuttled back round to the driver's side.

"Sorry," Alexander said a bit sheepishly, and Delysia laughed out loud.

"Are you hungry?"

"Not terribly, but I wouldn't mind something…"

Safe in the back seat of the cab, Alexander reached out and placed his hand over hers. She looked over at him, smiled, and exhaled shakily.

"You don't have to worry," he said simply.

She nodded.

The day had finally succumbed to dusk, and Delysia and Alexander were in the closed courtyard of the villa she shared with her mother. The older woman, Delysia had explained to Alexander earlier, was in Deira with an aunt, and would be back tomorrow—to cook Alexander *injera*, and vegetable stew, she promised in a phone call. "You couldn't get decent Eritrean food in the *city*."

Alexander looked pleased, then horrified. "She isn't clearing out the house for me, is she?"

Delysia laughed out loud. "She expects you to stay in the guest room, like a gentleman."

Instead of one of the glittering, luxurious haunts usually favored by social media stars in the Emirates, Delysia took Alexander to a small Turkish restaurant in

Sharjah's city center, one of her favorites. The ride was long, but worth it; they shared a platter of mixed grill and shawarma, and rice made rich and yellow with butter, saffron, spices that clung to and perfectly complemented the sizzling beef and lamb. Alexander seemed quietly content. He piled his bones neatly on the paper tablecloth and answered her questions about New York thoughtfully and told her, with one of those lightning-quick smiles of his, that he was being considered for tenure, and his roster for the next spring was already filling up.

"Alexander, that's wonderful!"

He'd nodded. "It is rather nice."

"And you've become a bit of a social media star," she said dryly, alluding to his many endorsements and the rush of followers that had come after she'd left. Their photo shoot's release had cemented it—and even Delysia was more in the public eye than ever before. Not that she cared about that right now. Her account was safe in the hands of interns who had enough content to keep up a continual stream for six months.

He chuckled. "Your fans miss you—the live videos, I mean. You aren't fooling anyone having an intern run your account, you know. I don't have an interaction without you being mentioned at some point."

"I know." Delysia's voice was wistful, even to her. Her posts in Dubai were much less frequent—only about once a week—and they tended to focus on more abstract things—art, poetry, inspirational things she'd come across. She missed the glittering part of her life, but the hiatus from the New York City social scene had been wonderful. It had been wonderfully healing to be Delysia Ephrem again, just a Tigrayan girl with a funny first name. Still, people had been reaching out. Just that morning a local Emirati influencer who made dance videos with his wife had reached out for a collaboration, and she'd been invited to several local dress shops…

She smiled and tucked a lock of hair behind her ear.

"Also," Alexander said, as if he were just remembering. "I'm to tell you that there's a spot open on the influencer circuit. Apparently Nicky Kim was busted for possession."

"What?" Delysia said, sitting bold upright in her chair.

Alexander was watching her, carefully. "Yes. He was caught making contact with his dealer. He managed to avoid jail time, but he's got a mother lode of community service, and his account's gone dark…how did you not hear this?"

Delysia sagged back in her chair. "I don't follow him." Her mind was racing—and she felt a sudden stab of guilt. She'd hardly been better than Nicky, but she had gotten away scot-free.

Alexander's lips compressed. "Delysia."

"Hmm?" She tried to clear her expression before meeting his eyes again.

"Don't. He had it coming."

"I know." And Faye had had it in for him, too, she thought, remembering the look of anger in her manager's eyes the night she'd come back to the *Gilded Express* so sick. She'd have to ask Faye one of these days if she knew how a man who was as good as covering his tracks as Nicky had been caught so easily.

Or maybe not.

Now they were back home, the light was growing dim, and she and Alexander were outside on deck chairs, drowsy and over-full in the heat, nursing glass bottles of

Coke that grew warm and slippery in the heat. It suited Alexander. He'd rolled up his sleeves, unbuttoned his shirt to reveal a sliver of skin that had tanned to a deeper hue since she'd left New York—his new life on social media had him outside way more, she supposed. It made his eyes more vivid than ever, almost catlike.

She could not stop looking at him.

"Do you like the city?" Delysia finally asked, just for the sake of something to say. She was twisting her curls nervously round her fingers, one by one.

"It's early yet, but I think so. The land might be old, but the city is young, shiny, and optimistic. Like you." Alexander's voice was low and possessed a husk that made her shiver; she remembered when she'd last heard it sound like that. She didn't even think he was doing it deliberately. There had been a palpable connection between the two of them for the longest time, since that night he'd kissed her in the doorway of that grimy club.

God. That had seemed a lifetime ago—and almost as if she had been a completely different person. But she wasn't. She was still Delysia Daniels, and her insides still turned to jelly when Alexander looked at her that way. It was funny; it was hard to predict the future, but she knew she'd spend a life without him wondering what could have been—and quite possibly, longing for it. She'd longed for him in those past weeks, hadn't she? As her mother had gotten stronger and the panic faded, she had time to remember. The memories weren't only tied to the way he kissed, or the rasp of his warm skin on hers—there was plenty of that, but that wasn't what stood out in her mind.

Love is a gift. It shouldn't matter if it was returned

or not. After Nicky she'd reached the point where she was too emotionally tired to try to make her heart happy anymore. Love had become secondary to survival, and became less important as the years progressed.

Alexander Abbott-Hill had upended all that.

Her cheeks warmed. She looked up and his expression had changed subtly; she could see it reflected in his eyes, see that what he'd said to her in New York was still true.

"Alexander."

"Yes?"

"How would this even *work*?" she found herself murmuring, and he smiled.

"Well, I'd exercise my right as an American to do visa runs every two months," he said dryly. "I'd work on my book, and perhaps call a couple of colleagues at NYU Abu Dhabi, see what the lay of the academic land is, and eat copious amounts of your mother's *injera*, and bask in this glorious heat, and film whatever videos Faye dreams up, as I'm as shameless an influencer as the rest of you now." His mouth tipped up, peered over his tortoiseshells. "I'm writing on the history of luxury. What better place to do that than Dubai?"

Delysia managed to smile. "It is pretty opulent. But—" She hesitated.

He raised his eyebrows.

"I'm not," she confessed, and laughed a little at her own foolishness. "Opulent, I mean." The words sounded ridiculous even in her head, but she said them anyway. She'd already resolved to never keep anything back from the man she'd grown to feel so strongly for in so short a time. "I don't want you to be too disillusioned with the real me."

He smiled at that, though he did not laugh, and his

hand crept out to grip hers. He did not speak for a long moment and when he did his voice was gentle.

"The real you is perfect," he said, "and the best days are yet to come. We'll build our brand, eat too much, travel…" He trailed off. "The possibilities are endless. And I miss you very much."

Delysia had to lower her lashes. She had never been able to hide her emotions from Alexander. Not well, anyway.

He continued in low, unhurried tones. "Delysia."

She looked up.

"Don't worry about me," he said. "It's fine if it's a no. I'm just glad to be with you today."

Delysia cleared her throat, then tucked a stray lock of dark hair behind her ear. "Is it okay," she said, "if I can't…say it, right away?"

"You don't have to say anything," he answered simply. "That changes nothing."

Delysia took a deep and shaky breath she hadn't known she'd been holding, then got up from her deck chair, bent over Alexander's, kissed him. Not hard, but sweet, slow, and intense. It was muggier now that the sun was setting, and she felt light-headed when she pulled away, drawing deep breaths of soggy air into her lungs.

The look he gave her was both soft and serious. "Come here," he said quietly, and drew her down into his lap.

Tonight, she knew, they'd make love with all the tension, the sweet urgency that was their hallmark; she ached for him already. She knew that she would say those words to Alexander, not tonight, but probably soon. Her heart had been in competition with her head since she'd met him in that ridiculous SoHo Lounge, and it finally was gaining ground.

Her fingers traveled upward, tangling in his curls. She closed her eyes.

"Thank you, Alexander," was all she said, and she felt a gentle squeeze around her waist as his lips met hers.

Chapter Fifteen

It was easier than Alexander thought to adjust to Dubai, although he suspected his relatives and his students would barely recognize him. He certainly didn't recognize the man who faced him in the mirror each day when he woke and pried the sticky window in his room open to the blazing day. His hair had grown out, and the curls rioted, dark and full, over his head; his already tan skin had deepened; a pair of aviator sunglasses dangled from his collar at all times, and he'd started wearing proper *cologne*. He attended pool parties. He went dune bashing, and loved it. He found himself having to designate strict time for study, something that hadn't happened ever, really.

It had been the first vacation that Alexander had taken since Cambridge, and the fact that it had an open-ended return date made things seem all the more leisurely. Delysia's uncle Abraham had laughed at the idea of Alexander's staying in a hotel or renting an apartment for his time in Dubai, and he had a ready-made answer for all of Alexander's polite excuses. Hotels were outrageously expensive, unless you wanted to be on the outskirts of Ajman and take two hours to get *anywhere*. Renting an apartment would be difficult for a non-visa holder; they'd rip him off. Any friend of Delysia's was family to him. It didn't take long for him to wear Alexander down, and he soon found himself enjoying his new role as a de facto member of Abraham's sprawling brood.

Delysia's twin cousins were absolutely star-struck, and he found himself escorted around Dubai in fine style by two *very* chatty girls, who were thrilled to have someone to pick up the tab everywhere. They'd followed his and Delysia's online love story and could recall it with encyclopedic detail, much to his embarrassment.

Delysia was different here, and yet exactly the same; almost an enhanced, richer, Technicolor version of the girl he'd met and fallen in love with in New York. Delysia Ephrem had none of the guardedness that made Delysia Daniels such an enigma. She laughed, and swore, and cried every single time they watched *Sabrina* together, and kissed Alexander at night with a heat that he felt long after she'd gone, with only the faint impression of her perfume on his pillows. He'd fallen in love with her in New York, but he was absolutely besotted here. He knew it would hurt like hell eventually, but it was worth it.

The two quickly fell into a routine, lulled into compliance by the easy rhythm of the Gulf. Alexander woke with the sun to study and write while Delysia took her mother to therapy. After, they either ate breakfast in Abraham's empty home after he and the twins had gone to work and school, feeling delightfully domestic, or went to one of the many beach hotels that littered Jumeirah Road for lavish spreads. They spent time with her mother, taking her to her favorite shops for slow promenades in air-conditioned comfort as she got stronger. He even spoke to Delysia's father on two occasions via videoconference; he was a thin, mustached man with a wicked sense of humor who even on camera had Delysia's extraordinarily large eyes.

Delysia did not attempt to document any of their time together for social media, though she technically was "back." This was for them, and it was deliciously private. He did not have to think of a narrative when he held her or kissed her or spoke gentle words in her ears, or breathed them on her skin. He could bask in the enjoyment of loving her, and doing little else.

That evening they'd agreed to meet at Reem al Bawadi, one of the tony restaurants on Jumeirah that the twins had dragged him to in the early days of his trip. The girls were rather snobbish about it, thinking it very typical of Arab dining establishments ("but we have to bring you here, you're a tourist").

However gauche it seemed to his teenage travel guides, Alexander quite liked the old-fashioned opulence of the dining room, with its twinkling lights and lanterns and shades of deep red. Delysia sweet-talked the hostess into a table by the window overlooking the skyscrapers of the city in all its brilliance, and they talked and laughed until the server brought their salads and hummus. They engaged in a bit of where-are-you-from (Alexander got Somalia, Sudan, and Egypt until he let the man off the hook good-naturedly) and then were finally left alone.

He watched Delysia look out the window, a dreamy, abstracted look on her face. Her mother returning to health had lifted much of the worry that had strained it in those early days he'd known her. She was makeup-free, her hair styled in long braids with wavy ends that fell past her waist. Her slim bronze arms emerged from the folds of a filmy dress that just touched the floor at her feet. She looked more beautiful to him than she ever had.

When she asked him what he was thinking about he told her frankly, and she flushed, but laughed. She'd grown used to Alexander's odd ways of speaking, and he'd grown used to being able to say what he was thinking.

It had, he thought, worked out quite nicely. Actually, this time in Dubai with her had been perfect in the way only films had been for him, before this. These were no carefully curated moments of perfection, but even failures felt wonderful with Delysia there. He raked his fingers through his hair, feeling them catch. He still wasn't used to having hair so long. He hadn't since he was a toddler, and his mother had tended his Afro jealously. Dubai seemed to be teasing out a part of him that had been dormant for a long time.

New York had never seemed farther away—not until an email from Dean McDermott landed in his inbox.

We've had, he said, an unprecedented amount of students requesting the History of Luxury class you taught in the fall. Might you consider coming back in September? We can revisit the tenure conversation as well, in light of the professional and creative pursuits you've engaged with over the past few months. We would very much like to ensure that your progress in these areas is both highlighted and rewarded.

Alexander read the rest of the letter once, twice, three times. Then he walked across the cool tiled floor in his little room in Abraham's house to take a shower, and go to meet Delysia.

The letter hadn't been wholly unexpected. His course evaluations from last semester read like glowing movie reviews, and he could remember each one: *"Wholly un-expected."*

"Exciting and fast-paced."

"Professor Hill is really chill and knows his stuff. Makes it interesting."

He'd basked in the glow of those compliments, more than he'd ever be able to admit to anyone but Delysia. It was really all he'd ever wanted, to be able to share what he loved with the next generation, and let them interact meaningfully with it. His students weren't apathetic, not really. Since beginning to engage in their spaces, he'd come to realize how sensitive and intelligent they really were. Even though he still didn't quite speak their language, he knew how to communicate with them, and that made all the difference in the world.

For the first time since he'd embarked on this career, Alexander felt as if he'd found his way, his voice. He wasn't trying to live up to his father's legacy, not anymore—instead, he was paying homage to the past, while creating his own future. Sometimes when all was quiet and still and he was alone with the pile of dusty books he'd brought to Dubai with him he thought, a little foolishly he supposed, that he felt the older man's presence, felt the warmth of his approval.

Seeing the letter was a bit of a jolt. It reminded him that despite what he'd told Delysia, he still had a life in New York. His job waited for him, as did the enormous house on Long Island, with its tours of the grounds and the wine harvest and other unpleasant things he had to sign forms for in person, if not supervise.

Dubai's golden warmth was as seductive as Delysia was—he'd fallen in love with it, too. Still, he had to make a decision, and make it soon.

When Delysia spoke, he blinked—he'd been completely lost in thought. "Sorry?"

"I was asking if you wanted to see *Aida*. It's at the Dubai Opera, starting next month." Her mouth dimpled. "I know that it may not be quite the standards of your aunt Sylvia, but it's a gorgeous production."

"Ah," Alexander said inelegantly. "I—when—?"

She said a date, but it was lost as he blurted out at the same time, "Delysia, they want me to come back. Southampton, I mean. To teach my luxury course again. I got some fantastic feedback, semester before this, and—"

She sat, staring at him, her mouth open a bit.

"I know I said…" He took in a frustrated breath, raked his hand through his hair. "I—"

Delysia was already shaking her head. "No, don't, Alexander. You have a job, and you've been here—what, the entire semester, just hanging out with me and my mother. Of course you need to go back. It'd be stupid not to."

"Delysia, I am in no way saying—"

"Alexander," Delysia cut in, and her smile was genuine, if a little sad. "You wouldn't have told me about it if you didn't want to go back."

They finished their meal in silence.

When they left the restaurant, Delysia gripped his hand in hers. She could not kiss him where they were, out on the open street, but she stood on tiptoe and let her lips hover over his ear. "Can we go to the Palm?"

Alexander's face bloomed with heat. He'd kept his studio at the hotel apartment he'd rented before her uncle Abraham had forcibly moved him in, mostly because he wanted a place to write that did not involve fourteen-

year-old twins having access to him, and because his
grant was paying for it anyway. He and Delysia used it
whenever they needed to be alone. There was a soft urgency in her voice that he recognized immediately, and
his body recognized even faster.

She said little until they arrived, rode the elevator up
to his apartment on the seventh floor. They were barely
through the narrow door before Delysia's arms were
snaking round his neck. There was something about the
way her body moved against his that night that reminded
him of that last, dark night on the *Gilded Express*, before she'd left. He shucked the yards of soft fabric up
her thighs to her waist, thumbed lace underwear aside
to trace soft downy skin with his fingertips. Her thighs
quivered with the effort of holding still.

"I want you inside," she whispered, and her fingers
began to fumble with the button of the trousers hanging
low on his hips. Most of his senses were beginning to be
reduced to the feeling of her hand on him, stroking and
thumbing him firmly, but there was enough left for him
to grit out words, on the tail of a breath.

"I'm not leaving tonight," he said firmly, pulling half
away and bending his head to ensure he was looking directly into her eyes. "Delysia—"

She would not meet them, not even when he was between her thighs, thrusting slow and sure, watching the
light play soft across her face.

Afterward they curled round each other like cats in
his narrow bed, both naked, covered with a thin sheen
of perspiration, and she told him that she loved him.
She said it quickly, as if the words would somehow be
snatched back into her mouth if she didn't speak them

quickly enough. Alexander's eyes were closed, and he didn't open them. He groped instead for the remote and flicked on the air-conditioning unit; they sighed as a waft of cool air covered them.

"Alexander?" Her voice was quiet, subdued.

He turned his head so that he faced her completely, but she rolled over and pressed her back against his chest instead. There was a dull ache in the center, similar to the one he'd had the night Delysia accused him of coercing her into a relationship. What they'd had since then had been the best experience of his life, but he'd been careful since then, careful to ensure she never felt cornered again.

"You don't have to say it if you don't want to," he said simply, bringing his hands down to cup the full heaviness of her breasts. Her nipples were hardening in the rapidly cooling air; they'd make love again, he thought a little sleepily, and this time in bed. Comfortably. Maybe then they would order something in for dessert, fall asleep in front of the flat-screen mounted on the wall that he rarely used. "I mean it."

Delysia squirmed just enough to anchor her hips between his legs. She made little sounds as he touched her, not necessarily sexual, but content.

It was worth it, he thought, if this was all he ever had of her.

"You should go back," she said finally. "We'll work it out."

The night Alexander left Dubai to go back to the States, Delysia was both mentally and physically exhausted—physically, from the effort of helping Alexander pack everything he'd managed to amass in three months of living in Dubai, and mentally from playing the part of the good, cheerful girlfriend. She drove him to the airport herself, managing to talk the twins into staying home, heartbroken at the loss of their American friend. She kissed him discreetly behind the tinted windows of their car and watched his straight back in its linen button-down until it disappeared in the crowd of passengers ready to make a long trek into arrivals.

Alexander was not one for long, drawn-out, public goodbyes, and neither was she.

She drove back home, slowly and soberly. It would still be several hours before he boarded. Alexander, in true form, arrived at the airport a full four hours before the flight. "I'll have plenty to do, it's Dubai International," he said cheerfully, seemingly unable to see her downcast face. Now, she was home, and she smelled *tsebhi* even before she reached the door; the rich meatiness had filled the compound.

Comfort food, and her mother knew it.

"You're not trying to cheer me up by fattening me up, are you, Mama?" she teased, but inside her heart was glad. Her mother had only begun slowly attempting housework in the past couple of weeks; this one was the first she'd attempted making a meal. Moving from Abraham's villa and back into her own home after her convalescence had plenty to do with it, as well—things were slowly, but surely, going back to normal for her. She hurried into the villa's small but immaculate kitchen, washed her hands. "And you shouldn't be doing all this."

"I'm strong," said her mother, shaking her shoulders as if to prove her words. She pressed a cool cheek to Delysia's, then began stirring the stew briskly in the pot.

"Besides, that young man of yours helped me prep everything this morning, while you were out cleaning the car."

"Oh," Delysia said a little too brightly, and took down plates. She finally prevailed on her mother to sit, and set steaming plates and water glasses, cloudy on the outside with condensation, in front of them. Her mother crossed herself briefly, and the two began to eat.

"How is Baba?" Delysia asked.

"Ah, fine. Spends his day sitting and gossiping with your uncles." Her mother chuckled. "Perhaps by winter I will be able to visit. Something to look forward to."

"If you're well enough," Delysia said, her mouth full, chasing pleasant spices round the surface of her tongue.

"I'll be well enough." Her mother looked her over with sharp brown eyes, then pursed her lips, took another bit of spongy *injera* and attacked the stew on her plate. "I will need your help to clean out the guest rooms," she said after a moment.

"For your trip to Eritrea?" Delysia was only half-listening.

"No, for your cousins' trip here. I've asked Iman and Amani to move in with me till I go to Eretria," her mother said, casually.

"What?" Delysia dropped her fork. "Why—"

"You've been here for almost six months, and I know you won't leave unless I'm taken care of." Her mother's face curved up into a smile. "They are two of the silliest girls I know, but they are strong and capable. Abraham didn't spoil them, and they're dying to get out from under his roof so they can gallivant all over Dubai, trying to keep up with their Instagram auntie."

"Mama—"

"You left a business over in New York, Delysia, to

take care of me. A thriving business, one that you've ignored since coming back. I follow you, remember?" her mother said acidly. "It's only that she-wolf you employed that's kept the whole thing afloat. She's recycling content at this point."

Delysia was dumbfounded. Her mother was right.

"You need to go back and see to your business, talk to Faye. If you want to continue, figure out how that will happen, and where that will happen. If you don't, shut things down properly, cash out, and come home." Her mother reached out and covered Delysia's hand with her own; it was cool, and the skin was dry, paper-thin, a hallmark of her long illness, as well as middle age. "Your Alexander, as well," she added, mouth curving upward. "Again. If you don't want him, shut things down properly."

Delysia could not speak even if she wanted to. There was an odd thudding deep in her chest, and suddenly the food she'd eaten seemed to rise, dense and high in her throat. She tried to take a sip of water, but her stomach closed against that, too, and she pushed her chair back a little abruptly.

"Do try to get some rest, my child," her mother said gently, and went back to her meal.

Delysia left wordlessly, went into the sitting room, closed the door behind her. Her heart was beating oddly—she could hear it in her ears. She picked up her phone, and against all reason, all *sense*, she dialed.

"Hello?" She was quiet for a long moment; she could hear Alexander breathing, softly. "Delysia?"

She swallowed hard. When she spoke, her voice sounded nothing like her. It was croaky and low, far from the full-bodied husk she used for her video content. "I'm here."

"Are you all right?"

I'm not, she wanted to say. But her mother was right. Things needed to be done properly; Alexander deserved that, at least. She cleared her throat, and when she spoke, it hadn't helped at all.

"Are you at the gate yet?" she asked.

Fifteen hours was a long time to be in the air, but Delysia barely felt the length, this time. Perhaps it was because this was the first time she hadn't made the flight alone, and being with Alexander changed the feeling completely. Faye had arranged the next flight for them, of course with the caveat that they produce content for both their pages, but it hadn't felt hard at all this time.

There was so much to say, so much to show, and the first video—she smiled to think of it, tucked safely in her own private files.

"We're in a dreadful mess right now," he'd said wryly to the camera, from where they were tucked in a little alcove in the first-class lounge of Emirates Airlines, sitting in front of a spread of fresh fruit and wine, ketchup and buttery-crisp french fries, on a little marble table. A screen in front of them gave an illusion of privacy, and the way Alexander looked at her kept her cheeks hot. All his natural reserve was completely gone, and he gazed at her as if she'd gifted him something he hadn't asked for but had needed desperately. She'd worn that expression more than once, but never had she had it directed at her. Part of her wanted to revel in it, and another part wanted to bury her face in his chest, hide until her heart stopped beating so fast and her skin was no longer flushed.

Then he spoke—and even when he was talking into

the tiny camera lens at the corner of her phone, he was looking directly at her.

"I'm not sure where we'll go after this, but everywhere you are is beautiful, and I want that feeling to linger forever." The words were quiet, simply said, and he had to clear his throat before continuing. "It's actually funny—we started out trying to put up with each other. Literally. We still do sometimes, I think. I still don't know how to Tik or Tok, and you still zone out when I discuss my work—"

"Correct," Delysia agreed, laughing. Her chin wobbled a bit. She was trying desperately to keep it together for the camera but wasn't doing a very good job. Only this morning she didn't think she'd ever have the courage to allow herself to be loved so recklessly, but with every word he spoke she felt that tight knot that had been in her chest for as long as she could remember loosening a little bit more, cracking wide open.

"I'm rather at a loss without you, in many ways," Alexander added, and then he did kiss her. It was whisper-soft and quick, but it resonated even more than the many he'd given her on the train journey, because this signaled the beginning of something that had no date of disembarkment. His words had her wiping her eyes in her seat, laughing and crying at the same time. They were everything she'd grown to love in him: funny, and generous, and tender, and true.

"Faye is *not* getting that," she told him firmly, after he lowered the phone, kissed her again, this time chastely on the cheek. They were words too intimate, too heartfelt for the world to consume, and she knew deep in her heart they were the foundation for years of happiness.

He shot her a wry smile. "It wasn't meant for her."

Their fingers were still laced. Delysia loved the way he touched her and looked at her with wonder, as if she were a precious thing that might be gone in an instant if he squeezed too hard.

It was a testimony to both his and her mother's personalities that neither seemed particularly surprised when she'd called, asked Alexander breathlessly if she could come back with him. He'd been silent for a moment.

"Why?" he'd asked, and for once Delysia did have an answer.

"Mama's fine now," she said quietly. "I'd like to— come with you, and worry about us a bit, if you'll let me."

Now that they were ensconced forty thousand feet above the gray-blue sea, with nothing but time in front of them, she was able to explain. "She had the twins move in with her," Delysia said, and wrinkled her nose. "She's already sick of them. She practically packed my bags and put me on the plane herself."

"So you're—" He took a breath, not sure how to ask.

Delysia lifted her slender shoulders. "I'm here. For the moment. My influencer base is in the city, and I want to maintain that. And—" She stopped, cleared her throat, and spoke so fast it was hard to understand. "We... I guess we can work out the details later, but I want us to be together. You've proven already that you'll move about for me, and—" She hesitated again, trying to find the words. "Home for us, I think, is wherever we are, together. And we'll keep making sure that happens."

He did not speak, but Delysia saw the answer shining bright behind eyes that were very suddenly so vivid they seemed lighted from within. He kissed her temple, and they spoke quietly of dinners and coffee shops and museums in New York and strolls along the Corniche and weekends in Oman, and other things they could do, now that they'd united and the world lay open before them, rich, bright, eager to be explored through the eyes of new love.

Faye's content was forgotten for the moment; in that moment, they were completely wrapped up in themselves, in the wonder that comes from complete surrender. They spoke through the drinks service, and the meal service, chatted softly as their fellow passengers ate their food, pulled on their loungewear, tucked plush blankets round themselves as the attendants circulated to soften the lights.

They listened to each other's words as if they were lines in a book, the kind that brought tears to your eyes, because the story, while not always happy, would be tender, sincere, and full of life's joy.

* * * * *

Author Note

Dear Readers,

I wouldn't be a very good research librarian if I didn't "cite my work," so I'd love to share a few of the books I read while researching and getting into the spirit of this novel. I'm quite sure Alexander has most if not all of them on his shelf! They are:

20th Century Limited by Karl R. Zimmermann

Luxury Trains of the World by G. Freeman Allen

Dining Car Line to the Pacific: An Illustrated History of the NP Railway's "Famously Good" Food, With 150 Authentic Recipes by William A. McKenzie

Mr. Pullman's Elegant Palace Car: The Railway Carriage that Established a New Dimension of Luxury and Entered the National Lexicon as a Symbol of Splendor by Lucius Beebe

I would also encourage my more visual readers to google the *Lilly Belle*, the last car on the Disneyland Railroad. It is plush and gorgeous, and simply marvelous. Another couple that inspired me were Great Britain's Royal Train and South Africa's Rovos Rail. All (excluding the Royal Train unless you're way more important than I am) can still be ridden on today!

Happy travels,
Jadesola

Acknowledgments

I would like to thank Stephanie Doig at Carina Press for the "like" that set this all in motion, and thank my editor, Mackenzie Walton, for her kindness, humor, and help. I'm also grateful to Carina Press for all the support at every step of the way.

Thanks to Fortune Whelan and Nikki for the late-night writing sessions and multiple beta-reads; you'll always be my writing siblings! Extra love to my real-life sisters, "J, F, T & D," who believed I could do this before I did. I love you four to eternity.

Finally: thanks to libraries I've loved and worked in, both big and small, both online and in person. I wouldn't know a thing about vintage trains without you.

About the Author

Jadesola James loves summer thunderstorms, Barbara Cartland novels, long train rides, hot buttered toast, and copious amounts of cake and tea.

When she isn't writing, she's a reference librarian and a scholar of American publishing. Her hobbies include collecting vintage romance paperbacks and fantasy shopping online for summer cottages in the north of England.

Find Jadesola and news about her upcoming books on Twitter at twitter.com/JJ_Nicola and on Facebook at facebook.com/jadesola.james.739.

Advertising mogul Laurence thought he'd escaped his past long ago. But when it turns up in the form of Kitty Asare...she stirs up not only long-buried memories but an inescapable desire. After she saves his life, Laurence is intent on repaying the favor. So begins a bargain where power, passion and redemption are all to play for!

Keep reading for an excerpt from Jadesola James's debut for Harlequin Presents, Redeemed by His New York Cinderella*!*

CHAPTER ONE

LAURENCE JAMES STONE hadn't eaten alone in a public dining room in years.

He had no idea why he'd chosen to do so tonight. The Park Hotel's quiet elegance, shrouded in greenery on the north end of a mid-Manhattan street, possessed the sort of shabby opulence that was no longer favored by the rich and young. However, the food was sublime, the service impeccable—and in a manner of hours, he would be hosting the biggest social event of the season here, in the Grand Ballroom.

His advertising firm, recently gone public, would be the talk of the evening. He and his business partner were so close to hitting the billion-dollar mark that he could taste it. That number had eluded him for years, and though his personal fortune was vast, this was different. He wanted to be able to *pay* himself that amount, created by his own hand.

This, in a way, was their debut.

Laurence had arrived and had been ushered to the Penthouse Suite with plenty of time to rest and dress for the evening's festivities after an eight-hour flight from Berlin, but his stomach started growling thirty minutes after his arrival. He was quite hungry, even though he'd been offered a bewildering assortment of food on the flight.

He showered and threw on a sweater and wool trousers, then took the penthouse elevator down. He looked forward this quiet meal; perhaps it was because he'd be forced to make small talk with hundreds of people in only a matter of hours, not to mention playing nice to a particular client he was hoping to sign...

He was dreading it like most people did the dentist.

"Oh, don't be such a snob," his partner, Desmond Haddad, said dismissively when Laurence had complained earlier. Desmond was everything Laurence was not—youthful, flashy and bafflingly optimistic. He was tall, slim and debonair in contrast to Laurence's solid, grave steadiness, and always up for a party, when all Laurence really cared to do was work. Upon their arrival at JFK, Desmond had seized his friend's laptop, tablet and work phone despite Laurence's protests, then waved him off to his room.

"It's for four hours," Desmond said mockingly, "and you won't go drinking with me, I know that, so you might as well get some rest, look fresh for tonight. Surely you can make do without looking at a single ad campaign for four hours. God, Laurence. I find it hard to believe you grew up rich. You work as if you're millions of dollars in debt."

Yes, fine. Laurence had grown up fairly well-off—after all, he'd met Desmond at Exeter. Hardly a school for the impoverished, although his senator father's fortune paled in comparison to Desmond's dynastic oil money. Still—he could not explain to Desmond, who spent his family coffers with gleeful abandon, the need to make a fortune that was completely his. And even when he *did* try to explain—

"Yeah, yeah, yeah, poor little rich boy, innit," Desmond said scornfully, his English accent cutting like glass. "Your problem, Laurence, is that you're too damned serious."

Well. Perhaps he was.

Laurence was relieved to see that the dining room was empty, except for a young woman seated alone at a table in front of a large stone fireplace.

"Do you mind, sir?" A harried-looking waiter ushered him to a table close to the young woman's. "We're short on staff right now, as there's an event taking place in a couple of hours. They've closed off most of the dining room."

"Very well." It mattered little to him, and as the waiter fussed about with clean linen and water glasses and a long, rambling recitation of a wine list, he found his eyes lingering idly on his dining-room companion. She was tucking into an enormous meal with so much enjoyment he stifled a smile. She hadn't skimped on quality, either. On her table he identified the remains of a caviar starter, oysters, a steak smothered in fresh mustard greens.

"Sir?"

He blinked, looked up. "A glass of whiskey and water, please. And those oysters—" he gestured at the young lady's table "—are they grilled?"

"Rockefeller style, sir."

"I'll have those, and the new potatoes in cream."

"Very good, sir."

The waiter swanned off, and Laurence was left to feel annoyed at the fact that he'd have to log manually into his email, since his rarely used personal line had none of the many apps he used to keep his work organized. He hadn't used it in a couple of weeks and he felt a rush of physical relief as he switched it on and began to scroll.

He was halfway through a report on viewing statistics for a motorbike ad when the waiter came back with a bread basket, dropped it off with little ceremony, and headed over to the young woman's table.

"Are we all set, then, ma'am?" he heard the waiter say solicitously. Laurence listened with about half an ear; he was curious to hear what such a voracious eater's voice sounded like.

"I am, thank you." She spoke quietly, almost inaudibly. Her voice possessed a low husk that, despite himself, made him look up; it was familiar, in that elusive way that nags until, finally, the brain identifies. He registered wide eyes in the clearest shade of brown he'd ever seen, a full bow-shaped mouth painted berry red and a dimpled chin before he looked back down at his phone.

Pretty, he thought idly. He'd look up again when she stood, see if the body matched the face. And there it was, that sense of déjà vu. Who could she possibly be? He'd gone to university abroad, so that was out. She looked far too young—and too broke—to be a client. Perhaps one of the many interns who filtered in and out of Laurence & Haddad each summer? No, it couldn't be that—he avoided them like the plague.

"Shall I charge it to your room, ma'am?"

"Oh, yes, please." Again, in that soft, cultured voice. "I'm in Suite 700."

"Ah, the penthouse. Very good, ma'am."

At *that*, Laurence did look up. He knew for sure that the woman wasn't staying in Suite 700, because that was his room. Brazenly, she signed the bill with a flourish and took a long last sip of champagne with every indication of pleasure before looking up.

She had the gall to shoot him a shy smile and lowered her lashes, touching the napkin to those soft, full lips.

Laurence was torn between being amused, annoyed and appalled. If the menu was any indication, she'd just charged at least a few hundred to his room, and the little grifter hadn't even blinked. He half considered going after her, but his phone buzzed just at that moment. His last impression was of subtle but definite curves, shrouded in soft faded denim as she headed toward the door, hips swaying gently. Laurence cleared his throat and looked away.

He glanced down at the message, and what he saw was enough to drive all thoughts of beautiful, dinner-scamming women from his head.

"What the *hell* do you mean, you're in Dubai?" Laurence hissed.

On the other end of the line, Aurelia Hunter—*his girlfriend*—yawned, and loudly. Laurence did the mental calculation; Dubai was nine hours ahead of New York. Most important, it was much too far away for her to show up that evening in formal dress as expected. "Aurelia!"

"Hold on." Aurelia sounded irritated now. He heard rustling—bedclothes, probably—and her soft, dulcet voice speaking to someone else. Then she came back, sounding only slightly more awake. *"What?"*

"You're. Supposed. To. Be. Here," Laurence said, emphasizing each word. "What do you mean, what?"

There was an incredulous pause, then Aurelia began to laugh. Loudly. "Are you serious?"

He was serious. He also was convinced that he now was missing something very, very important. "This is hardly a laughing matter," he snapped. "We're seated with the Muellers during coffee, Aurelia, and you know how important that account is—"

Her laughter finished on a gasp. "You really have no idea, do you?"

"Not unless you choose, very *kindly*, to fill me in. Why are you in Dubai?"

Aurelia's voice changed from incredulous amusement to something he was more familiar with—studied coolness. "I see you didn't get any of my messages. I know you didn't return any of my calls."

"Obviously not," Laurence snapped. He fumbled for the phone and opened his text notifications. Immediately messages began flashing up on the screen—messages that he hadn't checked. He squinted down at the screen, mouthing the words as he read them, then swore eloquently.

"Charming. I see you've seen it."

Laurence hated being taken by surprise, but this was outrageous in the extreme. He swore again. "You're— *ending* this?"

She sighed. "I'm sorry, Laurence."

"Via *text* message?"

She snorted. "How else was I supposed to do it? You've been ignoring my calls all week. Not much of a boyfriend, you are," she added sarcastically. "And as good as your assistant is at making you look genuinely busy, she isn't *that* good. I'm not going to fall for the 'in a meeting' line more than three times."

"But—why?"

"I met someone."

Laurence stared at the screen, struck dumb. His arrangement with Aurelia Hunter had lasted a year and had been quite a satisfactory one. As the head of a massive tech company she'd inherited from her father, she had no time to date, but plenty of occasions for which a date was needed. A chance meetup at a networking party led to a deal—he'd beau her around to her events, and she'd come to his, smile for photographs, be an escort he didn't have to worry about…or *call*.

That last detail had apparently been his downfall.

Aurelia spoke into the silence. "I'm sorry. It—it's kind of been happening for a month and came to a head a week ago. It—it's different. I don't want to do this anymore. I sent you a letter so you could make arrangements for the rest of the season."

Laurence scrolled through the letter, biting back another litany of curses. Were he calmer, he might marvel at Aurelia's tone; she sounded softer than he'd ever heard her, both in the email and now on the phone. *She's really in love.*

He'd be happy for her, he supposed, if she hadn't screwed him over so colossally.

"That's all well and good," he said sarcastically, "and I hope you're enjoying your desert getaway, but this is *appalling*, Aurelia. I'm courting a huge client tonight, I've got events coming up and—"

"Go solo." She was definitely awake now, and possibly enjoying this? He heard the flicker of a lighter, and Aurelia drew a long breath. He pictured her as she exhaled; probably swathed in something outrageously expensive, playing with the tendrils of hair on her shoulders. "And if you do find someone else to do this with, answer her calls, emails and texts, okay?"

"You really don't understand how badly you've messed things up for me, do you?" Or she had, until love had snatched all reason from her. Clients liked doing business with folks who were settled, committed. Couples were comforting. It made them feel as if their accounts were safe in the hands of someone who understood relationships, understood what it meant to make someone happy, to *care* for someone.

Laurence did not understand relationships, or want to—he'd given that up long ago. But he knew what they looked like, and he knew what he needed to play that role. The idea of pursuing a woman for romantic reasons was out—he had no time or inclination for that. Aurelia had been an ideal compromise. No strings, no sex, none of the messy aftermath. Still, the faithless woman had—

"Look, Laurence—"

Laurence hung up, then scrolled to her name and blocked her. It was childish, he knew, but he had a problem to solve, and Aurelia was no longer relevant. He could explain away her absence tonight, but the rest of the season still lay before him, with the galas, the dinner parties, the weekends away—

He swore under his breath again. She'd *met* someone. Women! They really were the most *ridiculous* creatures.

If Kitty Asare knew one thing, it was that lies were much more convincing when she half believed them herself. So, she recited them to herself over and over again as she stood shivering in the ladies' lounge at the Park Hotel. It was cold—colder than she'd anticipated, but then again, all she was wearing was a black lace thong at the moment.

She unzipped the small rolling backpack she'd brought

with her and extracted the silk dress inside, then held it up critically to the light. Last season's, of course, obtained from one of those designer-dress renting sites. It didn't look too terribly off-season, she told herself. It suited her lanky frame and deep coloring, and had enough oomph for tonight's soiree without looking out of place. It was also in her favorite color, a deep Lincoln green with a hint of brightness that made the rich tints of her skin glow.

Blending in was essential, since she wasn't actually invited. All that mattered was that she'd manage, for the fourth time that month, to run into Sonia Van Horn at a New York social event.

She was counting on Sonia's being in a good mood. The kindly older woman was definitely a low-watt bulb, but she was the current chair of the board of the Hunt Society, a social club that Kitty had been trying to get into for a year and a half. The small, unobtrusive group of the *ton* on the outskirts of Long Island was made up of a number of appallingly horsey middle-aged people, but it was one of the oldest, finest clubs in the state, and Kitty was determined to begin moving intimately with that group, or at the very least get an audience with them. There were simply too many potential contacts there to ignore—contacts with fat wallets who liked the convenience of contributing to a cause without getting their jewelled hands dirty.

Quality over quantity, she told herself as she shimmied the dress over her slender hips. As founder of a foundation that helped foster children transition to real life, Kitty had learned over the years that cold-calling and mass-mailing brochures were not enough. The charities she'd studied that did the most were either established by wealthy patrons or fronted by them, with endowments in the billions. A onetime donation was not nearly as beneficial as a lifetime supporter, and Kitty wanted those lifetime supporters.

She yanked the zipper up, trying to get her shivering under control. The dress fit okay, but narrow straps held up a draped bodice that was just a hair too big—Kitty would have to remember to stay upright.

Rich people, she thought with some disgust, and as she did, she saw the strong line of her jaw jut out from beneath the skin in soft relief. She'd have to take deep breaths, settle her face before she went in. She knew from experience that the grasping, greedy bunch inside would have spent months—and millions—planning their jewelry, their impeccably tailored wardrobes. Makeup and hair would have been done by professionals hours before, and they would have been ferried to the Park Hotel from their Manhattan penthouses and Long Island and Connecticut mansions to a party where champagne would flow like bathwater. Kitty, of course, had no such resources. She'd done her hair herself, cringing at the heat while she hot-combed her hair as close to her scalp as she could, and her dress would need to be dropped into a mailbox before noon on Monday if she wanted to avoid a fee from the rental company. There was no such thing as a fairy godmother, not for Kitty Asare. She had to make her own transformation.

Not that I care, she reminded herself. She didn't want to be one of them. Years ago she'd reached for the moon and fallen hard, and Kitty, if nothing else, was someone who learned from her mistakes. Hope was futile; so was depending on people.

She didn't need any of them. She just needed their money, and she needed plenty of it. Kitty had an encyclopedic memory for names, faces and stories, and she used them shamelessly. Acquaintances became donors much faster than strangers did—and though the glitter of these people were nothing but pretty facades to an aching emptiness, their money was extremely useful.

Other than that, the thought of the opulence and the waste all left a bad taste in Kitty's mouth. There were people only a few zip codes away who had nothing tonight, not even a bed to sleep in. There had been a time she'd been one of those people, and she'd been angry at the injustice of it, but now she chose to use what she'd learned over the years to take some of that money and funnel it to where it was really needed—to support the underrepresented, the underserved.

People like the girl she'd been.

Kitty took a deep and steadying breath. She could not think of that, not right now; thinking of what she lost and how she lost it made her stomach clench and eyes water, even ten years later. She would not be able to maintain her composure if she dwelled on it too much.

Focus, she told herself.

She looked the part, she'd dressed the part and she'd fortified herself with a meal fit for a king. She smiled, thinking of the meal she'd charged to the penthouse. t was immature, but it felt like sticking it to the Man, just a little, in a gloriously Robin Hood–ish manner. There had been another diner in the room, ordering a meal as lavish as hers had been. *He* probably didn't even finish it, Kitty thought with a mixture of wistfulness and disdain. He'd been shrouded in shadow from the soft lighting in the room, but she'd been able to make out broad shoulders, smooth skin, fine, tailored clothes. Someone accustomed to that sort of life. Probably handsome, too—they always were.

A glance at the time reminded her that she needed to head over to the Grand Ballroom, and now. Experience had taught her it was much easier to sneak into an event of this magnitude a bit late, when people were liquored up, guards were relaxed, and groups were moving in and out—groups that it would be easy to slip into. She looked in the mirror. She should have taken pleasure in her appearance; the dress skimmed over her slim figure, and her makeup was done to perfection. However, her eyes looked wide and anxious—too anxious. There was an odd prickling beneath her skin, as if something were about to happen.

"For God's sake, they're just people." Kitty picked up her beaded clutch. She'd stow her overnight bag with the concierge until the event was over and then stumble out to the subway to head back to Queens. She straightened her thin shoulders, set her face and clattered out the door, moving seamlessly into the group of well-dressed, heavily perfumed people heading for the ballroom.

The soiree, Kitty knew, was a "little dinner and dance" for clients of an advertising firm that Sonia's husband worked for. Enormous floor-to-ceiling prints and electric screens showcased what she supposed were the focuses of the firm: whiskeys, wines, a couple of luxury cars, perfumes, watches… Most of the women in the room wore gowns and cocktail dresses in deep greens and maroons and golds, echoing the runways of that year— she'd at least got that right.

Her mouth went dry as she identified several people she knew—well, not personally, but she knew of them. Page Six, the society columns—TMZ, even. She needed to find Sonia, and she needed to do it now. She pulled out her phone and shot the older woman a quick text message:

Hi, heard from a little birdie that you're at the Laurence & Haddad event tonight! Are you anywhere about? Would love to say hello. :)

She hit Send, knowing it was probably futile. The fifty-two-year-old matron barely knew how to turn the thing on, and Kitty was fairly positive she wouldn't have it out at an event like this one.

Suddenly she felt tired, and prickles of what felt suspiciously like embarrassment heated her neck, bit under her arms. It was the dreadful, suffocating self-consciousness of a person who didn't belong, and it would choke her, if she let it. Audacity was probably the defining characteristic of girls who were successful at this, and normally she had plenty. Tonight she didn't know what was wrong with her. Perhaps it was the heavy meal she'd had earlier. She tossed her head and lifted her chin, determined to overcome it, then she saw *him*.

The man from the dining room.

She'd seen him for only a few minutes before clearing out of the room to dress, but she certainly had noticed him—it was hard not to. Now that he was standing and she could see him from head to toe, she felt that same, almost involuntary, prickle of excitement, beginning at her scalp and blossoming down.

He was big and solidly muscled; the simple black tuxedo he wore created sleek lines from broad shoulders to a narrower waist. He was drinking champagne from a glass and surveying the room with a critical eye; he looked as if he did not quite approve of something.

She would not call him handsome; his features were too irregular for that. However, he was undeniably attractive, something that was unsettling for Kitty. She remembered the dark, heady gaze he'd directed at her from his table, and she swallowed, then gathered her wits and began to walk toward him. When she was close enough, she stopped and used the full battery of her eyes on him. "Hello," she said simply.

When the man turned and looked at her, Kitty experienced such a surge of unexpected warmth that she felt quite weak. The warmth was chased by panic when she looked at his face. She was now able to make out features, far sharper than the hazy impression a candlelit dining-room had left. Close up…

She knew him.

His was a face that was connected to her past, to things that still kept her up at night, even after ten years. Kitty felt her whole body go hot, all the way to her fingertips. She tried in one frantic effort to make her face stony, but she knew he had seen that moment of panic. She opened her mouth, his name on her lips, but he beat her to it.

This could not possibly get any worse.

"I'm Laurence Stone," he said, "and I think it's time for you to leave."

Redeemed by His New York Cinderella
*by Jadesola James, available October 2021,
wherever ebooks are sold.*

www.Harlequin.com